What readers are saying about previous books by

Ginny Aiken

"Captivating. I became a part of the story as it was unfolding."
—Jean Klusmeier, Pennsylvania

"Couldn't put it down! Ginny Aiken can tell a good story."
—Carole McAllaster, California

"Terrific. I laughed and I cried. But mostly, I just fell in love."
—Kay Allen, Oklahoma

"Wonderful. A novel with heart and soul involved."
—Shirene Broadwater

"Helped me through a bad time. I needed your wit and fun to help bring me out of it."
—KG

"Great book—thoroughly enjoyed each page! Easy to read, never slow, great plot."
—Cyndy Roggeman, Michigan

"Loved your characters. So much heart and emotion, not to mention an engaging story line."
—M

HEART
QUEST.

romance the way it's meant to be

HeartQuest brings you romantic fiction
with a foundation of biblical truth.
Adventure, mystery, intrigue, and suspense
mingle in these heartwarming stories of
men and women of faith striving to build
a love that will last a lifetime.

May HeartQuest books sweep you
into the arms of God, who longs for you
and pursues you always.

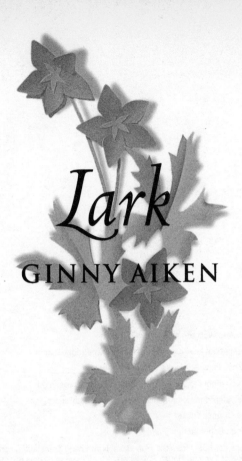

Lark

GINNY AIKEN

HEART QUEST

Romance fiction from
Tyndale House Publishers, Inc.
WHEATON, ILLINOIS

www.heartquest.com

Visit Tyndale's exciting Web site at www.tyndale.com

Check out the latest about HeartQuest Books at www.heartquest.com

HeartQuest is a registered trademark of Tyndale House Publishers, Inc.

Edited by Ramona Cramer Tucker

Designed by Melinda Schumacher

Scripture quotations are taken from the *Holy Bible,* New Living Translation, copyright © 1996. Used by permission of Tyndale House Publishers, Inc., Wheaton, Illinois 60189. All rights reserved.

Library of Congress Cataloging-in-Publication Data

Aiken, Ginny.
  Lark / Ginny Aiken.
    p. cm.
  ISBN 0-8423-3560-9 (sc)
  1. Women journalists—Fiction. 2. Dramatists—Fiction. I. Title.
PS3551.I339 L37 2000
813′.54 21; aa05 03-16—dc00   00-028701

Printed in the United States of America

06   05   04   03   02   01
9   8   7   6   5   4   3   2

To my sister,
Lou Schmitz, with whom, by the grace of God,
I have a wonderful relationship.

You are the light of the world—like a city on a mountain, glowing in the night for all to see. Don't hide your light under a basket! Instead, put it on a stand and let it shine for all.
Matthew 5:14-15

For though your hearts were once full of darkness, now you are full of light from the Lord, and your behavior should show it! For this light within you produces only what is good and right and true.
Ephesians 5:8-9

Acknowledgments

GRATITUDE AND THANKS TO:

My Lord Jesus	*—you are sufficient always.*
Claudia Cross	*the best agent on earth.*
Becky Nesbitt, Kathy Olson, and Jan Pigott	*editors extraordinaire.*
Ramona Cramer Tucker	*—you know why!*
Peggy Stoks	*for the years of sisterhood and her willlingness to read under fire.*
Karl Fieldhouse, Elizabeth Darrach, and Monica Doerfler	*for their constant support.*
Jeri Odell and Beth White	*for their friendship.*
George Ivan, Gregory, Geoffrey, and Grant Anikienko	*the four best sons a mother could want.*

And as always, to my husband, George,
who never bargained for a writer as a wife.

ONE

Bellamy, Loudon County, Virginia; Present Day

BRIIIING!

When the telephone rang at seven-thirty on Tuesday morning, Richard Desmond feared he'd hear an unwelcome—at that moment—New York accent on the other end. He'd spent the last twelve days wrangling around his latest contract tangle with his agent.

Storey Newburn, high-powered and much-envied in the literary world, couldn't understand why Rich, after the stunning success of his last two works, would balk at this latest offer. So what, he'd asked, if they wanted Rich to incorporate occultic elements in his next mystery play? So what if they insisted on some titillating sex scenes? These ingredients added to his already proven recipe would secure his place with the greats of the twentieth century and move him to the top as the first great of the twenty-first.

Briiiing!

Rich's spirit staged a revolt every time he considered his situation. As a Christian, he couldn't see how these so-called improvements—according to the powers-that-be—would honor anyone, much less God.

His head ached and his body creaked from hours of scrunching in his office chair until the wee moments of the morning, trying to reconcile his faith and his career.

Briiiing!

When he finally picked up the receiver and heard Bellamy police officer Cecil Wiggon's voice instead of Storey's, he knew nothing good would come of this call either.

"Wiggon?"

"That you, there, Rich?" asked the cop.

In spite of his troubles, and seeing as he lived alone, Rich grinned. "As usual, I'm the only one here. How can I help you?"

Silence ensued. Then, "Well . . . uh . . . ya see . . ." Another silence followed.

From their childhood days together, Rich remembered why the school bully had stuck Wiggon, a tall, earnest boy, with the nickname "Wiggly" way back when. Rich had hated the embarrassment and blush that appeared each time the mean-spirited nickname was used. He'd always stood up for his friend, even though Wiggon's occasional waffling did frustrate him.

"Hey, Wiggon, just spit it out so we can get it over with."

"You're right. My news ain't good, an' I hate to be the one to tell you, but it can't be helped. You'd best be getting on down to the station here. Your mama's got herself in a bucket of trouble."

"Mama?" Rich asked. "Did she run another stop sign? The last time she did that was five years ago, right after Dad died. I can't imagine what would make her so careless—"

"She's gone an' got herself arrested," Wiggon blurted out.

"*What?* Are you sure you're talking about *my* mother? Mariah Desmond?"

Wiggon huffed in his ear. "Of course, I'm sure. Mizz Desmond was my Sunday school teacher near as long as a coon's age. She's here, an' she's in an ugly situation. I'm . . . scared for her."

Rich rubbed his brow where the headache intensified with each word Wiggon uttered. "What are the charges?"

"Ah . . . er . . . well . . . you see, it's big stuff. I mean, the Secret Service agents were the ones—"

"*The* Secret Service? The guys who guard the president?"

"No other Secret Service I know."

"This can't be. Not *my* mother. You know her, Wiggon. All she ever does is sell her—" Rich winced in discomfort, as always—"*merchandise,* go to church and Bible study, and hang out with her Garden Club. She's a sweet old lady, an innocent among innocents."

"Humph! I dunno about those Garden Club ladies. An' your mama was thick as thieves with Miss Louella when she did her thing at her place. I dunno about all that 'innocent among innocents' stuff."

"Come on, Wiggon. They didn't wind up arrested during Miss Louella's home restoration, if you'll remember. Now you're telling me my mother's run afoul of the law, and you're hedging about the charges. Tell me what they are."

"Well . . . we can start off with credit-card fraud, conspiracy to defraud, grand theft, racketeerin', an' a couple of other biggies."

For once in his life, Rich was rendered mute. He, who was reputed to have a gift for words, for a turn of phrase, a brilliant way with the English language, couldn't dredge up a single syllable in response.

Then, "Mama? Racketeering? Theft? Fraud?"

Impossible. Laughable.

Except Wiggon wasn't laughing.

Oh, Father God, help me here. I don't know . . . anything.

Tamping down the fear that threatened to bloom, Rich

called upon his last bit of strength. "Have you spoken with my sister?" he asked.

Wiggon cleared his throat. "Ah . . . well . . . you see . . . the Cap'n felt it'd be better if he told Reenie. So, she's been called, only not by me."

Rich groaned. "Then you're right. I'd better get down to the station straightaway. Otherwise, who knows what mess of trouble you'll have on your hands—courtesy of the Desmond females."

"Ain't that the truth?"

Maureen Desmond Ainsley had been . . . predictably unpredictable since she'd raced to life six weeks prematurely. From the moment of her birth, she'd managed to keep the Desmond household in a constant uproar as they muddled through her childhood and adolescence. Matters grew worse after she made friends with the redheaded girl next door, Larkspur Bellamy.

Rich shuddered at the memory of years made miserable by the two of them. Especially Lark. He'd come to think of her as a bad case of arthritis. Not bad enough to kill you, but bad enough to make your days a pain.

Well, there was, of course, the matter of his prom. Just the thought of that night made Rich's cheeks blaze. When Suzanne Crandall, his date, had come down with mono seven days before the dance, he'd decided to ask shy, sweet Mercy Appleby instead. He knew none of the other guys would ask her, and he'd always admired the quiet girl's sharp mind. Mercy had been thrilled by his invitation, and he'd known he had made the right choice.

Naturally, he'd said nothing at home. He hadn't wanted Reenie—or Lark—to get a whiff of what had happened. His caution, however, had made no difference.

The snoopy redhead had found out about Suzanne's illness and told everyone he'd be escorting *her* instead—a notion concocted by none other than his little sis, who'd wanted nothing more than a romance between her big brother and her best friend. To make matters worse, Lark had shown up at the dance, mad as a red cape–teased bull, demanding to know why he hadn't come for her.

The brash teenybopper's words and the spectacle they'd brought about had shocked and hurt Mercy, who hadn't known she was Rich's second choice. And Rich's kind gesture toward a friend had become something to cringe over, even this many years later.

He also remembered Lark's embarrassment, not to mention the pride she'd donned as she left the dance, her cheeks scarlet in her otherwise white face, her chin tilted skyward.

He'd sighed in relief when he left town—not to mention Lark and Reenie—for the University of Virginia. He'd felt the same way later, when Lark went to college in Baltimore, and more recently, two summers ago, when he'd walked Reenie down the aisle and placed her hand in that of brave-hearted— or insane, depending on how you looked at it—Seth Ainsley.

Now with Mama in trouble, who knew what Reenie would do? Especially since the equally erratic, dogged, and truly frightening-in-the-quirks-of-her-fertile-mind Lark was back in town.

"Ah . . . Rich?" said Wiggon.

"OK, OK. Let me hang up, and I'll be right there."

"Well, that wasn't what I was gonna tell you, but yeah, get on down here. Your mama's gonna be needin' you. And your bankbook. Bail's gonna be sky-high. *If* the judge even says OK."

Rich's horrible morning turned into a black nightmare, promising only to darken as the day wore on. "Lord," he asked as he hung up, "what more do you have in store for me?"

Tat-a-tat-tat-tat-tat-tat! Tat-a-tat-tat-tat-tat-tat-tat!

It sounded like a woodpecker boring for lunch in a tree. Larkspur Bellamy buried her head in her pillow, too tired and too deep into dreamland to figure out what the sound was. But then the chatter grew more insistent, more immediate—louder.

"Lark!" called a voice from far, far away. It sounded like . . . her sister Magnolia. But it couldn't be. Maggie was busy with her pooch, her much-loved fiancé, Clay Marlowe, and her newfound career as business manager of Marlowe Historical Restorations.

"Would you *pleeeeease* open this door?" the voice begged in a distinctly Southern, super-sweet drawl. "I've been knockin' longer'n Noah sailed around with his critters, and you know you can't shake me off as easy as a dog does a flea by a long shot!"

Lark bolted upright, her heart beating faster than the woodpecker had pecked. As she fought to catch her breath, she realized she was where she'd crashed, oh, about two hours and forty-eight minutes ago—in her own bed.

Yawning, she dragged herself out from under the covers, tugged her Mighty Mouse sleep shirt kneeward, and trudged down the stairs to open the front door.

Maggie, Lark's junior by two years, marched into the house, lurching and stumbling uncharacteristically.

Lark yawned again, then mumbled, "Whatchadoin' here so early?"

"Why, honey, it's not early a'tall. I'm on my way to the office, you know."

Lark slumped into the vast wing chair across from the sofa Maggie occupied and tried to focus. Her effort didn't work. She rubbed her eyes, but it seemed that her dreams hadn't faded with her sleep. Something brown and furry and snuffly with saggy wings crawled across Granny Iris's antique Tabriz. She closed her eyes, and the seductive lure of sleep crept over her again.

Maggie would have none of it. "Larkspur Bellamy! What would Granny say about your behavior? Why, here I've come bearin' a gift, and you fall right asleep on me. Where are your manners?"

Lark winced and cracked open one eyelid. She'd been up all night compiling the latest issue of *Critic's Choice,* her recently launched-to-much-success literary criticism magazine. Her sister's shriek hurt.

"Keep it down, willya? I just put the magazine to bed."

"And you, too, it would seem."

"Mm-hmm . . . so, if you don't mind, I'm going back where I belong. In bed."

"Not yet, you don't. I have a present for you. I know how lonesome I was until I met my Clay, and I also know what a difference Buford made in my loneliness."

"Ah, Mags," Lark groaned, "I don't want your dog."

"I wouldn't dream of givin' you my darlin' puppy. That's why I brought you your own. Here."

Before she knew what was happening, a weight landed in Lark's lap and a rasping slurp scraped her cheek. "What in the world . . . ?"

"Meet *your* new dog," said Maggie as she smartly—and wisely—hurried to the front door. "Enjoy him!"

Lark wrestled with the . . . *thing* in her lap—a dog, as Maggie had said, droopy and drippy, at that—and yelled, "Get back here, Squirt! You can't just dump an animal on me like this. What am I going to do with it?"

The door opened with its characteristic squeak. "How many times did Granny Iris warn you about name-callin', Larkspur Bellamy?"

"About as many times as she warned you about calling me Radish-top."

Stepping out to the porch, Maggie sniffed. "Well, I'm not callin' you that now. And as far as *your* dog goes, Lark, all you need to do is love him. He'll do the rest. The Lord bless you this day, sis."

"Wait!" Lark cried as the door clicked shut. The squirmy critter in her lap slithered off and began to howl mournfully, tugging on the leather leash Lark had grabbed when Maggie had thrust it her way.

To Lark's amazement, the pooch sniffed the Tabriz, then, nose to the ground . . . er . . . rug, took off in Maggie's wake. The animal yowled again, snuffled the floor some more, then scratched at the door, determined to follow her sister.

Now what?

Lark had never owned a pet. Camellia, the youngest of the three Bellamy sisters—Bellamy's Blossoms, as everyone in town called the three florally monikered siblings—was the one who'd brought home every stray that crossed her path. Lark had been too busy planning, plotting, thinking, imagining.

What was she going to do with the pooch?

And why did lousy, sleepless nights always end in weird ways for her? Did this doggy encounter mean the rest of her day would follow suit?

As she yawned again and held tight to the leash, the phone rang. "Hello?"

"Lark?" asked her best friend, Maureen Desmond Ainsley, in a shaky voice. "Lark, is that you?"

"Who else?"

The dog wailed. Reenie's voice dropped to a whisper. "Are you all right? Do you need help? Should I call the cops?"

That was all she needed, professional bloodhounds to go

with her . . . what *was* the thing, anyway? Beagle? Nah, too big, no patches. Bassett? Not *that* miserable looking.

"Lark. Are you there?" Panic shrilled Reenie's voice. "What have they done to you? You can tell me. I'll help."

Lark blinked to full alertness—at last. "No, no. I'm fine. This is just Maggie's idea of a joke. A bad one. I'll tell you all about it later. I'm all right, but you sounded terrible a minute ago. What's wrong?"

"Oh, Lark. The worst thing's happened. An' you're the only one who can possibly help." Reenie's mellow Southern accent ate up letters at a ravenous pace. "You have to investigate this an' get to the bottom of ever'thin'. I simply cain't bear to watch 'em lock 'er up an' throw 'way the key."

Lark blinked. First the woodpecker, then Maggie and her beast. Now Reenie at full throttle. On only two hours and forty-eight minutes of sleep. "Slow down, willya? Who's going to lock up whom and throw away what key?"

"It's . . . it's Mama, Lark. She's been arrested."

Now Lark knew she was dreaming. The whole thing—Maggie, mutt, and Maureen's call—were mere morsels of her overworked imagination. If she pinched herself hard enough she'd surely wake—

"Ouch!" Later on she'd have a bruise on her forearm.

"I just knew that awful noise meant trouble," Reenie said. "I'm comin' straight over, an' helpin' you with whatever's goin' on."

"Hang on, willya? What about your mom? Or didn't you call with some crazy story about her in jail?"

"Oh. Well. Yes, I did, but if you're in trouble, we have to get you out of it 'cause you're the only one who can help Mama. She's in jail 'cause the Secret Service nabbed her. You've got to find out why they're framin' her, an' for whose sake."

Lark thought this over. "Your mother's *really* in jail?"

"What've I been tellin' you, Larkspur Bellamy?"

"Where is she?"

"At the Bellamy police department."

"Did you call a lawyer?"

"Of course, Lark. I'm not *that* dizzy—no matter what Rich says."

As usual, Lark's cheeks burned at the mere mention of handsome Rich Desmond, on whom she'd had a monumental and embarrassing crush from the moment she met him in elementary school to the day she left Bellamy after graduating high school. A very public, object-of-everyone's-comments crush. "Does he know?"

"The chief said Wiggon would tell Rich."

"Will he be at the station?"

"Come on, Lark, mah big brother doesn't bite. An' besides, it's for *Mama*."

Lark had always loved gentle, sweet, cheerful Mariah Desmond. For the lady who'd taken her under a loving wing after the deaths of her parents, she'd swallow her dread of coming within ten miles of Rich Desmond. But only for Miss Mariah. "Oh, all right. Hang up so I can get dressed. I'll be there in five."

"Thank you, thank you!"

After Lark hung up the phone, two things happened. The dog at the end of the leash bayed loud enough to blow out her eardrums, then had a very wet, acrid-scented "accident." Right on the beautiful oak floor of the Bellamy family's ancestral home.

Yep. The day was shaping up in its usual, crummy disaster-after-the-sleepless-night way. And as had often been the case, Lark, the oldest sister, had to clean up the mess.

Literally.

Even when the greater mess wasn't one of her own making. Or even of her sisters' making—this time. It was a bona fide imported catastrophe, likely to hurt a woman Lark had always loved.

With Rich Desmond thrown into the mix, Lark suspected the worst was yet to come. At her expense.

Rich ran up the cement steps of the Bellamy PD, convinced Wiggon had made a mistake. Or something.

No way could his mother be in jail. Even the mention of Mariah Desmond's name and racketeering in the same breath proved the questionable condition of Wiggon's brain.

Still, a corner of Rich's mind hadn't quit piping up during his split-second shower and the run into town. *What if Wiggon's right?* it had asked. *What if Mama has been arrested? What if something's gone wrong somewhere?*

To his relief, even that corner of his mind wasn't stupid enough to consider Mariah Desmond breaking a law. It all had to be a mistake. One he'd straighten out. Quickly.

With a prayer for strength, Rich pushed open the finger-smeared glass door and stepped into the main lobby of the age-and-exhaust-darkened brick fortress. Thoughts of his mother foremost in his mind, he didn't notice the tarp spread on the floor to his right. He did, however, hear the warning from above. "Heads up down there!"

Looking ceilingward, he found Horace Hobey, the best masonry contractor in the county and probably well beyond, perched on a scaffold, repairing the mortar of the faded-to-pink inside brick wall. "Hey, Hobey! How're you doing?"

"Praise God, just blessed to bits, son. 'Bout you?"

The reason for his presence at the station wiped the smile right off Rich's face. "Not so good. Wiggon says Mama's been arrested—if you can believe it."

"Izzat how come Mizz Mariah came in here with that stream a'suits awhile back?"

"According to Wiggon."

Hobey waved a trowel tipped in glop. "That boy's got honeybees hummin' in his head. Ain't no way Mizz Mariah's done nothin' wrong. Why, your mama's a true saint."

"Thanks. But remember, Hobey, she's buddies with Miss Louella and the rest of the Garden Club."

Hobey's broad ruddy face turned puce all the way past his nonexistent hairline. "I tell you, son, them gardener ladies do come up with some wild notions, all right. Why, I was fit to be hog-tied over that bidness at the Ashworth Mansion."

"Exactly. And Mama was right in the thick of it."

"Hmm . . . seein' as that's the case, well then, Wiggon might have hisself a point there. Who knows what kinda trouble Mizz Mariah mighta got herself into now?"

A terrifying thought struck Rich. "Was Louella Ashworth with Mama?"

"No sir," Hobey said, dabbing mortar between two bricks. "Ain't seen no other wimmen but your mama an' them police ladies we got us these days. Miss Louella's done learned her lesson, she says. Why, she gave her testimony at church last Sunday. Spoke real pretty about all the good Lord's taught her through that craziness at her house."

Rich grinned, picturing the scene. "I went out of town last weekend. Too bad I missed that service. I'll bet the Bellamy Community Church was sizzling."

"Bunch a red-faced wimmen there at the BCC, all right. But God taught 'em all but good. An' your mama was one of 'em, I'll tell ya. Blushin' an' praisin' God for his mercy and forgiveness. Still . . . maybe Wiggon ain't wrong. Maybe your mama's done gone an' got herself in trouble again."

"That's what I'm afraid of." Rich sighed in resignation.

"There's no getting around it. I'd better see what's happening. Will you be at tomorrow night's Bible study?"

Hobey turned away, his shiny pate reddening again. "Ah . . . well, I'm a mite busy tomorrow night—all Wednesday nights for a spell, so I ain't signed up for this new study. I—I'll see you 'round town, though. God bless you, an' see what's what with your mama, OK?"

Bewildered by this normally straightforward man's strange and evasive response, Rich nodded. "The Lord's blessing on you, too, Hobey. Take care."

"Oh, hey," added the older man. "Since we're speakin' on trouble, how 'bout that Larkspur Bellamy? Can you believe she's come back home? Moved into her Granny Iris's house again—smack next door to you. An' her a famous newshound an' all."

Rich didn't answer. His thoughts on Lark Bellamy, her return to town, and especially her news-sniffing talents weren't the kind he wanted to share.

Hobey went on. "There's some what say that there new magazine of hers is some kinda right smart bit of work, but the ones I take a gander at don't make much sense. Wadda you make of her comin' home to do her magazine here instead of in Baltimore?"

"Oh, the magazine's good," he said, making his voice light and relaxed, "as good as her reporting was. Lark's smart, all right, but you're right about another thing, too. She's trouble, and I refuse to think what kind she'll dig up now that she's back in town."

The mason's deep-set eyes twinkled. "You reckon she's still sweet on you?"

Before he could swallow the words, Rich fervently said, "Oh, Lord God, no."

Hobey gave one of his booming laughs. "She's right pretty,

though. With them green eyes an' red curls of hers, why, she's near as pretty as an angel."

"One with her halo throttling her. Trust me, the woman's trouble, and I want nothing to do with her." He gave his friend a farewell salute. "I'm off to see about Mama."

"The Lord go with you," Hobey answered, turning back to his mortar and bricks.

As Rich stepped up to the main desk, the brass-and-glass front door banged against a wall, startling him.

"Hey!" bellowed Hobey.

"Watch out," called a frighteningly familiar female voice. "Coming through!"

Refusing to turn and find what he'd hoped to avoid, Rich gritted his teeth and closed his eyes—tight. Trouble had just stormed the Bellamy Police Department.

A clackety skittering, snuffling, and panting, plus a cacophony of rushed footsteps, grunts, and desperate "hold ons" approached. He'd known it would sooner or later come to this, but he'd prayed for it to be later. That prayer hadn't been answered.

Marshaling his patience—not to mention his strength—Rich said, "Hello, Lark. What brings *you* down here today?"

TWO

WHEN LARK'S RESPONSE DIDN'T MATERIALIZE, RICH SLOWLY turned around and stared.

Hobey hadn't been kidding when he'd said Lark looked like an angel. The ten years she'd spent away from Bellamy had been kind to her. She'd grown, bringing her to within two or three inches of his own six feet. But whereas he was broad and sturdy, built like his late father, Lark was slender, willowy, and feminine, with an air of the wood sprite about her.

Her hair, once a wild, fiery red, had mellowed to a burnished mahogany, deep and glossy, livened with curls. And her green eyes had always been riveting, even when they'd followed him with the puppylike devotion that had made his childhood and adolescence a mortifying misery.

Now, though, Rich found himself thinking that a man could get lost in those forest green depths—a man bent on exploring their spark of mischief, their glow of intelligence, their gleam of exuberant life.

He noticed that the sprinkle of cinnamon over the bridge of her nose remained, despite the many times he'd watched her submit to Reenie's "beauty" treatments. He'd never understood why Lark had hated those freckles with such intensity. He'd found them the most appealing thing about her. They seemed totally and utterly normal—unlike her.

Lark was—and always had been—different. Unpredictable. Spontaneous. Curious as the worst cat, stubborn as the best mule, smart as the next Einstein, and sharp as a porcupine's quills. About that comfy, too.

As if to prove his assessment true, she was at this moment performing the most bizarre jig before him, her eyes glued to his face, her lips slightly parted, a dumbfounded expression on her face. She lurched. She bucked. She dipped.

Still, those green eyes stared at him, rendering him incapable of tearing his gaze from hers. Until a lance of pain in his right big toe brought him back to earth. "Ouch!"

Glancing down, Rich found a dog gnawing on his brand-new leather loafers, growling and tossing its head from side to side as it tried to rip a chunk out of the expensive Italian hide.

"Hey! Where'd this thing come from?" He tried to pull his foot free and maintain his dignity. But as he caught sight of the animal's collar and leash, he knew. The ferocious beast had come with trouble—Trouble, with a capital *T*. Otherwise known as Larkspur Bellamy, erstwhile Pulitzer-prizewinning reporter for the *Baltimore Sun* and current literary-magazine mogul. His once-upon-a-time and, unfortunately, once-again neighbor and nemesis.

With her in sight, there'd be no dignity for him.

Praying for patience, he gritted his teeth. "Will you please get your dog away from my shoes?"

The green eyes snapped with temper. "Can't you see I'm trying? Besides, it's not mine."

One, two, three . . . ten. "Then why have you brought it to the police station?"

"Because your mother needs me."

Rich shook his head and backed away—right into the main desk. "Ouch!"

He rubbed his spine. He'd have a bruise in the morning, but such things were to be expected when Lark was around. "My—mother—does—*not*—need—you."

The beast nuzzled up to his foot again and chomped down, catching another of his digits. Rich relinquished his last hope of dignity and hopped sideways to evade the creature's sharp little teeth. "Get your mutt away from my feet while I have toes left."

Lark yanked on the leash; the dog released its hold. "This thing's not mine, and I have to help your mom. Reenie asked me. I promised."

"The chief told Reenie I'd take care of everything. She doesn't need to worry—much less call in the press."

"Shows how little you know." Lark tugged on the pooch's leash as it approached Rich again. "I'm no longer the press. I'm a businesswoman in my own right."

The dog howled its objection to her restraint, and Rich raised his voice to be heard over the din. "You haven't lost an ounce of your nosiness, though, have you, Snoop?"

She pulled herself upright, her gorgeous curls vibrating with energy. "The name's Scoop, and I'm proud of it. Few reporters ever got the jump on me, while I got the jump on them all."

"Yeah, yeah. I'll concede you're a fine reporter, but there's not much to report in Bellamy. Let's see how soon you get bored, pick up again, and hare off on a loony-tunes search for some weird and unusual bit of trivia."

"Trivia!"

The dog let off with another earsplitting, mournful wail, and the police station fell silent. Only then did Rich realize every eye in the building was fixed on them. A couple of knowing smirks made him groan again.

Great. The rumors and comments about Lark's endless passion for Rich would blaze through town before lunchtime. The thought of his adulthood turning into the personal torment his childhood had been as a result of the selfsame woman was more than he could bear.

Rich turned his back on Lark. "Go home. I have things under control. Tell Reenie I'll call her as soon as Mama and I are done here."

"I'm not going anywhere until I see Miss Mariah."

Glancing over his shoulder, Rich caught a glimpse of the tipped-up, squared-off chin. There was no budging Lark when she got into one of her moods. He'd seen them enough times.

Then she fell. Dropped straight down onto the floor.

So maybe she could be budged. Only not by reason or common sense. It seemed only like could move like.

Because at that very instant, smack on Lark's stomach, a very appropriate dog sat slurping her face. The only kind that would ever suit this girl-next-door. One that matched every aspect of her troublesome personality. One that reminded him of the greatest detecting nose of all time. For Lark had always viewed herself as heir to Sherlock Holmes's sleuthing talents.

Rich now had a pretty good idea what the immediate future held in store for him. He just wasn't sure God had had anything to do with it. It came courtesy of Scoop Bellamy, ace reporter.

At a time when he couldn't afford any distraction—his mother in jail, his career in crisis—the woman behind him posed the kind of distraction that meant only calamity.

A scant half hour later, Rich wrote a check that nearly brought him to his knees. To bail Mama from jail, he was wiping out his longtime savings. It wasn't the money that hurt so much—in fact, he thanked God for the financial blessing that would allow his mother to remain free—but rather the years and the hard work it represented. All for the sake of a ridiculous accusation.

Mariah Desmond was no racketeer. She was a devout Christian, a Sunday school teacher, a person sincere in her faith. But she was also a bit naïve, dangerously trusting, always seeing the world through hope-tinted glasses.

When Wiggon and Percy Baker, her lawyer, escorted her from her cell to the lobby, she said, "Hello, dear," kissing Rich on the cheek. "You shouldn't have troubled yourself comin' on down here. This is just a misunderstandin', you know." She smiled and patted dour Mr. Baker's arm. "Percy here will straighten these boys out, and I'll be back on my way to work."

Rich ground his teeth. "Mama, you're in serious trouble. You've been accused of . . . well, of being a mobster. This is serious."

Mariah waved. "Oh, no, Richie, it's not serious. It's up-and-down hilarious. No one in their right mind would think I'd do somethin' like that. You just go on home, and don't give it another thought. Everythin's goin' to be fine. After all, you know 'God causes everything to work together for the good of those who love God and are called accordin' to his purpose for them.' And the heavenly Father has called me to bring comfort and ease to women everywhere. He wouldn't let a silly mistake keep me from carryin' out my work."

He gritted his teeth again. He had no argument with the Scripture; sooner or later the mess would be straightened out. He just knew it wouldn't be the piece of cake Mama assumed it would be.

"Here," he said, handing the clerk at the desk the plain blue slip of paper that transferred his life's savings to the government. He was glad he still had his movie-deal money in two certificates of deposit. He could always pay the penalty to withdraw those amounts should the modest sum his late father's general store brought in not cover their needs until he agreed to a new contract.

It could get dicey, though, if the chasm between him and the powers-that-be didn't close soon. Desmond's Country Store had never been a moneymaker, but he'd kept the store after his father's death as much from loyalty and tradition as for more personal reasons. He wondered how much Mr. Baker's defense would cost.

Then his mother squealed with delight. "Lark, sugar! Come give Mizz Mariah a great big hug, honey. I haven't seen you in way too many days."

The tension in Rich's neck and shoulders set off a blunt throb at the base of his skull. He'd prayed Lark would leave, but as usual, she'd remained contrary.

"Reenie called me," the redhead said, her voice muffled in his mother's embrace. "I came down as soon I could. What's going on?"

Good question, Rich thought, one he hadn't voiced, since he'd hoped to discuss matters in the privacy of Percy Baker's office. Scoop, of course, had no concept of privacy.

"Pure foolishness," Mama said. "Somethin' about credit cards and stealin' and my foundations—you do know about my Dream Squeezes, don't you?"

"Just that you've become the sole distributor of some kind of girdle. Tell me about it."

As the two women headed toward the door, Rich turned to Mr. Baker. "Can she leave?"

"Just to go home," said the lawyer in his usual dry tone. "She can't leave town, you understand."

"Not even to go to work?"

Mr. Baker arched a colorless brow. "She doesn't work in town, does she?"

Rich's nerves curdled with dread. Nothing had kept Mama

from her distribution center near Leesburg since she'd gone into business. Keeping her in Bellamy would not be an easy task. "I'll see what I can do," Rich said.

"No," said the lawyer, his manner gaining pomposity. "You *will* keep her in Bellamy, or you'll lose the bail you've posted and Mariah will go back to jail for good—until her trial's over. You don't want that, do you?"

Stupid question. "Fine. I'll keep her home." Somehow. Then Rich heard the rumblings of further disaster.

"How's your magazine goin', sugar?" his mother asked his nemesis.

"Fine, Miss Mariah, and it's going to go better."

"How's that, honey?"

"Well, you know that hot playwright, Des Richter?"

"The one who wrote that mystery movie with that darlin' Australian boy, Mel somethin'-or-other? You know, the one with the blue eyes."

"*That* playwright," Lark answered, a petrifying gleam burning in her forest green eyes. "Well, he's never given an interview, you know."

Mariah nodded. "I read that in *People* magazine not so long ago."

Adding to the chaos in Rich's day, the bloodhound bayed again, plastered its nose to the police station floor, and yanked on its leash in an effort to follow a trail. Who knew what trail?

Rich knew craven fear in his heart.

"Hold on there, you mangy thing!" Lark cried, fighting a losing battle.

"Why, honey," Mariah chided. "He's not mangy at all. He's a darlin' little pup. He's goin' to make you the most wonderful friend when he grows a tad. Where'd you get him?"

As the "darlin' little pup" struggled to answer his instincts,

Lark lunged in his wake. "I didn't get him," she yelped, obviously in her own defense. "Maggie showed up with him this morning and dumped him on me. She has some dumb idea that I'm lonely, and this is her answer."

Mariah bustled to Lark's side. "Well, are you, dear?" she asked. "Lonesome, I mean."

"Of course not. Besides, if I was lonely, this beast wouldn't be the answer. See what it did to Rich?" She pointed at his foot.

His mother glanced at the mangled shoe and clucked in sympathy. "Well, it's only a shoe. One can't put too much value on earthly things. Remember Matthew 6: 'Wherever your treasure is, there your heart and thoughts will also be.'"

Rich smiled despite his unease. There was a certain comfort in a mother who remained constant and true to herself and her faith regardless of the circumstances. He thanked God for her example.

Then Lark said, "Yes, well, I'm not giving this dog any more thought than how to unload him. The only thing on my mind until Reenie's call this morning was sniffing out Des Richter's whereabouts. I'm going to get the first interview with the guy for my magazine. Don't you think it's suspicious how desperately he's hiding? I wonder what he's really protecting with his alleged scorn for publicity. People like that always have horrible stuff to hide. Maybe he's an ax murderer on death row. Or maybe it's a pen name for . . . England's Prince Charles."

Rich fought a laugh at Lark's flights of fancy.

"Nah," she said, stumbling when the dog tried to nose open the station door. "Not the Royal Chuck. That's too crazy. I'll bet Des Richter lives a Clark Kent life as far as his neighbors know. But I'm going to find him and sniff out what he's really up to."

Ice flowed through Rich's veins. Why had Lark come back?

And moved into the Bellamy family home—right next door to him?

Surely God knew the danger she posed him. A woman as snoopy as Lark was the single most impossible neighbor for a man like Rich.

A man leading a double life.

A short walk later, Rich slammed the front door shut as he sought sanctuary in his home. He'd known the peaceful existence he'd built for himself would be peaceful no more when he first heard Lark Bellamy was back in town.

He'd been forced to hear it from everyone he met. If he spent two hours behind the counter at Desmond's Country Store, he'd hear no less than twelve times that his sister's best friend had returned to Bellamy in a blaze of career glory.

The members of the Bellamy Garden Club were the worst offenders. When each older lady came shopping, she'd make a point of mentioning Lark's single state and how much the redhead had always fancied him—not to mention her beauty.

"This is your chance to get yourself a good Bellamy wife," Miss Louella Ashworth, current president and ringleader of the gardeners, had said.

"She's always loved you," Sarah Langhorn, the owner of The Blissful Bookworm, the local bookstore, had added.

Savannah Hollings, wife of the president of Bellamy Fiduciary Trust, had offered, "You could do much worse."

The elderly choir had made Rich wonder if he'd been nuts to come home after finishing his degree. But he loved Bellamy. He loved its smallness, its quaint provincial atmosphere, its old houses and lushly treed streets. He loved knowing everyone who lived in the area, and knowing they'd known his family forever and a day.

But there were times . . . like now that Lark Bellamy was back . . .

Those times, the intimacy of living in a town of less than eight thousand residents grew too great for a man as reserved as Rich. Then he considered moving elsewhere. Anywhere. Just someplace where his privacy wouldn't be threatened, where he could simply be the quiet guy who minded his business and bothered no one while no one bothered him.

But Mama was in Bellamy. Reenie was in Bellamy. Rich's roots and his heart were in Bellamy. He'd learned while at the University of Virginia that he belonged in these hills. They'd nurtured him through childhood and adolescence, and even as he'd relished every ounce of knowledge his college years had afforded him. He'd come home for good only hours after receiving his diploma.

He'd settled into the quiet existence of a country retailer, helping his father run Desmond's Country Store. When Dad died five years ago, it had been an easy decision to keep the place running.

Oh, he knew everyone in town wondered why he'd settled for so little. The neighbors had even questioned his parents' decision to fund his expensive education when all he'd ever done with his degree was store the diploma in his desk. But Rich had his reasons. Excellent ones. Especially now, when things were—

Briiiing!

He groaned. Was that Storey calling again? To badger him some more? Or was it someone about Mama's case?

Reluctant to go another round with his agent, he stared at the phone as it gave another peal, but then common sense won out. It could be Percy Baker or Wiggon or Mama herself.

"Hello," he said with trepidation.

"So, Des. You seen reason yet?" asked the New York voice.

He should have let the phone ring off the hook. If he hadn't picked up, though, Storey would have had another excuse to lecture him on what he termed the absurdity of Rich's refusal to use an answering machine. But answering machines weren't for him.

"I've seen reason all along." He prayed for patience and strength. "And Des is just a pseudonym that makes you lots of money. I'm real—Rich Desmond is real. Please use my name."

"Sure you're real. And that's another thing. All that reclusive artist stuff's a bunch of—" Storey caught himself— "hooey."

Rich smiled. At least something he'd told the man had sunk in. Foul language made Rich uncomfortable, and during the early years he'd asked his agent—time after time—to refrain from using it when they spoke.

Hmm . . . maybe repetition was the way to reach the guy. "No, Storey, it's not hooey to me. I've explained my reasons for my anonymity, and they haven't changed."

"Yeah, yeah." Rich pictured the rotund gent at the window of his cluttered office, cordless phone glued to his ear, wiry gray hair tufting around the device. "I know about your religion and all. But your public, Des—"

"Rich."

"Yeah. Rich, your public is dying to meet the guy with the brain. You've touched them; you've reached them with your work."

"As I've said before, I haven't touched them, but God through me has touched them. And that's how it's going to stay. I don't want the glory that belongs to the heavenly Father."

Muffled mutters struck Rich's ear. He moved the receiver a foot away. "I'm no longer listening."

"Sorry, sorry, but you know I don't buy your argument. Anyway, about this new contract. There's nothing so bad about it."

"There's plenty bad about it. I've told you many times that the project the powers-that-be want conflicts with my conscience and my faith in Christ. I've asked you to tell them that from the start."

"I told them, I told them. They think you're too uptight. It's not as if they want you to reject your religion or anything."

"No, but they want me to add occult-flavored horror, violence and gore, plus graphic, gratuitous sex to my stories. That's not what I do. Mystery is my medium. Remember, you're the one who said my cerebral, intricate plots are what keep everyone guessing until the end, then coming back for more."

"But a little horror, a little slashing, a bit of titillation will get you more fans."

"It will also 'get' my conscience. Dabbling in the occult is forbidden by God, horror and violence are abhorrent to him, and sex is holy and to be kept private. It's not to be flaunted for its prurient effect on the public."

"But—"

"No. I won't do it."

"Then you might just be kissing the contract good-bye."

"So be it."

"Whatcha going to live on?"

"God will provide." Rich rejected the pang of apprehension that shot through him in light of this morning's events.

"I sure hope so, because I can't guarantee you this sale."

"I haven't asked for any guarantees. I gratefully consider the offers you bring me."

"I may not be bringing you another one for a while."

"As I said, so be it."

"You're nuts. Think about it some more. You've got to see reason sooner or later."

"It doesn't matter how long I think about it, Storey. My answer will remain the same. Take care, now."

Rich hung up, then unplugged the phone and collapsed onto his leather recliner. Each bout with Storey drained him. He'd thought of finding a new agent, but loyalty held him back. Storey had hung in there with him during Rich's slow beginnings. He also was considered the best there was.

But Storey was also as high energy as they came, exhausting even at the best of times. And today Rich had started with an energy deficit. The episode at the police station had taken its toll.

The news of his mother's arrest had shaken him. Then the enormity of the charges against her had alarmed him. Finally, hearing Lark voice his greatest fear had shredded his nerves.

She was after him. Not only was Lark snoopy and curious, but she'd also been blessed with a bloodhound's accurate nose—its tenacity, too. She'd always been a force to reckon with. Now she'd decided to go gunning for Des Richter, Rich's literary alter ego.

He feared that, like her unwanted pup, Lark would sniff out the trail that led to him and bring his house of cards down around his ears.

THREE

AFTER STUFFY MR. BAKER AND THE EVEN-STUFFIER RICH led Miss Mariah away from the police station, leaving her and the mutt behind, Lark went home.

Who did that turkey think he was? And how could two siblings turn out so totally different? Reenie was human. Rich wasn't. But he sure was attractive and intriguing, if infuriating.

Lark had stared like a starstruck teen when they'd come face-to-face at the police station. She could hardly believe what stood before her eyes. Rich was still the boy she'd loved in third grade, and at the same time, he wasn't.

Back home in her living room, Lark dropped onto the couch. She propped her feet over one arm, stuffed the loose pillows under her aching head, and held tight to the dog's leash.

The image of Rich remained fixed in her thoughts.

In the years since she'd left her Blue Ridge hometown, Rich had matured, become a man. He'd broadened even since she saw him at his father's funeral five years ago. He now looked like a younger version of Mr. Desmond. He wore his dark blond hair thick and straight, in that same short style his father had favored—classic, well groomed, clean-cut.

His eyes, though, as always, hinted at secrets that called Lark to explore them, awakening the sharpest curiosity she'd ever known. What went on behind those gray orbs? What kinds of thoughts kept Rich so serious, so uptight, so . . . reserved?

The older boy had always fascinated Lark, and from her first visit to Reenie's home, she'd known he was special. To her, if not to everyone else.

He'd seemed so wise to her young mind, involved in school activities, working with his father at the store. Rich had paid no mind to the two girls, but Lark's attention had rarely strayed from him.

Everyone had noticed. Everyone.

She could still relive the merciless teasing she'd endured when, as a budding adolescent, she'd worn her tender heart on her sleeve.

But no more. Lark Bellamy was a different person now. A woman. She was no longer the girl who'd mooned after Rich Desmond all her life. She was no longer the "odd" Bellamy Blossom. She was no longer the girl who'd been voted "Most Likely to . . . What?"

Lark had become a career woman, an acclaimed journalist, and a businesswoman. She was now the editor in chief and owner—not to mention chief cook and bottle washer—of what would soon become *the* lit-crit magazine in the U.S. She would get that exclusive interview with Des Richter.

But how?

Her bravado deflated when she realized she hadn't a clue. But she knew she'd come up with something between this issue she'd just finished and oh, say . . . the next ten thousand. And she'd do it before anyone beat her to it.

She sat up tall. "Not for nothing did they call me Scoop at the *Sun*," she informed the dog, who stared morosely at her. Or at least that's what the animal's expression seemed to say. The creature gave a mournful howl, then dropped its muzzle back on its paws.

A knock at the kitchen door interrupted the canine/human noncommunication, and Lark perked up. Maybe her visitor would want a dog. Free.

As she turned the knob, the door flew inward. Lark leaped aside to avoid getting squashed. Reenie raced in, as usual, speaking a mile a minute.

"Tell me everythin' that happened at the PD, Larkspur Bellamy. I cain't believe that brother of mine made the police chief make me promise not to go to the station. She's my mama, too! An' here I don't know what's happenin' to 'er." She pressed Lark onto the living-room sofa, then sat at her side. "But I know you'll tell me everythin'. Y'always have."

"When I had something to tell."

Reenie tapped her toe against the polished oak floor. "Now what does that mean?"

The dog's long ears twitched, its right eye opened, and its nose wiggled. Then it wailed.

Reenie squeaked, "What was *that?*"

Lark pointed.

"Oh, what a darlin' little pup!" Rushing to the creature's side, Reenie knelt to pet him. "An' why didn't you tell me you'd gotten a dog?"

"Because I haven't."

"He's here, isn't he?"

"Oh, yeah. He's here, all right. And at the PD, too."

"Why'd you take 'im with you?"

"Because I didn't know what else to do with him after he . . . um . . . messed on the floor, is why."

"Oh, no! Your granny's beautiful floor!"

Lark nodded, then shrugged. "I cleaned it up, but you can see why I couldn't leave that beast here alone. Who knows which of Granny's treasures he'd have attacked next. As it is, I owe Rich a new pair of shoes."

"Rich?" Reenie paused in her play with the dog. "Shoes?"

Lark regretted her slip of the tongue. She didn't want to remember the episode in question, much less recount it. But she knew Maureen Desmond Ainsley well enough.

"That 'darlin' little pup' ate one of your brother's shoes while we were at the station. Rich was no happier to see me now than back when we were kids. And it wasn't even my fault this time."

"Well, you did take the dog inside the police station."

"Yeah, but I never wanted a dog. I didn't buy myself a dog. I just got stuck with a dog."

"Huh?"

Why did these things keep happening to her? "Maggie showed up this morning and dumped the thing in my lap. So now I don't know what to do with it."

"Why, you just feed 'im an' walk 'im an' love 'im, is all. There's nothin' to it, Lark. You'll see."

"I'm too busy, and you know it, Reenie Ainsley. I have my magazine to work on, I have to find that mysterious mystery writer, Des Richter, and I have to make sure your mother doesn't wind up behind bars for life."

Reenie's gray eyes, identical to Rich's, widened. "No! Oh, no, no! We cain't let Mama die in jail. We cain't even let her go back for a minute. Who knows what might happen to her? You hear the worst stories about prison life. My mama wouldn't survive that. An' I need her. Especially now."

"Now?"

Her friend blushed. "I just found out for sure right before I came over. I'm pregnant, an' my baby needs its granny to cuddle it once it's born. You have to find out what's goin' on,

Lark. What's *really* goin' on. You know an' I know Mama didn't do any of those things they're sayin' she did."

A strange feeling crossed Lark's heart at Reenie's announcement, but she couldn't quite place the emotion. "Congratulations. I knew you and Seth wanted a family. And you're right about your mother. I know Miss Mariah's no racketeer. Somehow, I'm going to prove it."

"Maybe that's a better case for you to work on than chasin' after that playwright. I mean, you know Mama, an' you want to help her, but you don't even know who Des Richter is."

Lark narrowed her gaze. "Oh, I'm going to get to the bottom of these accusations against your mother, all right, but I'm also going to find Des Richter. And I'm going to publish that interview, too."

She had to. She had to clear Miss Mariah's name, and she had to make her magazine a success. She had to prove to everyone in Bellamy they'd done her wrong by mocking her as they had while she was growing up.

She'd worked too hard for too long to fail now.

After Lark had calmed Reenie, the two friends decided the puppy's downcast mood would probably improve if they fed the poor thing.

Lark donned her Birkenstock sandals again. "Isn't this just like Maggie?" she asked rhetorically. "My sister hasn't a practical hair on her blond head. When she catches a notion between her brows, she just dashes ahead without thinking about the repercussions or permutations."

"There you go again, talkin' in five-dollar words. You're so much like Rich, I cain't figure why the two of you haven't made a match of it yet."

"You bite your tongue, Maureen Desmond Ainsley. I don't

even want to remember what a fool I was when I was young."
Taking the dog's leash in her right hand, Lark opened the
door, ushered Reenie outside, then locked up behind them.

"Like you're so old now, Methuselah." Reenie's gray eyes
danced with mischief. "I still think the two of you were made
for each other. An' maybe, just maybe, that's why neither one
of you has married durin' all these years."

"I'll have you know I haven't married because I've been
focused on my career. I haven't had the time and energy to
waste in looking for a man. Besides, who says a woman needs
a man? I'm sufficient unto myself, just as I am."

"Just you wait, Lark. Some guy's gonna come along an'
knock you straight for a loop. I'm willin' to bet that guy's
gonna be my big brother."

Lark's insides cringed as she remembered the times a friend,
a neighbor, the class tease had taunted her about her innocent
feelings for Rich. "Never, you hear? Not in a million years."

Reenie chortled. "God works in mysterious ways, you
know. Every time you an' Rich come within miles of each
other, why, sparks worthy of a lightnin' storm singe the air. I
cain't wait to see what's gonna happen now that you're back
in town."

"Nothing," Lark muttered, briefly regretting her decision
to come home, despite her youngest sister Cammie's unexpected widowhood and pregnancy, and Maggie's propensity
for blundering headlong into trouble. Since she could
produce her magazine anywhere, the decision had been
simple. Now she questioned her actions.

"Nothing," she said again, this time with extra starch.
"Absolutely nothing's going to happen between your brother
and me."

"Yoo-hoo! Lark, Reenie. Mornin', girls," called Miss
Louella Ashworth as she approached down Main Street.

Groan. If her mind hadn't been on that miserable man,

Lark would surely have noticed—and avoided—the older woman. Miss Louella was Bellamy's most notorious Cupid, and she'd had her eye on Lark and Rich for years.

"Hi, Miss Louella," Lark said, quickening her pace.

"Hey, there," added Reenie, slowing to chat.

"Lovely summer day the Lord's given us, don't you think?" asked the older woman.

Lark stepped away from the other two. "Mm-hmm."

"Well, I wouldn't say that," countered Reenie, planting her heels for a long chat. "Why, Mama's been accused of all kinds of horrid things, Miss Louella. An' none of them are true. None. You know Mama."

"I heard, and yes, honey, I do know my dear housemate. So what are we doin' about this fine mess?" A canny smile curved her lips. "You all know I have not only knowledge but also experience with investigations. . . ."

Fear tightened Lark's middle. Miss Louella was fond of a fictional secret agent named Marvin Pinkney and had recently landed herself—not to mention Maggie—in trouble due to her interest in the 007 clone's methods. The last thing Miss Mariah needed was Miss Louella's "help."

Lark gave an arch wave. "You needn't worry. Everything's under control. Miss Mariah has Percy Baker to handle legal matters, and I'm investigating what's behind that false arrest."

Miss Louella's laser gaze raked Lark's face. "Will you be workin' with our dear Richie?"

"No way. I work alone. Always have, always will. I don't need anyone's help."

Miss Louella's well-preserved features turned sad. "Now, honey, don't you go makin' that mistake. The dear Lord put us all on earth to help each other. Life is mighty empty if you insist on livin' all by your lonesome."

"I'm fine," Lark said, "and not lonely. I'm too busy to be lonely. In fact, maybe you could help me. Want a dog?"

Miss Louella looked startled. "A dog? Me? Whatever for?"

"Well, you're alone. . . . "

"Nonsense. I'm not alone. I have the Lord with me at all times, and besides, didn't you know? Now that the Ashworth Mansion's well on its way to becoming our town's Historical Society Museum, Mariah, Sophie Hardesty, and I have rented the Hormel's nice little colonial down on Maplewood Drive, seein' as they built that big place outside of town. We're havin' more fun than a litter of puppies. You're the one who needs the dog."

As Lark sputtered her objection, she caught a familiar, speculative spark in Miss Louella's eyes. "Time to go," Lark said. "We need puppy chow. See you soon, Miss Louella."

"Of course, honey," said the older woman. "As I'm sure you'll be seein' Richie, too. I heard all about your . . . encounter at the police station. I think it's so excitin' that even after all this time, the zing is still there."

Lark grimaced and tugged on Reenie's arm. Her friend refused to cooperate.

"Do tell, Miss Louella," said the female Benedict Arnold with a glare for Lark. "My best friend here was awful stingy on details."

"Well, sugar, it's just like I've always said," Miss Louella started. "Put your brother and Lark in the same town, and things get downright hot straightaway." The scamp gave a wink. "Whooee! Did things ever sizzle downtown today. We could've warmed the town during all February with the sparks these two set off. Seems to me, life is sure to get mighty interestin' in Bellamy now. Just hold on to your hat, and watch the fireworks show."

Mortification blazed through Lark hotter than any confrontation between her and Rich Desmond, more searing than the fieriest of pyrotechnics, more tormenting than the worst memories of her youth.

Reenie cheered.

The traitor.

As Lark started to refute Miss Louella's words, the hopeless romantic continued. "After all, girls," she said, while Lark wished the sidewalk would open before anything more was voiced. But she had no such luck. Nothing ever stopped Louella Ashworth, president of the ever-present, ever-curious, ever-nosy Bellamy Garden Club. "Lark didn't nab herself a foreign husband out there, so what could be better for her than a homegrown boy?"

Without waiting for an answer, Miss Louella added, "Why, Bellamy's single most eligible bachelor."

Reenie crowed. "I told you, Lark. Didn't I just finish tellin' you? Everyone knows what's what. You an' Rich are made for each other. Just watch. You'll see. Life's sure gonna be fun now that we're gonna be sisters soon enough."

"Wait!" Lark cried. "That's never going to happen—"

"Hear, hear," said Sophie Hardesty, appearing as if from nowhere.

"Oh, yes," sibilated Philadelphia Philpott, a chronic whisperer who always overdressed—in multiple layers of garments, not in glamour and elegance—as she sidled up to Miss Louella. "True love always wins out."

Joining the group, Sarah Langhorn sighed. "Like Tristram and Isolde, Cleopatra and Mark Anthony, Lancelot and Guinevere, Romeo and Juliet."

"Yeah, right," Lark countered. "More like the Roadrunner and Wile E. Coyote."

Would Miss Louella run true to form? Had she really set her mind on striking a match between Rich and Lark? After all, the woman claimed credit for Maggie's romance and upcoming marriage, one Lark wondered about. Her sister's fiancé was an ex-con, and thanks to Miss Louella, even Maggie had landed in jail.

If the woman turned her doubtful talents on Lark, what disaster would visit *her*? What new mess would she have to mop up?

Especially since she'd come home to take on Cammie's predicament, only to find her other sister in as terrible a bind. Would Lark have yet another calamity to clean up? One of her own? Involving Rich?

She hoped not from the very bottom of her leery heart.

By the time he got home from the disaster at the PD, Rich didn't have the motivation to do more than slap two slices of bologna between Wonder bread and call it lunch. He munched away, his mind on weightier matters.

Percy Baker didn't exhibit much along the lines of feelings. Sure, he was pompous; but as far as reading the guy's opinions, Rich might as well stare at the Sphinx.

While he had this free moment, he should probably check in with Mama's operations manager. He dialed the familiar number. After three rings, Frank Vallore picked up.

"Dream Squeeze Distributors. May I help you?"

"Hey, Frank. It's Rich Desmond. I suppose you've heard—"

"Heard! I was here last night when the Secret Service raided us. Kept me until 4 A.M. answering their questions and digging up documents for them. How's your mother?"

Rich rubbed his temples. "Oh, you know Mama. She's spent the morning quoting Scripture. Now you and I know she'll eventually be proven innocent, but no one seems to be able to impress upon her the seriousness of her situation."

"Sounds like the lady. Did you just call to tell me the news?"

"'Fraid not. I have some questions for you."

"Shoot."

"Do you know what kind of evidence the authorities have against Mama? Or even what she could have done to make them suspect her? arrest her?"

"I'm not sure, but they took copies of a bunch of our records. And they talked about some heavy-duty thief she does business with."

"That's it?"

"Mm-hmm."

"So how am I going to prove she didn't do whatever they seem so sure she did?"

"Beats me. But listen, Rich. You just worry about helping Mariah through these stupid accusations. I've got the company under control. I'll take care of everything here."

"Thanks, Frank, I appreciate your commitment. I guess we'll be talking again soon."

"No problem. And take care, OK?"

Sure, Rich would take care of himself—and his mother. But as he washed down his last bite with a glass of milk, he faced a painful reality: he had no idea how to go about helping her.

True, he'd become a whiz at research—as long as the information could be found in a library or on the Web. He'd done his share of interviews, but those had been to learn about specific careers, mechanical or scientific data, locations, customs.

How was he going to excavate clues? How was a playwright and small-town shopkeeper going to coax germane details from crooks or witnesses? Especially if he had to deal with organized crime, notorious for their cohesiveness.

More to the point, how was he going to do all this while keeping professional newshound Lark at bay?

He closed his eyes and ran rough fingers through his hair. One thing he knew: he couldn't count on Reenie for help . . . for *anything*. He loved his younger sister, but he knew her shortcomings only too well. Mama didn't need the combustible combination of Lark and Reenie at this time.

So what was he going to do?

Rich went to the sink, washed his milk glass, and tossed the napkin that had served as a plate into the trash. Glancing out the window, he groaned. As she'd done for decades, Reenie dashed up the Bellamy walk, darted around the far side of the big white house next door, and didn't return. Dread joined the sandwich in his gut.

Trouble was brewing. At least he knew it was coming. He went to his computer, set up in what had once been the dining-room bay, and turned it on. He hoped his years of experience dodging Lark's and Reenie's loony behavior would hold him in good stead now.

His mother needed him.

His mind a million miles away from the Alaskan setting of his work-in-progress, Rich absently scrolled down to the end of the last scene he'd written. A sense of futility swamped him. Why bother writing any more when he doubted Storey and the higher-ups would accept the project as he intended to write it?

He skimmed the page and eventually caught the excitement of the tale. This was why he wrote—not to rake in zillions of dollars, not for the acclaim so many pursued to the detriment of every other aspect of their lives. He wrote for the joy of collaborating with God to produce something that entertained, challenged, perhaps even taught. That was what he loved about his occasionally burdensome gift.

"Lord," he asked, "am I right? Or am I overzealous, as Storey says? You know I don't want to push anyone toward baser responses with my work. Violence exists, and I know it, but do I need to give it play to achieve my goals for my audience? And what about the sex bit?"

Rich sat in silence, love for the Lord foremost in his mind.

He sought only to honor the Savior and knew he had to stand firm. But if he did, would he simply disappear from the public's awareness and lose whatever value he brought them through his work?

"Is that what you want, Father?"

Then there was his anonymity. Rich wanted all the glory to be for God, not for him. He wasn't the one who created the tales; he only wrote what the heavenly Father inspired him to tell. He didn't want to claim kudos for the work; it was God's workmanship. Rich wasn't a self-centered, proud man.

"What do you want from me, God? How do you want me to proceed?" In the ensuing silence, Rich concluded that God wasn't speaking at the moment.

The unfinished play encouraged him to keep writing. So he asked for the Holy Spirit's guidance, as he always did before even keying a letter. Then he lost himself in the joy of his art.

As the afternoon wore on, Rich typed furiously, producing a prodigious amount of rough material. Finally, at half past four, the scene in his head had flowed onto the screen, his fingers had cried uncle, and he'd realized he had to show up at the store, if nothing else, to close the place.

He'd called Sophie Hardesty, the Country Store's manager and Mariah's housemate, from the police station. He'd asked the dear but dotty lady if she'd cover for him that afternoon, since he doubted he'd make it in. Mrs. Hardesty, a surprisingly sharp saleswoman and organizer, had of course agreed. But if he didn't wander in before five, she'd likely flutter off in a dither, fearing the worst had happened to Mariah. Rich sighed at the thought of having to keep another zany female on an even keel.

He saved and backed up his afternoon's work, turned off the computer, and locked up the house. He debated whether to drive or walk downtown, but the summer afternoon was so spectacular—bright and clear and fragranced with roses, carnations, sweet peas, and other blooms—that he opted to walk.

Bad move.

No sooner had Rich stepped onto the sidewalk than a brown missile dragging its carrottopped cargo at the speed of light rushed past him. It zipped straight to the bed of marigolds Mama and Reenie had planted for him that spring and deposited an odoriferous "present" in the blossoms' midst.

As Lark panted and Rich counted to a jillion, the pup finished its production and began sniffing the flowers. Apparently it took a shine to—or offense at—a particularly full clump of dark gold blooms, and, with a single tug, uprooted the plant.

Forget counting. "Would you do something about that beast?"

"What exactly would His Nibs want me to do?"

"Scoop the poop, for starters." He watched the canine pluck every petal. "Then replace the plant. Oh, and a new pair of shoes would be nice."

Fiery red rushed up her fair cheeks as Lark studied him, then the dog. She thrust the leash at Rich. "Here. Take the dog in trade. Value for value, I'd say."

Too stunned to do anything but grab the leash, Rich caught the gleam of devilry in her gaze as she spun and trotted toward her home.

He took off after the gleeful escapee. "No dice. The pooch is *yours,* Lark. A bona fide menace, just like his owner, and not something I care to mess with."

She spun around and glared at him. "Now you know how I feel. Maggie showed up this morning and dumped the critter in my lap. I never wanted a dog; I never needed one. So show the world you have a heart and take it."

Rich reached out for her hand. He tugged it up despite her resistance, pried her fingers open, and wrapped the leather strap around them. "Yours, you hear? So take responsibility for your pet. And keep him out of my life." *Yourself, too.*

Disdain curled her lip. "Sure, Rich. I'll take the dog. And you can go back to living your secluded, superior life. I wouldn't dream of making the haughty and imperious Mr. Desmond dirty his hands with something as humanly normal as cleaning up after a dog. You're much better, loftier than the rest of us folks."

Lark stalked toward her house—her head of dark red curls bouncing, the dog trotting at her heels—leaving Rich with an open mouth and a host of troubling thoughts in his head.

She couldn't be right. Could she? Then why had she voiced the same things Storey had brought up a time or two?

Rich wasn't a proud man. Was he? He was a Christian. Pride was a sin.

And Lark was just nuts. Wasn't she?

Shaking his head, Rich took off toward the store. One thing had become perfectly clear during that little tussle. He had to steer clear of Lark Bellamy. And not because of her troublemaking dog, either.

Lark's imagination was working overtime, as her accusation showed. Rich couldn't afford to lose his focus. He couldn't let her shake him from his path. He knew himself. He knew where he was going.

He stumbled.

He *did* know where he was going.

Didn't he?

FOUR

THE INSISTENT RING OF THE PHONE FORCED LARK TO DRAG her head out of the fridge and glare at the beckoning slave master. What would it be? Phone? Food?

With all that had happened today, she'd forgotten that marvelous thing called lunch. Now her stomach was berating her for her inattention. But the phone's persistence beat out her growling guts. "Hello?"

"Oh, Lark, I'm happy as a puppy gnawin' on a bone to find you home. You won't believe what's happened."

Lark dropped into a maple kitchen chair. She wasn't ready for another of Maggie's onslaughts on this, the longest day she'd ever lived. "Try me."

"It'll be kinda nice. We'll get to be a cozy pair of peas in a pod, you and me. It'll give us that chance I've been prayin' for to get closer'n a shadow."

This time, Lark couldn't ascribe her confusion to anything else. Maggie was its source, and the non-hunger wriggle in Lark's middle told her the news wouldn't strike her as "kinda nice."

"Back up, Mags. I don't know what you're rambling about."

"I'll have you know, Larkspur Bellamy, I do not ramble. What part of this conversation do you not understand?"

Taking the receiver from her ear, Lark shook it, scowled at it, then listened again. Deafening silence came from her mind-boggling sister. "Try all of it."

"You just aren't payin' no never-mind to what I'm sayin' to you. Like always."

Lark glanced out the blue-gingham-curtained window over the sink at the elm tree she'd considered her private domain while growing up. She cared for her sister, and concern for Maggie was one of the reasons Lark had returned to Bellamy in the first place, but this middle Bellamy Blossom tried her patience sometimes and confounded her all others.

"OK," Lark said, conceding the point in the interest of expedience. "Let's say you start at the beginning and tell me again—and don't leave out a *thing*. This time I promise I'll pay utmost attention."

"Why, it's just as I said. The apartment buildin's goin' condo, and it makes no good sense for me to move to a motel a country mile away from town for the few days till my weddin'. Not with you just rattlin' around in Granny Iris's house like a snake's ol' tail all by your lonesome."

"Now wait a minute—"

"Didn't you just say you'd listen to me?"

"Yes, but—"

"Why, then, hold your horses while I beat around this bush and make my point."

"Which is?"

"Why, that Buford and I'll be movin' in with you until the weddin'."

"But—"

"It'll be more fun'n a barrel of monkeys, the two of us—

well, the four of us, when we count our little loves. Just think, we can share all the things we've been too busy to discuss. You know, just be sisters."

Sisters. That should be interesting.

If it worked.

Which Lark doubted . . . yet wished it could.

Suddenly the wedding she'd worried about seemed more desirable. A lot more desirable. And the ex-con fiancé looked more like a lifesaver than a prescience of doom.

"I work here, Mags," she said. "One dog's too much for me to handle, never mind two in the house at one time. It's not as if you can help, either. You leave early for Clay's office, and then what? I'm stuck."

"Oh, fiddle-faddle. It won't be a spit of trouble, Lark. I'll just keep bringin' Buford to work with me. That'll give you and . . . what did you name him, anyway?"

Now Lark knew for sure the noisy creature was a male. "I haven't."

"What do you mean, you haven't? D'you just call him 'Hey you!'? Why, that's pathetic. My goodness, surely a reporter can do better'n that!"

"But I don't know this animal, Maggie." Lark's words sounded lame even to her, so she went on the offensive. "Besides, you're the one who got him in the first place. Did I ask for a dog?"

"No, but—"

"Did you check to see if I wanted a dog?"

"No. But—"

"And did it occur to you I might absolutely despise dogs?"

A gasp. "You don't . . . do you?"

Lark sighed in exasperation. "Of course not. I just don't need a dog right now."

"But, Lark, you're all alone in that big house, without a soul around you. And I remember when I didn't have my

Buford or Clay; why, it was downright depressin'. I'd hate for you to be all lonely like that."

A strange pang zipped through Lark, but she forced herself to ignore it. She could only handle Maggie at the moment.

"I like being alone," she said. "I need to be alone to concentrate on my reviews, coordinate the stories my contributors submit, consider the advertisers I'm willing to work with. I can't be mopping up accidents all the time."

Maggie's chuckle made Lark wonder about her sister's sanity. "What a relief, then," the middle Blossom said. "That won't be a problem. He's housebroken, you know."

"Wanna make a bet?"

"You mean he . . . ?"

"Yep. On Granny Iris's oak floor. Right at the front door, too."

"Oh, dear."

Lark thought she heard the gears in Maggie's guileless mind grind away. Hoping to derail her sister's sales pitch, she said, "Well, I gotta go—"

"You know, Lark, it's like with the bathwater," Maggie said, imparting her own brand of wacky wisdom. "No one dumps a baby just because it soils its diapers, right?"

"Yeah, but—"

"There you have it. You can't get rid of your puppy just because he messed—it was a mistake, I'm sure, and he's surely sorry for it. It's only right to forgive a repentant sinner."

Again, Lark shook the receiver, then stared at the collage of family pictures on the far kitchen wall. Ordinary gene pools like those of her mother and father couldn't possibly produce such diametrically different offspring. Maggie had to be an alien changeling.

The chatter continued on the other end of the connection and, remembering her promise to her sister, Lark brought the earpiece back to her ear. To her regret.

". . . so I'll be movin' most of my things into Clay's new place little by little. And I'll bring my regular day-to-day stuff over to Granny's house—"

"But—"

"Oh, I can't wait for us to get to know each other better. It's what I've wanted for longer'n Miss Louella's memory."

"B—but—"

"God's hand is all over this one. It's surely the answer to my prayers."

"But . . . but—"

Maggie's disconnecting click cut off Lark's objections.

An explosive bang jolted Lark out of a blissful—and mercifully dreamless—sleep the next morning. The critter at the foot of her bed let go one of his astounding, mournful yowls.

Lark glanced at her bedside clock. Six-forty-four. What was happening at such an inhuman hour of the night—and after a torturous day?

A loud thump shook the house.

Burglars.

Lark was alone. *Uh-oh.*

Wishing she had the phone book nearby, or at least the PD's number memorized, she dialed Myrna Stafford, Bellamy's gossip par excellence and closest equivalent to the big-city 911, on her nightstand phone. The widow had always been Scoop Bellamy's most reliable source.

"It's Lark Bellamy," she whispered when Myrna answered. "Call Wiggon. I don't have his phone number, and someone's broken into my house."

Myrna began firing questions. Lark murmured answers and prepared herself for what might happen next.

With her free hand, she tugged down her gargantuan,

faded-to-delicious-comfort, knee-length Penn State sweatshirt with ripped-out sleeves, then grabbed the baseball bat with which she'd won the Bellamy Bantams' division title game her senior year in high school. Thieves grew more outrageous each day. This bunch wasn't even trying for surreptitiousness.

"What do you mean, how do I know it's burglars?" she asked Myrna, bat in one hand, cordless phone in the other. "Someone's crashing and banging around Granny's house before the McAvity's rooster's even crowed."

"All my chickens are flutterin' around the yard an' have eaten awhile back, I'll have you know," countered Myrna, then resumed her barrage of queries.

As Lark opened her bedroom door, the dog darted out before her. Fear for his safety twisted her middle. "Hey, you. Get back here. It's not safe out there. . . ."

Lark's admonition trailed off as the pooch raced down the stairs with more verve than he'd ever displayed and with which he'd made her night a misery.

Myrna's questions sharpened.

A scraping sound from the rear of the house tightened the knot of apprehension in Lark's belly. "Would you please hang up and call Wiggon, the chief, the volunteer firemen— anyone who can help me?"

"My, my," Myrna chided. "Aren't we testy this mornin'?"

To Lark's bewilderment, the galloping dog produced no sound beyond the clacking of his nails against polished hard-wood floors. Figures. When she needed him to howl, he didn't. Ah, but when she needed silence . . .

"You'd be testy, too," she said to Myrna. "I collapsed in bed at nine-thirty. By midnight, this pup—"

Myrna needed to know about the dog. Lark offered a pinky-nail sketch of yesterday's events. Then Myrna asked for more details.

"Well, he yowled and scratched for release from his prison

in the upstairs bathroom—ceramic-tile floor. Sucker that I am, I took pity on him. To my regret. By quarter to two, he'd jabbed his icy nose under the covers and zapped me awake to demand room on my bed. At two-thirty, he progressed to sharing my pillow—doggy-biscuit breath is less than appealing. I shoved him toward my feet and dropped off again. But at three-twenty-seven, he wailed at the door. Tinkle time. Then, at five-o-three, the squirrel who lives in the elm came to visit its favorite windowsill and turned the bowwow into a baying beast. As far as I can tell, that squirrel's life isn't worth the proverbial plugged nickel if the two animals ever come within chomping distance."

As Lark came to the end of her blithering discourse, she realized she was more frightened than she wanted to admit. She'd been babbling at Myrna to feel less alone in the scary situation.

But she had intruders in Granny Iris's house. And the dog remained perversely silent.

"Mrs. Stafford," she said, nerves shrilling her voice, "it's been nice talking to you, but I really need help. Since I've just come back to town, I don't remember many phone numbers, so call Wiggon or the chief. Please, please help me."

Punching the off button before Myrna could ask another thing, Lark flung the instrument onto her bed and fought the tremor in her hands. She strained to catch the sound of a siren.

And heard none—too soon, of course. She counted to twenty. No siren. Yet.

But a creaking floorboard in the foyer sent her heartbeat into overdrive.

Had Myrna fallen down—for the first time ever—in her mission to spread every drop of news to every soul in Bellamy in as little time as possible? Was she merely gossiping? Had she called for help? Where was Wiggon?

No matter. Lark couldn't afford to wait. Granny Iris's antiques had to be protected, regardless of how scared she was. As the oldest Blossom, she had to take charge of the situation. Fear had no place in her life. She could handle this; she could handle anything.

Tiptoeing down the stairs, the blood pounding so loudly in her ears it nearly drowned out the intruders' noise, Lark forced herself to face whatever awaited her.

She hefted the bat high over her shoulder, ready to crash it down on the first offending head she met, and stepped onto the foyer floor. At that second, the front door swung open and Rich Desmond strolled in. As if he owned the place.

Lark had to forcibly restrain herself from following through on her batting instinct at the sight of her nemesis. "What . . . are you doing here?" she asked, her voice embarrassingly high.

"Scared you, did we?"

Lark cursed the blush that blazed up to her hairline. "Not at all. Just taking sensible precautions. A woman alone never knows what kind of lowlife might saunter in and take advantage of her."

His silver eyes twinkled.

She narrowed her gaze. "Don't think you're so sharp, buster. You can't divert my attention from my question with one of your own silly queries. I asked what you were doing here at such a ridiculous hour of the day, and I expect an answer."

In response, he hefted higher the pair of suitcases he carried.

Lark wished she functioned better in the morning. "Pink luggage? And why are you bringing it here?" she asked, wondering if Rich's mind had some heretofore unnoticed deficiency.

"Larkspur Bellamy," called a reproving female voice, "you're a mess."

Lark closed her eyes. It was too early to deal with Maggie. Then she remembered an alarming detail. She pried open one eye and spotted a box-laden Clay Marlowe, her sister's intended, grinning as goofily as Rich from over Maggie's shoulder.

"You're . . . moving in . . ." she concluded weakly.

"Why, of course I am. I told you so yesterday. Run upstairs and do somethin' for yourself."

The reason for Rich's and Clay's amusement dawned on Lark. She loved this particular sweatshirt because of the myriad washings it had undergone in its long lifetime. Its color had once been a rich navy blue but now hovered somewhere around an ashy indigo. And she knew what her hair looked like when she crawled out of bed—or was unpleasantly forced out, as the case might be.

She tipped her chin. "Don't you think you could have warned me of your imminent invasion?"

Maggie's jaw dropped. "What do you think my call yesterday was all about?"

Lark cranked her chin a notch higher. "You said nothing about this morning."

Planting small fists on the hips of her fashion-right, plum rose, linen suit, Maggie radiated impatience. "Did you think I'd dillydally around until the new owners of my apartment shoved me out in the street?"

"No, but letting me in on the secret of your moving date would have helped."

"What secret?"

"That I had to rise with the chickens after being up all night with that . . . that dog-fiend you foisted on me."

A choked bleat caught Lark's attention. Rich's cheeks glowed scarlet from his obvious effort to avoid laughing.

"Ladies," he managed to murmur, then lost the battle and

howled with mirth. Which, of course, set off the furry howler again—now that there was no danger.

The pounding in Lark's temple grew intolerable.

Anything that involved Maggie was maddening by nature; adding Rich to the mix was insanity-affirming. And much too much for this early hour.

"I'm outta here," she said and headed back up the stairs. "You guys do what you have to do."

"Hey, Red," called Rich, inciting Lark to mutiny. "You're awfully cute in the morning."

At her glare, he chuckled some more. "No, really. You're the only woman I know who does great things for an ancient Penn State rag. And don't let anyone tell you otherwise."

Lark growled in response to the masculine laughter—and the feminine titter accompanying it. Slamming the door to her room behind her, she stalked to her dresser to assess the damages in the mirror. Then she howled loud enough to match her dog. And Rich.

She grabbed the wildly boinging mahogany corkscrews at her temples, yanked, and stared in dismay. With a little dirt and a cart of bizarre possessions, she could pass for one of Baltimore's bag ladies.

Why did Rich always have to catch her at a disadvantage? And why did it bother her so much, even after all these years?

After taking a flash shower, then running downstairs, water-darkened corkscrews dripping copiously, Lark had only enough time to wave good-bye to her invaders.

As she watched, Clay and Rich indulged in one of those male ceremonials she'd never really understood. At first, Maggie chattered and the two guys eyed each other, mistrust in the set of their broad shoulders, the jut of their jaws, the tilt of their heads. Then Maggie must have said something both liked, since they grinned and began the manly hand-shaking, followed by hugging, succeeded by the heavy back-slapping that always left Lark befuddled.

She hesitated in the doorway, trying to hear what they were discussing, but they'd reached the sidewalk—too far for her to catch more than the occasional chuckle.

Finally, she heard the siren as the patrol car approached. Oh no. No, no. She couldn't handle any more embarrassment before her morning ginseng tea.

Fortunately for her, the bosom buddies out front took care of Wiggon, their male chuckles impelling Lark to shut the door quickly.

Although Rich struck her these days as nearly too perfect, Lark knew he was honest and decent. Clay Marlowe . . . well, her jury was still out on him. Yet the way Rich had taken to her sister's future husband spoke well in Clay's favor. Rich was no fool, and Lark had never had reason to mistrust his instincts about people. Well, not about people in general. Just about her in particular.

At least his last glimpse of her this morning had been more acceptable than his first. Now she didn't look like a bag lady, just . . . drippy.

Which reminded her of the dog.

If she didn't do something about him—and soon—she'd be cleaning a less-fragrant drip than the shampoo-scented droplets dotting her forehead, cheeks, and shoulders.

"Hey, you!" she yelled, then bit her lip.

Maggie was right. Lark sounded pathetic calling the puppy that. What should she name him? She'd never named a dog before. But she'd heard a lot of stupid pet names.

As Lark hooked the leash to his collar, she studied the shorthaired brown dog. "Well, at least you're safe from the dreaded Fifi." She rolled her eyes, and he shook and sneezed.

"Plus, no one in her right mind would christen you Snowball."

As soon as she opened the door, the critter took off at a speedy gallop.

"Slow down!" she hollered, hoping not to trip over her own feet. "How about On-Dancer-on-Cupid-on-Prancer-on-Blitzen? You could pull Santa's sleigh—single-handedly."

Nose to the ground, the hound snuffled and trotted around the base of the shrubs that separated the Desmond property from the Bellamy's, evidently weighing the merits of various spots. Lark tried to summon the patience to watch the procedure, but noticed something far more intriguing in Rich's driveway.

"Would you look at that?" she asked the oblivious dog. "It's a brand-spanking-new white Jaguar. Too bad those temporary tags mar the sleek perfection of the vehicle's rear window." The sad condition of her little Escort inspired Lark's sarcasm.

From the driver's side of the killer car, a round little man with tufty, wiry hair disembarked, lovingly closed the door and, bulging briefcase in hand, climbed the porch steps.

"Hmm . . . even though his tie's askew," she told the heedless dog, "even from this distance, it looks like Italian silk, as does his wrinkled suit. What does that tell us about him?"

Calling on her reporter's powers of observation, she continued chatting with her canine companion. "He's distracted by something he considers even more important than his expensive wardrobe. And look at his shoes. I'm willing to bet you a case of Milky Way bars—I'd win them, too—that those shoes started life in the boot-shaped peninsula."

The puppy ignored her comments, having finally found an acceptable spot.

Lark stared at the man pounding on Rich's front door. In all, his ensemble could buy a replacement for her Escort, yet it unfortunately did nothing for his rumpled appearance. Something big was bugging him.

Who was he? What was he doing in Bellamy? Did he have business with Rich? What kind of business?

As the dog scraped his paws on the grass after finishing his deed, Lark tugged on the leash. "Now, listen, pooch. You're not going to make a peep, you hear? Something's cooking at Rich's, and after his and Clay's chummy hugs, I want to make sure it's all aboveboard."

Then she groaned—almost. She caught the sound as it made its way up her throat. Maggie was a menace. She even had Lark talking in clichés now.

But it was for Maggie's sake that Lark needed to check out her neighbor's visitor. What if . . . ?

"After all," she told the now-happy hound, "Rich's mama was just accused of racketeering. And although there's no chance that Miss Mariah's guilty, who's to say her son hasn't gone bad?"

The strange little fellow pushed his way past a clearly reluctant Rich. Lark then hurried to the sidewalk and rounded the hedge, canine at her heels. The solid young beast trotted along agreeably, his nose still glued to the grass.

She shook her head. "I can't figure out your fascination with the ground, dog. But I can't afford the time to think about you right now. Who knows what's going on inside the Desmond home?"

Hmm . . . Reenie might. If Lark didn't get enough info through snooping, then it was time to buy the future Ainsley heir a present and go visit its joy-filled pregnant mom.

"Yessss. We have a plan."

Watching for anything on the ground that might cause her to betray her presence on private property—like twigs, uncoiled hoses, rakes, anything that might make noise—Lark crept to the nearest living-room window.

"Rats." Her disappointment was acute. "I can't believe this, pooch. I can see the stranger's red face and waving arms—hey, and get a gander of Rich's oh-so-stoic and stubborn expression."

But try as she might, Lark couldn't catch a word they were saying. The hum of the central air just ten feet beyond her explained why.

"Bummer."

The dog cocked his wrinkly head at her, then woofed.

"Shhhhh, you traitor. Be quiet, or Rich'll come out and skin us both. I guess it's time for plan B. Even though I hate shopping and have no idea what a newborn needs."

Beating a hasty though judicious retreat, Lark dragged the recalcitrant canine through the hedge, up the porch steps and around its circumference to the kitchen door, through the back rooms, whose floors were covered with nearly indestructible linoleum, then hefted him in her arms to climb the stairs. Despite his objections, she dumped him in the bathtub for good measure and shook her finger at him.

"Now, you listen to me. I have to do something, and I need you to behave. The drain's at this end—" Lark pointed in the appropriate direction—"and the pillow I sacrificed is at the other."

For a moment, the sad, sad eyes tempted her to relent, but then she remembered the mess he'd made of Granny Iris's floor. She bolstered her resolve. "No way, bud. I'm not falling for the poor-me routine. See you later—not more than an hour max."

Then she closed the bathroom door, slung her wallet-on-a-strap across her torso and ran to her ailing red Escort. She'd invested so much in her magazine that now she couldn't afford to replace the vehicle—not without a loan, and interest was something she refused to do to herself.

Coaxing the car to life, Lark headed toward Main Street.

She couldn't believe her luck when, as she neared Lullabies and Dreams, a meter—with a half hour left on it—became vacant. Lark nodded a grateful farewell to the driver and slipped into place.

Minutes later, butterflies in her stomach, she stepped into the unknown universe of infants.

"Did you see that?" asked Louella Ashworth, clutching Mariah Desmond's arm in a death grip while jabbing her chin in Lark's direction. "Well, praise the Lord, and amen an' amen. Didn't I tell you all that child needed was a nudge in the right direction?"

Mariah took in the scene before her with a glimmer of hope and a ton of skepticism. "Louella," she cautioned, "I don't know if Lark and Rich are even on speakin' terms. Don't you think you're gettin' a mite carried away?"

"Where's your faith, woman? Haven't we been praying and praying for those two to come together since near the moment she was born?"

"Well, sure, but just because the girl's shoppin' at a baby boutique doesn't mean she's lookin' to settle, much less with my Rich."

"Pshaw! It's a cinch those two are made for each other. And I was very subtle yesterday in planting the right romantic seed in Lark's soil. Why, if I were you, I'd start drawin' up my guest list for the reception."

The glimmer of hope in Mariah's heart turned to a flicker. "Do you really think . . . ? Well, maybe. After all, all things do work for the good of those who love the Lord. . . ."

Louella smiled. "Haven't I just been tellin' you that? You just leave it up to me. I'll get the Garden Club to help—I'm not president for nothin'. Those two haven't got a chance."

FIVE

LARK'S VISIT TO REENIE PRODUCED NO RESULTS — ASIDE
from the expectant mother's rapturous coos over the eyelet
layette her best friend had brought.

Disgruntled, Lark returned home and read three submis-
sions that had come in the morning's E-mail. Only one
would make it into the next issue of *Critic's Choice.* The other
two were blatantly biased: one pro, one anti-interactive art
because of its similarity to drama. She preferred more
balanced, judicious consideration of literary pieces for her
magazine, not disquisitions on an art form she wasn't even
sure she considered legit. Besides, she was determined to write
the next piece on a play based on her own interview with the
elusive, reclusive Des Richter.

Lark's frustration over her fruitless — as yet — search for the
guy made her shut down the computer and stare out the
window. How was she going to find the man? Would she
have to do a criminal-type investigation? Check DMV files,
the Social Security Administration, FBI records?

As she worried the prospect to bits, she saw Rich exit his

front door and turn on the water faucet at the corner of the porch. Seconds later, underground sprinklers painted rainbows above the lawn.

"Wow," she said to the pup, who'd come nosing up to her leg. "Desmond's Country Store must be doing better than I thought. That system didn't come cheap."

The dog snorted.

"OK," she said. "Who knows what Rich has been up to lately? And how does the guy with the pricey Euro-wardrobe play into it?"

Pooch-Face whined.

"Well, of course, I'm going to find out. Have you forgotten who your new owner is? They don't call me Scoop for nothing."

He'd made progress with the script but none with Storey, despite the man's unexpected visit that morning, not to mention his irate demands for Rich to use some sense.

Which he was doing. However, Rich had learned early in his walk with Christ that often God's sense displayed not one iota of what men considered common sense. And the more Rich thought and prayed over his situation, the more certain he became that he couldn't capitulate to the powers-that-be. The only power he bowed down to was God's.

With a glance at his watch, Rich realized it was time to relieve Sophie at the store. He backed up the scenes he'd worked on and shut down the computer. Then, noting a hint of browning on the lawn, he headed outside to turn on the sprinklers.

He scooted to the gate in the picket fence to escape a drenching, shook his head to dislodge a few droplets, then grinned. "Hey, Maggie. Taking off early from work today?"

The middle Blossom smiled. "Why, yes. I'm as thrilled as

a piglet in a wallow to be back in Granny's house. Now that Lark's home, I've been prayin' we can finally . . ."

Rich waited for her to finish her sentence. When he saw a certain wistful expression on her beautiful face, he prodded, "You finally . . . ?"

She waved a delicate hand. "Oh, never mind. I'm just . . . woolgatherin'. And where are you off to?"

He leaned down to rub the wrinkles on Buford's forehead. "To the store. If I don't get there soon, Miss Sophie might just call out the Special Forces to save me."

Maggie's cheeks warmed to an elegant shade of shell pink. "Those ladies sure do have wild imaginations, don't they?"

Remembering Maggie's recent misadventures, aided and abetted by his mother's cronies in the Bellamy Garden Club, Rich laughed. "You should know."

Darkening to a deep rose, Maggie took a step toward the Bellamy home and gave a fidgety tug to Buford's leash. "Well, now, Rich, I'd best let you be on your way. Wouldn't want to set Miss Sophie off like a house afire again, would we? I'll see you in less'n a twitch of a puppy dog's tail, since we're gonna be neighbors again. Yessir, this is gonna be good as gold, right as rain, and you can bet your boots it'll be even better'n havin' my cake and eatin' it too."

Rich winced at the cavalcade of molasses-rich clichés that, as he'd learned through their families' long acquaintance, revealed Maggie's discomfort and embarrassment. He had to admit she possessed a goofy Southern charm—unlike Lark, who'd fought tooth and nail to eradicate any hint of Dixie from her words.

That non-Southern voice yelled, "Watch out!"

A series of earsplitting howls followed her cry, and Buford took up a response, dragging Maggie by the leash. Seconds later, the sidewalk became the scene of a dogfight, something Rich had never expected to face.

He debated which blurred dog-part to grab to stop the fray. "Now quit it!"

"Buford, baby," chided a chagrined Maggie, pulling with all her petite strength.

"Pooch-Face," grunted the frowning Lark as she dragged her beast a scant two inches from her sister's pet. "I thought you had business to take care of."

The yowls and growls and howls continued. Rich girded his courage and leaped into the canine quarrel, grabbing for Lark's hound, since Buford topped the pup by at least sixty pounds.

"*Grrrrrr,*" both curs chimed in response, turning their ire on him. He hastily backed away, the beasts resumed their battle, and Rich noticed something he'd missed until then. Neither animal was doing any real harm to the other; instead, they looked cheerful, excited, alive, vigorous, and healthy.

Lark's hound lunged up onto Buford's tall shoulder and grabbed the bullmastiff's neatly bent dark ear for a nip. Buford shook his massive head, easily freeing himself from his attacker. Then, in retaliation, the hundred-plus-pound animal rolled the youngster onto his back and planted a platter-sized paw on the puppy's chubby belly. The pup wriggled and bayed as Buford seized his throat.

The combatants then broke apart, shook themselves with profound dignity, and sniffed each other end to end.

The two sisters stared in openmouthed amazement. Lark, predictably, recovered first. "Does this mean . . . they're not going to kill each other?"

Rich glanced at the dogs and, from their heaving rib cages and lolling tongues, deduced that whatever conflict the two males had faced, Buford had resolved it by pinning the young upstart to the ground.

As he let the tension ease from his shoulders, Rich said, "Looks to me like both of them know who's boss now and might be ready for a bowl of cold water."

Maggie sent him a reproachful look. "My goodness, a bucket of it might've helped while they were fighting."

The oldest Blossom frowned. "It only lasted a few seconds, Mags. I doubt Rich would have had enough time to find a bucket, much less fill it and douse the dogs."

Maggie faced her sister. "You're right, but why did you let your puppy out when I was walkin' home with Buford? Don't you know you need to introduce dogs cautiously to prevent territorial battles and injuries?"

"Er . . . well . . . I . . . um . . . didn't know you two were coming up the sidewalk."

How unusual, thought Rich. He'd never known the snoopy redhead to stammer . . . unless she was hiding something. Or fibbing. He studied her. What was Lark up to?

"Well," Lark said to her sister, "since you're almost there anyway, come on home." She glanced at Rich. "See you later."

The sisters left Rich feeling unsettled. Maggie was right. Why on earth had Snoop-Scoop let her dog out just at that precise moment? Was it mere coincidence? Or had she wormed his secret out of . . . somebody?

Rich kept his gaze glued to the dancing mahogany curls atop the most frightening, maddening, and irritatingly fascinating—to his mortification—female head.

Was Lark onto him already? Or was she still determined to "help" his mother?

Faced with those two rotten choices, he didn't know which one to hope for. He didn't know which option was worse.

🌿

"Shut the door behind you," Lark said as she trotted through the hallway and into the kitchen in Pooch-Face's wake. "I'll get water for the dogs."

"Thanks," called Maggie. "Ooh, it's so nice in here. Cool. It's hot as a griddle fryin' this cat's feet on that tin roof of a sidewalk out there."

Lark rolled her eyes. As long as she could remember, Maggie had talked in that weirdly mangled, clichéd, somewhat Southern way, driving everyone in her vicinity crazy. Lark, instead, had worked to eliminate her drawl even before she'd left for Baltimore. She loved Bellamy, and she also loved her sisters, but she suspected the accent made others see them as weak Southern women, people to discount.

She'd had enough of that growing up. Being the "odd" Bellamy had been sufficient burden to bear. Once she'd escaped her legacy, she'd wanted no remnant of the taint.

"Hey, Buford," she called. "Water's ready."

The large dog ran into the linoleum-floored kitchen, his dignity dropping when his claws skittered and he lost his footing. The pup slurped in joy, his tail whipping through the air.

"I'm *famished,*" Maggie said, her high heels *tap-tapping* into the rapidly crowding kitchen. "Since I'd packed, all I had for breakfast were some dry Froot Loops—no milk, no coffee, no Tang—and lunch never happened. I had to juggle more calls'n honey does bees."

Lark gestured toward the fridge, trying not to wince at her sister's choice of breakfast beverages and cereal—if one could call those devitalized, multihued, crunchy doodads cereal. "Help yourself."

"Thanks." Maggie's blond curls dipped into the appliance.

Out of habit, Lark turned on the radio, set as usual to her

favorite classical station. The eloquent notes of a violin-rich concerto soared through the room. She braced for one of Maggie's comments, seeing as how the sisters' taste in music differed.

"What," Maggie asked in a horrified voice, "is *this?*"

"Haydn."

"Not the squallin' cats on the radio. This mess."

Lark glanced over and said, "Oh, that's sea-veggie soup. It's great. Help yourself."

A glare at the glass jar, a disdainful sniff, and a "not in this lifetime" followed.

Unease wriggled down Lark's back. Did this portend oncoming misery?

"For goodness sake, Lark. You don't have a thing to eat in here. Weeds! Bags of weeds an'—what are these? Sprouts?" Maggie's voice implied she'd come face-to-face with raging bubonic plague.

Taking a deep breath, Lark sought forbearance. "They're bean sprouts. Fabulous food—lots of enzymes and great protein. Put some on an avocado sandwich, and sprinkle it all with tamari. It'll do you good."

The refrigerator door slammed shut. "You're a health-food freak."

Lark met Maggie's accusing eyes. "No, not a freak at all. Just concerned about my health. You ought to try it. Life lasts longer without congested arteries. All that saturated animal glop . . ."

Maggie's jaw dropped. Then she stumbled to the table, pulled out a chair, and collapsed on it. "You're not."

"Not what?"

"One of them."

"One of who?"

"A *vegetarian,*" Maggie spit out in a gust of aversion.

"As I said, you ought to try it, sis. And there's absolutely nothing wrong with being vegetarian. I'm here, I'm healthy, and I'm sparing the lives of animals. That should please you, seeing how much you love dogs."

"I never!"

"You never what?"

"I've never eaten a dog in all my born days. And you know it, Larkspur Bellamy."

Had Lark entered one of those weird mirror houses in a circus? "That's not what I said. Not even what I suggested. It's a comparison. Sorta. I don't eat animals since I can eat plants, be healthy, and not kill anything to do so. That's all I meant."

"Fine, but I'm surely not eatin' your weeds. Why, I'm marchin' straight to the grocery and buyin' myself some real food. Come on, Buford. I don't relish starvin' right before my weddin'."

A reluctant Buford rose from where he'd curled up around Pooch-Face and followed his mistress. When Lark heard the front door slam, she took a seat. Why did every encounter between her and her sisters have to end inevitably in friction?

She'd returned to Bellamy knowing she could help both younger Blossoms. Then Maggie had become embroiled in a terrible mess—despite Lark's repeated warnings, maybe even as a result of ignoring Lark's admonitions. Cammie remained in an impossible situation—pregnant and taking care of a houseful of strangers. Who knew what those people were really up to? With her simple faith in God, Cammie was too easy on others, making herself a perfect target.

Why couldn't her sisters realize Lark had so much to offer them? That she really had a handle on the world? That she knew what was best for them?

After all, she'd handled everything life had thrown her way in Baltimore and succeeded. True, she bore a scar or two . . . or twenty, but she could handle anything, anyone. "And I'm going to help those two figure out their lives if it's the last thing I do. I know what they need."

Her pup snuffled.

"You got it, Pooch-Face. Those two don't have the sense you do."

Lark rose, took a glass from an open-fronted cabinet, and headed for the crockery stand holding a five-gallon bottle of purified, filtered water. As she poured herself a drink, her gaze flitted toward the Desmond home. Yesterday's dapper stranger was again pounding on the front door.

"Yessss." Forgetting her drink, she flung open the door. "No one's home, Mr. . . . ?"

The chubby man turned and offered her an unobstructed view of today's outfit. He'd gone British in his Saville Row dove gray suit, white-on-white striped shirt, and regimental tie—askew again. Lustrous wing tips encased his feet. "So where is he?" the slightly off-kilter dandy asked.

"Probably at Desmond's Country Store, Mr. . . . ?" When he again failed to fill her in, Lark continued, "I can take you there, if you'd like. I have nothing pressing right now."

The guy's small black eyes narrowed, nearly disappearing behind his full cheeks and the overhang of frizzled brow. "Nah, just tell me how to get there," he said in his knife-sharp New York accent.

"No, really, I can get you there. It would be no bother. Wouldn't want you to get lost."

"In Bellamy? Lady, just tell me where to go."

For a moment, Lark's frustration got the better of her, and thoughts of jumps into deep, deep lakes danced in her head. But her determination to get to the bottom of the Jaguar driver's presence at Rich's house proved stronger. In brief words, she gave him directions, then watched him buzz his honey of a car out of the driveway and toward town.

She didn't bother following; Rich would never talk to the guy with her in the vicinity.

But what if she made an overture toward her nemesis? In the interest of overcoming their awkward past, of course. Maybe they could build a new, more normal, mature, neighborly relationship. And then she could go in for the kill, using her legendary interrogation methods to get what she wanted.

Grinning, she headed for the kitchen, wondering if Maggie had any chocolate chips, butter, sugar, and white flour in the box she and her movers had left under the kitchen table that morning. They always said, *The way to a man's heart—*

Ooops. Wrong destination. What she wanted was this man's secrets. Still, she could always pave her way there through his flat stomach. She just hoped Rich wasn't allergic to chocolate. They had too rocky a past to overcome without adding anaphylactic shock at this stage in the game.

Later that evening, Rich opened the door and saw his future: He knew he had to run away from home. He had no alternative.

Bearing a plate of what appeared to be—and smelled like—chocolate chip cookies, Lark stood on his porch, ear-to-ear smile on her face. He'd seen that adoring-bovine expression before, too many times.

Lark. After Storey, who had hounded him up and down the Country Store's aisles for the better part of two horrific hours.

The silence grew painfully long. "Yes?" he asked.

"I made these for you."

Rich glanced at the goodies, back at her, then pointed at the chunks of chocolate embedded in the baked batter. "Can I trust that's chocolate—real chocolate? No booby traps or love-potion-number-nine or anything stupid like that?"

"Just for *that,* I should've used Ex-Lax. Of course, it's choc-olate—real chocolate. Nestlé's Toll House chips."

"Hey, *I* was the one with stomach cramps for a week after *your* love potion backfired on me. Naturally I'm looking at any food you bring me with a jaundiced eye."

Lark's lips tightened to a white line. She planted a palm in the middle of his chest, pushed him against the door and out of her way, then marched into his living room. "Boy, I'll bet there isn't a kid in this town who ever gets away with any-thing in your store."

"And that's a bad thing?"

"No, but I'll bet they don't come in to hang out with you either."

Lark's words brought back a vivid image. All through Rich's growing-up years, his dad had been the pied piper of Bellamy. School-age kids had crowded into Desmond's Country Store every afternoon during the school months and from breakfast to supper in the summers. Rich's friends had envied him his fabulous father.

When Dad died, those same kids had joined Mariah, Rich, and Reenie in mourning a man they'd loved like a member of their own families. The pain of loss cut through the poi-gnancy of memory, and Rich glared at the woman who'd reminded him of those days darkened by grief.

Especially since she was right. Kids *were* conspicuously absent from the store these days. Had he—Rich—chased them away? Was he too harsh? Then again, his father had never had a problem with the kids. That was something to think about later.

He lifted his hands, palms out. "Truce, OK?"

Lark plunked the plate down on the coffee table and plopped onto his couch. "Fine," she said, giving no sign of a quick departure.

Rich listened as his computer hummed in the dining room.

He had to keep her out of that room. With one glance at his screen Snoop-Scoop could strip him bare.

"So . . . ," he said, sitting across from her and searching for a topic, "how's the magazine?"

"Great new issue coming out next month." Her green eyes darted around the room, apparently not missing a single detail.

Since when was Lark Bellamy interested in decor? He tried another subject, since that last one had died fast. "How're things going for Maggie's wedding?"

"Beats me."

Swell.

The hairs at the nape of Rich's neck rose in alarm. "What did you name your dog—"

"How's Miss Mariah doing? Has Percy come up with anything? What did the Secret Service have to say? Have you dug any info out of Wiggon? What's really going on?"

By the time she spewed her last word, Rich's eyebrows had burrowed into his hair. "Man. They ought to consider renaming Uzis. Seems to me 'Larks' would be a better name. No wonder you have a Pulitzer under your belt."

"Everyone's got a gift. I guess that's mine." She leaned forward, those emerald eyes shining brighter than the display at Adams' Fine Gems on Main Street. "So, what's up?"

"I thought you'd brought cookies. I never dreamed I'd opened the door to the Trojan horse."

"Rich, your sister asked me to help. I love your mom, and I'm worried. Especially since I know nothing about what's going on. Even worse, nothing—you got that?—nothing has appeared in the papers about her arrest. Explain that to me, will you?"

Over my dead body. "It's all under control." He hoped.

"Baloney. If everything was under control, Miss Mariah would've been at her warehouse today rather than shopping downtown with Miss Louella. I saw them strolling into Babette's Boutique at a quarter to one. Your mother's never around at that time. She's too committed to her work."

Committed. Now there was a concept. One from which a too-nosy reporter—one who wreaked havoc faster than her dog dug up marigolds—might benefit. As long as said commitment included iron bars.

Rich asked God's forgiveness for his mean-spirited, fear-inspired thought. "There's not a whole lot to know. Mama was falsely arrested, and her lawyer's taking care of the matter."

"So what exactly are the charges?"

"Reenie said she told you. Racketeering, credit-card fraud—"

"Details, Desmond. Details are sorely lacking from your vague little commentary."

"Perhaps because discretion is sorely lacking from the mind of a nosy, award-winning reporter."

"That's only the opinion of those who have something to hide."

Rich froze. His lungs failed. His heart stopped.

She knew.

When she didn't say anything further, cardiac tissue resumed its work, beating so hard he feared the muscle would explode from the violent pumping.

Did she know?

"I have nothing to hide," he said in a voice that convinced neither of them.

A dark auburn brow arched gracefully, and coral lips tipped up. "Do tell."

Boom, boom, boom tympanied his heart. "No, really." Man, what a wimpy attempt. Even he knew he was only making her more curious by the minute. "Well," he said, coming to his feet, "I have a ton of paperwork to do, so . . ."

She laughed at him.

Rich was tempted to ignore the sixth commandment and go for her pretty neck. The only thing that stopped him was the summons of the doorbell.

As he went to answer, Lark murmured, "Saved by the bell," and laughed some more.

To make matters worse—impossible though he'd have thought that to be—his mother stood on the porch, poised to knock.

"What took you so long, Son?" she asked, worry on her soft and youthful face. "Are you havin' trouble with your current script—"

"No!" He hoped he'd drowned out the dangerous word. "I-I have company." Taking his mother's arm, Rich led her into the living room.

As usual, the older woman threw him for a loop. Instead of alarm at her near miss, delight filled her features. "Lark, honey," she said. "Just the woman I wanted to see."

Rich's redheaded albatross ran to hug his mother. After a quick spritz of the usual hello-how-are-yous, Mama led Lark to the couch again. Why couldn't she have arrived one minute later? He'd have had danger headed back to her own house by then.

"Sugar," his mother said to Lark, "you won't believe the foolishness of our law-enforcement agencies. Not to mention our lawyers."

"Wanna bet?" Lark quipped, excitement flaring in her eyes. Ah, yes, the bloodhound was on the scent. And Rich was in trouble again.

"No need for wagerin'," Mama answered. "It's a sin against God, Lark, honey. As is their latest? Why, sugar, those sadly befuddled men say they caught me on tape using stolen credit-card numbers to supply a gang of retail thieves with—of all crazy things—girdles!"

Lark's smooth forehead creased. Apprehension flooded her eyes. "Miss Mariah, that's serious. A tape?"

"Oh, yes," Rich's mother answered, then laughed. "Of course they can't have any such thing. I've never seen a stolen credit card, much less used one. And I don't sell my girdles to crooks. I sell to stores where women buy the comfy foundations they deserve—"

"Back up a minute," Lark urged. "Where do the thieves come in?"

"Why, honey, that's the wildest thing Percy told me. The Secret Service says they've been stealin' department stores blind by stuffin' merchandise into the Dream Squeezes they wear. An agent claims one woman even stuck seven women's suits—hangers and all—into her Squeeze. Now I know they're great girdles, but seven suits? And hangers. That just goes to show how silly this whole thing is. Besides, what do girdles have to do with protectin' the president?"

Lark's moan drove fear into Rich's gut. The shake of her head made him send a wordless plea heavenward.

"No, Miss Mariah," Baltimore's best said, "it's not silly at all. The crime you just described is called *boosting,* and for the last year there's been a ring of shoplifters operating like that in the mid-Atlantic region. The FBI and the Secret Service are on that case. If agents say they have tapes, I'm afraid they've filmed you doing something that looks suspicious. And girdles have nothing to do with the president. The Secret Service is the agency in charge of credit-card fraud."

Blood curdled in Rich's veins. If Snoop-Scoop knew about this, chances were it was real. Serious. And his mother was in the thick of it.

"Well," chirped Mama, clearly unmoved, "Frank has the office under control, so I haven't a thing to worry my head about. I'm innocent."

Lark gripped his mother's shoulders. "I know you're innocent, Miss Mariah, but you've got to understand. You could go to jail for the rest of your life over this. You're in serious trouble."

The bottom dropped from under Rich. He'd known there'd be nothing but trouble the day he heard Lark was in town. He just never expected his mother to be the catalyst.

SIX

"This meeting of the Bellamy Garden Club will now come to order," Louella Ashworth proclaimed, beating her gavel on the table.

Some of the gathered ladies heeded her call; others continued gabbing as if they hadn't seen each other for years—if not decades.

"Ladies, ladies," she further admonished, punctuating her words with additional wooden clunks.

The multigarmented Philadelphia Philpott scurried in. She met Louella's gaze, then hissed at the other gardeners, "Shhhhh."

To Mariah's surprise—and Louella's astonishment—the group fell silent. Well, the entire group except for Myrna Stafford. Bobbing her purple, sausagelike curls in a pseudo-sage fashion, she murmured something in the ear of the woman to her left.

Mariah shook her head. Myrna's obsession with gossip grew worse each day.

Clearing her throat, Louella banged her gavel one more

time. "As your duly elected and installed president, I now declare this meetin' called to order—if Mrs. Stafford will cede us the floor, of course."

With a sniff and a jut of her pointy chin, Myrna sat up straight and crossed her arms across her flat chest. "Deliver your words of wisdom, Louella," she said. "Some of us have important matters to attend to after we're shut of your bossiness."

Louella closed her eyes, and Mariah joined her friend in offering a brief prayer—asking forgiveness for her impatience toward Myrna as well as for a softening of the woman's heart.

"As you all know," Louella began, "summer will soon be over, and we must begin thinkin' on fall. It's bulb time again. How many shall we order? What varieties do we need? What suppliers shall we deal with?"

The Garden Club added to the floral beauty of Bellamy every year, enhancing seasonal displays judiciously. Fall planting was considered their most important contribution, since many of these plants came into blossom year after year. What should they add this year?

Thinking over the past few months, Mariah had an idea. "Delphiniums," she suggested. "I fancy them, and since Lark has come home, it would be a lovely idea to honor her return with a display of larkspur at the town square."

Myrna offered another trademark snort. "Will we then have to buy magnolias and camellias for the other two Bellamys, too?"

"That's not a bad idea," Mariah said, "now that you mention it. We have that lovely Iris Bellamy Garden by the library in honor of their granny, and the beds of aster at the police department for their mama. Why not the girls? Especially now that Maggie's marryin', and Cammie's expectin'. The Blossoms are the last of the town's foundin' family, after all."

Louella frowned. "We might be able to get away with a couple of magnolias over by Langhorn Creek, but I don't reckon tropical camellias will fare too well in our neck of the woods."

"Well," said Mariah with the same persistence that had catapulted the Dream Squeeze into position as the nation's best-selling girdle, "there's no good reason we can't just dig up a chunk of granite off the library's lobby floor where City Council installed the skylights. We can plant some bulbs for that little girl—her a widow and expectin' and all."

"Hmm . . . ," Louella murmured. "You know, we could dedicate the plants to the Blossoms the day of Maggie's wedding. After all, she listened to me and didn't let that darlin' Yankee of ours get away from her."

"She's been a loyal Bellamy resident all along," Rosemarie Melbourne, the Right Reverend Stuart Melbourne's wife, said.

"So has Camellia," added Sophie Hardesty.

"But Larkspur?" asked Myrna with yet another snort.

Elvira Morgan, the aging town clerk, stood. "Ain't she the odd one?"

Seated four ladies to Mariah's right, Norberta Robbins, the postmistress, nodded her bottle-black bun. "And her an unwed vegetarian, at that . . ."

"Is she one of us even?" wondered Eloise Dubbs, the voice that sent fears through Bellamy's residents when she called "Next" at dentist Ken Walters's office.

Myrna erupted from her chair and in her stentorian bray challenged the group. "How do we know that flighty miss is gonna stay in town oncet we've spent money on her tribute?"

Louella *tsk-tsked.* "Why, of course, Lark's stayin' in town. Don't you all know God's brought her home to match her up with Richie Desmond? Tell the girls, Mariah. Tell them what you found last evenin' in your old home."

After a reproving glare at her friend and housemate, which Louella ignored, Mariah told the gardeners of visiting Rich

79

only to find Lark settled on the sofa, sharing with him a plate of chocolate chip cookies.

"See?" Louella said. "And that after their sizzlin' encounter at the police department."

Myrna wagged her purple-sausaged locks. "We've all been there'n seen that, Lou. That crazy Lark's been chasin' Rich Desmond since she was a brat. Ain't nothin' new about it. Oncet she gets tired of the quiet life in Bellamy, she'll be off to some far corner chasin' one of her exclusives."

Mariah met Louella's questioning gaze. She firmed her shoulders and took a determined breath. But before she could formulate an adequate answer, Louella sallied forth.

"Lark can't go," she declared. "The Lord's brought her home, and now it's up to us wiser women to make sure she doesn't rebel against his will. We're goin' to make sure that match is made good and strong. What do you all say we make them the Garden Club's next project, even more urgent than the bulbs?"

Early the next morning, Pooch-Face made Lark rise early and take him outside. He sniffed every inch of the Bellamy lawn and lifted his leg to mark every shrub he found, before finally allowing her to return to bed.

Except the phone didn't cooperate then. She eyed her bed with longing as she answered it. "Hello?"

"Lark, honey," said Miss Mariah, relief in her voice, "I'm so glad I caught you home. I was afraid you'd be off and gone by now; you're such a busy thing."

Lark chuckled. This early in the morning she normally kept busy with her pillow, blanket, and dreams. "I'm here, all right. How can I help you?"

"Sugar, that's one of the things I like best about you.

Straight off, you're askin' what you can do for another.
You're such a blessin' to your friends."

Miss Mariah's son didn't see her that way, Lark thought.
"Thank you. Is something wrong? I mean, something besides
the obvious."

"Well," the older woman said, unusually hesitant, "I have
an appointment with Percy Baker this mornin', and I was
wonderin' if you'd . . . if you weren't too harried . . . would
you come with me?"

Yesssss. "I'm not too busy to support a friend in need," Lark
answered, thinking Rich would about die if he learned of this
development. Well, she wasn't likely to tell him.

"Thank you, honey. I have to admit, that bit about the
videos does have me a mite perturbed. Mind you, I'm not so
much afraid, seein' as I did nothin' wrong, and, you know all
things work to the good of those—"

"Yes, yes," Lark cut in. Miss Mariah's faith reminded her
too much of Granny Iris's and contrasted with Lark's own
lack thereof. "Would you like me to pick you up?"

"Could you?"

"Of course. What time's your appointment?"

They made arrangements, and Lark hurried to shower.
Now she'd get some info, she thought, lathering her hair,
since Rich wouldn't be smack in the middle of the picture.
Satisfaction ran through her, and she hummed as she dried
off and dressed.

Gulping the last bite of her scrambled tofu sandwich, Lark
faced her first dilemma of the day. From his conspicuous
absence, she inferred Maggie had taken Buford, as she'd said
she would, to the office. That left her to deal with Pooch-
Face.

"What am I going to do with you?" she asked the mourn-
ful-looking pup, whose tail resembled a hyperactive metro-

nome. "I can't leave you by yourself. Who knows what I'd find by the time I got back."

He cocked his brown head and emitted a snuffle.

"I don't believe you," she said, picking up her car keys. "I have a chewed-up sock upstairs to prove I can't trust you."

Pooch-Face flopped to the floor, his muzzle on his paws, dark eyes on her face.

"Don't give me that poor-me look," she answered, searching for the leash. "You have to play by my rules. I'm sick of picking up after everyone's messes. If you want to stay with me, you're going to have to toe my line. I know what's best, so you do what I say."

She clicked the leash to the dog's collar and tugged him toward the door, thinking how great it would be if her sisters were as easy to manage. Why couldn't they just accept that as the oldest—and wisest—Lark knew what was best? She had more experience than they did. She'd succeeded in freeing herself from the provincial Southern ties they still dragged around with them.

But no. Maggie insisted on marrying that questionable contractor, and Cammie . . . well, Cammie was too pie-in-the-sky innocent for words. Lark would just have to be stronger than her younger sisters. She had to make them see reason.

After she straightened up the Desmond mess.

When Lark arrived at Miss Mariah's home, she left the dog in the car and went to the door. "I'm so sorry," she said when the older woman came outside. "I'm afraid we're stuck doing business with my dog alongside us."

"Don't you go apologizin', now. I just love dogs, and yours is a darlin' little baby."

After a few minutes' drive, they reached Percy's office. Lark killed the engine and scrambled out. Grabbing the leash that had launched her into pet ownership, she glared at her canine companion. He cocked his head, a quizzical look on his mournful features. Against her better judgment, she chuckled. "You're pathetic, you know that?" The dog didn't respond but trotted amiably at her side.

Surprised by the lack of comment from the usually talkative Miss Mariah, Lark glanced over. White-knuckled hands clutched the elegant handbag as if it were a lifeline.

Lark transferred the dog's leash to her left hand, then placed her right on Miss Mariah's arm. Her friend jumped, and Lark's heart squeezed.

"It's going to be all right," Lark said, struggling against her own fears. She tamped down her own disbelief, and for the woman's sake, added, "Remember your Scripture: 'God causes everything to work together . . . '"

The grateful smile on Miss Mariah's lips didn't quite make it to the silver eyes Reenie and Rich had inherited. "I know, dearie, but there's so much evil in this fallen world, and God's children aren't spared the pain. I just hate to become a burden to Richie and Reenie at this particular time, with both of them so busy with their own situations and all."

Lark gave her friend a one-armed hug. "They love you and would never see you as a burden. Besides, what am I? Chopped liver? I'm here to help, and you've always been a joy to me. I'm honored you called me. Now, buck up." She opened the mahogany door bearing the name Percival Baker on a brass plate.

"What are *you* doing here?" Rich asked as Lark, the dog, and Miss Mariah entered the law firm's waiting room.

It figured he'd be in on the interview, too. Rats. She tipped up her chin and met his gaze. "Your mother asked me to accompany her. She seemed to feel the need for my supportive presence."

"But I'm here."

Mischief made her say, "Precisely."

"Children, children," Miss Mariah admonished. "I need you both. Rich, you know a lot about business, what with your caree—"

"The store, of course," Rich cut in, making Lark wonder what had gotten into him. A hint of something—could it be fear?—had sharpened his normally resonant voice.

But fear? Rich?

She glanced at his mother. Miss Mariah's eyes had widened. "Of course, son," the older woman said. "The store. And Lark, why, she's an experienced investigative reporter. She can certainly bring needed expertise into this matter. Besides—" she placed a soft hand on Lark's leash-holding fist—"she's my friend."

Rich's eyebrows crashed over the bridge of his nose. "And I'm not?"

"For goodness sake, Richie, of course you are. But Lark's a woman, if you hadn't noticed. And I need a woman friend right now. Especially one with her special talents."

The moment Miss Mariah raised the issue of Lark's womanhood, Lark felt Rich's eyes on her face . . . her hair . . . her figure. The intense scrutiny to which those silver stilettos subjected her made currents of unwarranted heat shoot through Lark. When his eyes met her own gaze, they unnerved her with a shock of—she didn't exactly know what—and her breath caught in her throat.

Had Rich noticed she'd become a woman? And what did he think of her as one?

The moment grew long, the air electric. Seconds ticked by on the sluggish beat of her heart. Lark knew she should look away from Rich, since it was the smart thing to do. But something kept her gaze tangled in his, her every nerve ending exquisitely aware of his presence merely inches away.

He'd always had some odd power over her, Lark thought, as she stared into his intriguing gray eyes. Her breath had always done strange things in his presence, her insides melted, her common sense vanished. Even when she'd been too young to know what attraction really was.

A memory sped through her thoughts. A painful memory. One of many—dozens, hundreds: "First comes love, then comes marriage, then little Richie in a baby carriage. . . ."

The childish voice burned through the haze of . . . who knew what? Pheromones, maybe. The thought yanked Lark back to reality and the present. Her pheromones had no business responding to Rich. Even less in a lawyer's office, his mother at their shoulder, smirking as they . . . what? Admired each other? Challenged each other?

She shook her head, hoping to shed the cobwebs of Rich's spell. "Where's Mr. Baker?" she asked.

"In there," Rich answered, tipping his sandy head in the direction of the lawyer's private office. Lark noted the roughness of his voice and felt a measure of comfort in knowing he'd been affected as well.

"Don't you think we should go in?" Miss Mariah said, sudden strength in her expression.

Lark wondered if her friend's renewed vigor had anything to do with what had just transpired between her and Rich. Miss Mariah had never made a secret of her wish for Lark and Rich to, as she always put it, make a go of it.

Fearing the trap of her youthful feelings, Lark chose to escape. "Of course," she said. "That's what we're here for."

As the dog led the way, snuffling along the carpet runner, Rich asked, "Then what's your beast doing here?"

"What would you have me do with him? I can't very well leave him in Granny Iris's house all alone. Who knows what calamity I'd find when I returned."

"You have to give Maggie credit. She chose the most appropriate pet for you. Not only does he have your nose, but it seems Calamity Jane just met her Calamity John."

Lark crossed her arms. "Who do you think you are, insulting my nose? The high and mighty captain of the Bellamy High School Bantam football team? That won't wash after this many years." She moved to block the doorway to Mr. Baker's office. "You owe my nose an apology."

Rich laughed.

Which only made Lark nuts. "You are the most insulting, self-righteous, pompous, supercilious—"

"Stop!" He held a hand out like a traffic cop, his laughter only slightly diminished. "Are you telling me you don't know what kind of dog that is?"

Lark stared at Pooch-Face, who chose that instant to let off one of his most woeful howls. "A miserable one, of course."

Rich leaned against the wall, laughter still getting the best of him. "I can't believe . . . I've caught Snoop-Scoop out . . . of the loop. You really don't know . . . what breed that monster is?"

Calling on all her bravado and some of her pride, Lark said, "Of course, I do."

"So what is he?"

"A . . . a . . . Transylvanian Border Melancholy!"

Rich howled some more. Her traitorous dog joined him.

"What is the meaning of this . . . this outrage, Miss Bellamy?" asked the always uptight Percy Baker.

Drawing on her dignity—what little Rich hadn't already shredded—Lark entered the room, dragging Pooch-Face in her wake. "I'm not exactly sure what Mr. Desmond's problem might be. However, Mrs. Desmond and I are here to discuss the progress of her case."

Behind her, the door closed with a slam. No longer laughing, Rich stalked past her to claim one of the three brass-studded cordovan leather wing chairs in front of Mr. Baker's desk. As he grazed her shoulder, he murmured, "Later."

"Later," she echoed.

"Well, Mr. Baker, Lark is right," Rich said, and her jaw nearly dropped onto the blue-and-cream wool Aubusson rug underfoot. She would have to remind him that he had once in his life said she was right. Later, as he'd promised.

Mr. Baker rounded his immaculate desk. Sitting, he removed his rimless glasses, then polished the already gleaming lenses. He pulled the chain of the green banker's lamp in the front middle of the desktop despite the sunshine pouring through the office window, and sat back, withdrawing a paper from a drawer at his left.

"It would seem, Mariah, you've really gone and done it this time. The Secret Service here says they've got the goods on you."

Lark's eyebrows rose. She'd never in her twenty-eight years heard Percy Baker speak anywhere near that close to normal.

A line bisected Miss Mariah's smooth forehead. "But they're wrong, Percy. You know that."

"Maybe so, maybe no, but there's little one can do to fight hard evidence."

Rich leaned forward. "Couldn't someone have faked the tapes?"

Mr. Baker peered over the top edge of his lenses. "Why would the Secret Service do that?"

"To frame Miss Mariah," Lark said, "that's why. It wouldn't be the first time—"

"Or the last," Rich cut in and glared at Lark. "Anyway, you know Mama better than that, Baker. You know she hasn't done a thing wrong."

"As I said," replied the lawyer, his voice resuming its usual haughty tone, "that may be the case, but the Secret Service has her on tape, approving charges to stolen numbers and supplying the thieves with their preferred tools. It's mighty hard to fight those facts."

Turning to his client, he added, "Now, if you'd plea-bargain—"

"Never! I'm not sayin' I did any of those horrid things, because, as I walk day-to-day with my dear Lord Jesus, I didn't do any of them."

Mr. Baker got up. "I was afraid you'd say that, Mariah."

"Well, at least you know somethin' about me."

"I'm afraid you're too much of an idealist, which also makes you a bit of a fool."

"Wait a minute," Rich said. "You can't call my mother a fool—"

"I'm her attorney," Mr. Baker argued.

"*Woo-ooo-wooo-ooooo!*" the dog countered.

"Apologize!" Rich demanded.

Miss Mariah sagged in her chair, a sob escaping her lips.

Lark brought four fingers to her mouth and gave an ear-shattering whistle. The room silenced. "That's better," she said. "What's next in getting Miss Mariah out of her predicament? And no more male posturing, please, gentlemen."

Rich glowered, but Lark ignored his disapproval. She'd had years of practice doing that, years that were now coming to her aid. She forced herself to focus on the lawyer, who turned his back to them and stared out his office window.

As the silence lengthened, Lark asked, "Well? What are you doing to get her out of this mess, Mr. Baker?"

He took a shoulder-hefting breath, then turned around. Without meeting anyone's gaze, he said, "I'm not doing another thing. With the evidence mounting against her, and the list of witnesses the agents have produced, I'm afraid there's nothing I can do for Mariah since she won't bargain. I must withdraw from the case."

Miss Mariah gasped.

Lark took a step back.

Rich planted his large fists on the desktop. "Come again?"

Lark knew the power of his steely stare, and for a moment, she felt sympathy for the scrawny elderly lawyer. But only for a moment. After all, he'd just—

"I quit, Mariah. You'll have to find yourself another lawyer to fight this mess. I've not gotten this far in life by fighting lost causes, and that's what yours is. I can't afford to let my name be tarred by losing a case this huge."

SEVEN

LARK AND POOCH-FACE FOLLOWED A SUBDUED RICH AND Miss Mariah out to the sidewalk. In contrast, Lark's insides bubbled with anticipation. She loved nothing better than to champion the cause of the underdog.

Pooch-Face bayed.

Well, the underdog of the human persuasion. "Hush, now," she hissed.

"We need to talk," Rich said.

"I'll say," Lark concurred.

"Not you."

"Yes, me."

"Children, children. This isn't the time for such nonsense. Why don't we all meet at home and mull things over? Louella went shoppin' yesterday and made a lovely chicken salad. It's right near lunchtime, and I always think better on a full stomach."

"No," said Rich, his voice firm. "We're not discussing your legal situation at your house. Not with Miss Louella and Sophie there."

Miss Mariah looked wounded. "Son, don't you trust my dearest friends?"

"Since when did you think me a dimwit, Mama?"

"Why, never, Richie. What are you talkin' about?"

"Remember Louella and the Ashworth Mansion?"

Blush roses bloomed on Miss Mariah's cheeks. "Of course, and I also remember her repentance, son. The Christian thing to do is forgive her. It would do you good."

"It's not a matter of forgiveness, Mama. It's a matter of caution. We can't have her deciding to help us with your situation. It's bad enough that you plunked Snoop-Scoop right into it. I had plenty to deal with, but now I've also got to keep her from bounding off on one of her half-baked schemes."

"Ahem," Lark interjected. "I've been highly decorated for the success of my—as you call them—half-baked schemes. You could come off your high horse and accept my experience. It can only do your mother good."

"Exactly," said Miss Mariah, marching toward Lark's Escort. "And if you object to discussin' strategy at my house, why, then we can head on to yours, son. We'll meet you in ten minutes. You ready, Lark, honey?"

At the "honey," Rich gave a disgusted snort. "I'll be there in ten."

"I love my son dearly," Miss Mariah said for Lark's ears only, "but sometimes I have to wonder where he got that stuffy, inflexible—"

"Self-righteous, prideful, obnoxious, offensive, macho attitude," Lark filled in, opening the passenger door for Miss Mariah.

"That bad?"

Lark trotted around to her side of the car. "You don't know the half of it. And he seems to get worse as time goes by."

"What my boy needs is a good woman to shake some sense into him."

Slamming the door felt good. "I'm not going there, Miss Mariah. Been there, done that, and didn't enjoy one second of it."

A soft hand landed on Lark's fingers as they gripped the steering wheel in a choke hold. "What you need, dear," her friend said, "is to seek God's will for your life. He's brought you home, but I don't reckon you know what for yet."

"Of course I know what I came home for. I came home to straighten out the mess Maggie and Cammie made of their lives. And to make my magazine number one at the same time."

As Lark turned the key in the ignition, Miss Mariah remained quiet. Considering silence better than further nudges on the matchmaking front, Lark kept her peace, too.

Then, "Honey, where did you get the notion it was up to you to manage your sisters' lives?"

"I don't want to manage their lives. It's just that I can see where they've gone wrong. It's so clear to someone older, wiser, more experienced than they."

"Two extra years' worth of livin' gives you that great an edge over Maggie? Four over Cammie?"

Lark clicked on her turn signal. "The age helps, but I think the greatest advantage comes from having shaken Bellamy's Southern dust off my shoes. I saw a lot and learned much more while I lived in Baltimore. It's a matter of perspective."

"But whose perspective, Lark? Man's or God's?"

"With all due respect, Miss Mariah—"

"I think, since you're so mature and all now, you can drop the Miss on my name, don't you? Just call me Mariah, dear. And continue your thought."

"Well," Lark said, not yet able to call her best friend's mother by her first name, "God dumped on us when he took Mama and Daddy so soon. And he sure didn't offer me any protection from the meanness of everyone in town. Then

Granny died, too, and there was no one to look out for the other two. I went off to school, followed by work, and just look at the mess they're in now. I've always had to clean up for them, and I came home to do it again."

"I have to wonder if you're not takin' on someone else's responsibilities."

"I'm the oldest."

"That doesn't mean you have the right to make their choices for them. The good Lord gave each and every one of us the gift of free will. Would you like your sisters comin' along to straighten out your life?"

Lark grinned. "What's there to straighten out?"

"Oh, my, child. I had no idea things were that bad. You have some hard knocks ahead of you if you don't make your peace with the Father soon."

Lark lifted her chin. "We've made our peace. He goes his way, and I go mine."

When Miss Mariah remained silent, Lark glanced her way. The older woman's head was bowed, her eyes closed. Sadness lined her attractive face, and Lark realized her friend was praying for her. That knowledge jabbed an uncomfortable twinge through her. After all, Mariah Desmond was the one in trouble, not Lark. Mariah was the one in need of prayer, not Lark.

Wasn't she?

With relief, Lark turned into her driveway. "We're here. Let's go figure out what to do next—and drive Rich batty doing it."

After a thank-you for the ride, Miss Mariah made her way toward Rich's house.

As Lark waited for Pooch-Face to do his thing, she shoved aside the unease Miss Mariah's words had brought to life. Her friend was wrong, and Lark was anxious to get going on the investigation.

"Imagine," Lark said to the dog, "someone in the Secret Service cooked up a false video to incriminate Miss Mariah in a major fraud case. Wouldn't it be cool if the agent who did it turned out to be the head crook?"

Pooch-Face lifted a leg.

Lark again hummed with the thrill of the hunt for truth. "Wow! Could I ever go to town on a story like that. I could sell it to any paper in the country. And you know, I wouldn't turn down another Pulitzer."

The dog kicked up grass with his hind paws, evidently done. And unmoved by her zeal.

Excitement pulsing through her, Lark rounded the hedge between her yard and Rich's. Then she saw it coming. Hurricane Rich.

"Not so fast, Snoop—"

"Give it up, Rich. The name's Scoop, and I earned it. Besides, you need help, and you know I'm your best bet. Why are you so opposed to me? Do you have something to hide?"

Although his movement was minute, she saw Rich recoil. His lips pressed into a tight line, and he refused to meet her eyes.

Hmm . . . had she hit a nerve? Did he have something to hide? Just who was the rumpled fashion plate with the white Jag he kept meeting with?

Lark stepped forward, formulating questions.

"Now, children," Miss Mariah said, poking her head out of Rich's door, "come on in. We don't really have time to fritter, do we? I have to get back to my work, and until this mess is straightened out, there are millions of American women doin' without their Dream Squeezes. Richard? What do you have to eat around here?"

Deciding to hold her questions until after Miss Mariah left,

Lark followed her dog to the front porch. Rich joined them, his eyes shuttered, his lips a slash.

"This gets more and more curious," she said to her pup, then stepped inside the Desmond home. The dog objected.

"Come on, Pooch-Face," she urged, tugging on the leash. "Miss Mariah needs our help."

The hound remained rooted in place, his nose glued to the gray floorboards of the wide wraparound porch. He strained against the leash, endangering Lark's foothold. "Hey, you. I'm the boss, and I say we're going inside."

A rumble of laughter told her Rich had dropped his kill-'em-with-a-stare stance—again at her expense.

"Is that the best you can do for a dog name?" he asked. "Hey, you? Or is the lovely and lyrical Pooch-Face your Pulitzer entry?"

"You're a pain, you know that?" she asked, yanking on the leash with all her might, finally gaining her recalcitrant pet's attention. "I have to find just the perfect name for him. He's a flawless specimen."

Rich crossed his arms over his broad chest. "Of what?"

"What do you mean, of what? Of dog."

A familiar, mischievous twinkle in his eyes warned Lark of impending danger to her dignity. "What kind of dog?"

She tossed her head in that bubblebrained way so many women used—and she deplored—to get around difficult men, then said, "I already told you. He's a . . . Midget Manchurian Maudlin. Golden brown, at that."

Rich guffawed.

Why had she thought she could pull it off? And why hadn't she asked Maggie what kind of dog she'd bought?

She headed toward the kitchen. "Miss Mariah! Can I help with lunch?"

"You don't know, do you?" Rich asked in a teasing tone.

Standing in the doorway, she said, "Does it matter?"

"In this case it does."

"Why?"

"Take a look at your dog, Lark. A good look."

She turned to study Pooch-Face. His large size and saucepan-sized paws indicated he'd grow into a solid animal. The pup's golden brown coat, short and smooth, bore a tint of red. He had an abundance of wrinkles over his forehead and the sides of his face, and a baggy dewlap at his neck, too. His lips hung long and low, and his ears were thin and soft to the touch. As Pooch-Face cocked his somewhat pointy head, his hazel eyes stared back at her, intelligence manifested in their quizzical expression. All in all, these features gave him a somewhat noble look, contrasting with his puppy exuberance and mischief.

As she stared at the animal, a hint of recognition pierced her memory. "I know what he is," she said slowly, digging into her mental archive of facts, searching for the detail that danced just out of her reach. "I've seen one before. I just can't remember where."

"Want a . . . clue?"

"Sure."

"Who was your fictional hero while you were growing up?"

The memory jelled. "Sherlock Holmes, of course, but . . . you're kidding. You mean, this is a . . . ?"

"That's right. He's a bloodhound. Just like his mistress. Nosy to a fault."

Lark dropped to her knees and took the canine face between her hands. Pooch-Face's ever-present drool slicked her fingers, but she ignored the inconvenience. "So you're the real thing, are you?"

The pup blinked and snuffled her hands.

Warmth flooded her heart. "What a thoughtful gift she gave me," Lark murmured, thinking of the sister she often considered a total flake. "I never would have expected it of her."

Rich joined her on the floor, scratching the pup's now

offered belly. "Maybe you've sold her short. It looks as though she knows you better than you thought she did."

A stab of guilt bit at her. "You're right. And I need to apologize to her."

With an exaggerated look of amazement, Rich said, "Who would have thought Snoop-Scoop would see the light?"

She pushed against his rock-solid shoulder. "Hey, can I help it if I'm never wrong?"

"Whooeee! There you go again, Red, proving yourself wrong and me right instead."

"No, I didn't. I'm not wrong."

"You were about Maggie."

"But not about other things."

"How do you know?"

"I know . . . because I know. OK? I've been doing things my way and succeeding. I even have proof—my Pulitzer is hard to deny."

"That only applies to business, Lark. What do you know about people? about life?"

Since she didn't want to think about his questions, she countered by asking what a small-town grocer knew about the greater scheme of things.

As they bantered, Pooch-Face bounced his head back and forth, following the volley of words. He yipped, then stood and ran in excited circles.

Lark swiveled, trying to catch him before his hard-swinging tail knocked over a piece of furniture.

Rich dove for the leash.

The dog evaded their efforts, and the two humans landed in a tangled heap on the floor.

The yowls and howls faded into the background. Heat singed Lark everywhere she came in contact with Rich. The hand flattened against his chest. The ankle captive beneath his knee. The elbow cradling his head.

Her eyes saw flames in his, mere inches away. She couldn't move. She couldn't breathe.

His face approached.

Her heart pounded. Her palms grew slick.

His lips came within a simple kiss from hers. Fear and excitement surged through her. Was Rich Desmond about to kiss her?

"What on earth is goin' on?" Mariah said into the charged atmosphere. "Why is this puppy gnawin' on Richie's shoe while the two of you wrestle on the floor?"

"Nooooo!" Rich rose and clamored much like a tsunami. "Give me back my shoe, you miserable, mangy mutt. You've already demolished one, and I'm not ready to feed you another."

Lark stood, moving slowly, as though she'd just been thawed by the heat of Rich's proximity after she'd spent an eternity in deep freeze. A jumble of thoughts rioted in her head, and somewhere in her heart she felt searing disappointment. What would Rich's kiss have been like? Then she realized what she'd just thought.

No. She couldn't do that again. She couldn't let the powerful attraction she'd always felt for him drag her down that embarrassing road again.

Pouncing on her misbehaving dog's antics as a lifesaver, she charged him. "Give me that shoe, you dumb dog. I can't be supplying this guy with new footwear—"

Lark fell silent as she gripped the slobber-damp shoe. What was small-town shopkeeper Rich Desmond doing with hand-sewn Guccis? Where had the money to lavish on *haute couture* footwear come from?

Who was the guy in the white Jag?

What was Rich Desmond hiding?

And how did it all play into the Secret Service's investigation of the girdle business?

Was Rich behind his mother's woes?

"So," she said, eyes flying to Rich's handsome face, "what's our next move on Miss Mariah's behalf?"

"This meeting of the Garden Club will come to order," Louella said, banging her gavel.

Goodness, Mariah thought, *Louella really likes that little hammer. It gives her instant command of the situation. Now if she could only gain that kind of response from Lark and Rich. . . .*

Just minutes after she'd found the two tangled on the floor, they'd gone back to sniping at each other. And when she'd told Louella about it, her housemate had felt such behavior called for more drastic measures on the Garden Club's part.

Louella cleared her throat. "The bulbs have been duly chosen and ordered, and the City Council has no objection to our change for the library foyer. The dedication of the Bellamy Blossoms' gardens will go forward on Magnolia's weddin' date as planned."

She took a sip of water, then continued. "Which brings us to the second order of business. Lark and Richie are just as hardheaded as they've ever been. We need somethin' to get them to quit sparrin' and start spoonin'."

Myrna rose. "I didn't join this club to run a lonely hearts' bureau. I can keep an eye on them—just in the interest of stayin' abreast of what happens in our fair town, y'know."

Chuckles rolled through the room.

Her white, Gibson girl hairdo a-bobbing, Sophie Hardesty said, "You just want to keep sniffin' out what's happenin' between them all on your own so you can spread the tidbits. My goodness, Myrna Stafford, gossip's hardly the Christian thing to do."

Sage nods accompanied additional titters.

Alarmed, Mariah stood. Louella waved her to the podium. "I must say," Mariah began, "that it doesn't seem quite right to mess between two people. On the other hand, I just know the Lord's always meant those two children to end up together. They're just stubborn and ornery sometimes."

Louella nodded. "That's why I think they need gentle nudges here and there. The good Lord'll do the rest, don't you all think?"

More nods ruffled the gathering.

"Well, then," Louella went on, "I have just the thing. Magnolia's darlin' Yankee, Clay, was called away, as you all know, on a job a couple of weeks ago. He comes back to town as work allows, so she's runnin' the office by her lonesome. She's a mighty capable woman, but she's awful busy. Poor thing hasn't been able to go to Leesburg to pick the flowers for her rehearsal dinner tomorrow and the weddin' Saturday. The warehouse is willin' to rush the order as a special favor to me. You all know how expensive it is for the wholesalers to deliver fresh-cut flowers for an event, and it'd be a blessin' if she could save some on delivery at least."

Myrna sniffed. "So what's your point, Louella? You're jawin' up a storm, an' we're no wiser here. What are you cookin' up now?"

Triumph brightened Louella's face. "Since in desperation Maggie asked me this mornin' to choose and order the flowers for her, I say we let Lark do it. Richie can drive her to the wholesalers. He can use the Country Store's refrigerated truck."

Mariah gave Louella's hand a grateful squeeze. "I think you're brilliant, Louella."

Louella bowed her head in modesty. "Well, one tries to follow one's callin', you know, dear. And I truly feel called to help others. Especially my dearest Iris's granddaughters. Why, those three little girls are alone in the world, their mama and daddy long dead, and Iris gone these many years."

Turning toward the members of the club, she clacked her gavel to regain their attention. "So, ladies, what do you think? Do we need further discussion, or are we set to vote?"

"Vote!"

"Very well," Louella said, grinning. "Philadelphia, dear, as the newly elected secretary, are you ready?"

"Of course," whispered the tiny woman from the depths of her blouse, under a sweater, under a shawl, above a skirt, over stockings and orthopedic shoes.

Minutes later the matter was approved; all were in favor— except Myrna, who looked much like a child who'd dropped her penny-candy stick in a puddle of mud.

Louella checked her agenda. "Excellent, ladies. We're truly makin' progress tonight. Now, on to our third, and last, piece of new business for this evening. A future member has been proposed, and we have to evaluate her qualifications and desirability, then vote on whether to offer membership or not."

"Forget it, Louella," Myrna said sourly. "None of them Bellamy Blossoms of yours has a civic-minded hair on her head. We've tried before to lead them in their granny's an' mama's footsteps, but they just ain't interested."

Louella glared at the eternal dissenter in their flock.

Mariah wondered if there was something other than prayer they could do to help sweeten the woman's disposition. She'd have to discuss the matter with her housemates.

After a weighty silence, Louella returned to the business at hand. "None of the Blossoms have been nominated, Myrna. We're considerin' dear Mariah's daughter, Reenie. What do you think, ladies? And remember proper procedure. Sarah, as parliamentarian, please keep us honest, would you, dear?"

The owner of Bellamy's favorite bookstore, The Blissful

Bookworm, nodded her trademark bob. "It's my job, and I'm honored to do so."

"Well, Reenie's settled now," offered Pastor Melbourne's wife, Rosemarie. "And she and Seth are bein' especially blessed in the near future. So, since her mama's been such a loyal member, and Maureen's matured into a lovely wife, I say we'd do right fine to invite her to join."

Mariah smiled, thrilled to hear praises of her girl. Louella grinned as well. They'd often discussed how Reenie would bring a much-needed influx of young blood into the group and might someday lead the Blossoms into the feminine fold, Louella's ultimate goal.

Sophie waved. Louella acknowledged her.

"I love what Reenie's done with her own garden," she said. "Very imaginative use of wood and stone in her landscapin'. She's ideal for us, and I've loved her to pieces since the day she was born."

The general consensus was pro—until Myrna stood again. "Well, if you must know, I think Reenie's dizzy and flighty and can't be trusted to know what's what. Besides, she's always gettin' herself in trouble with that odd Lark. We can't afford to have her unseemly behavior taint the good name of our club. I say we watch her closely and see what she's gonna do now that Lark's back in town rufflin' things up."

"Oh, Myrna, hush," urged Savannah Hollings, wife of the president of Bellamy Fiduciary Trust. "You just want another excuse to go watchin' and spreadin' gossip."

Savannah turned from Myrna, whose purple hair rolls quivered indignantly, to Louella. "I say we take our vote. Let the chips fall where they may, but I'm sure we'll soon be welcomin' Reenie right into our midst. Just think, ladies, she's Lark's best friend. Surely she'll be instrumental in makin' sure things work out right between her brother and her bosom buddy."

Savannah's words clinched Reenie's acceptance—and further sealed Rich's and Lark's immediate future. Matchmaking was on. In full bloom.

EIGHT

"TELL ME AGAIN HOW AND WHY YOU AND I GOT ROPED INTO today's little hike," Lark said on Friday morning as Rich started the Country Store's refrigerated truck.

"Beats me how, and as far as why . . . that's not too clear in my mind either."

"Then why are we doing this instead of solving your mother's case?"

Rich reined in the impulse to smack his head against the steering wheel. By now, he should know better than to have anything to do with Lark, even if he had agreed to go along with the Garden Club's request so as to keep an eye on Snoop-Scoop. It was all in his—and his mother's—best interests, of course.

But for him to have thought—if only for a second—that something as minor and inconsequential as her sister's wedding might divert Lark's dogged attention from where it didn't belong. . . .

"Maybe," he said, hoping to lead her from verbal land mines toward more secure territory, "because I own the only refrigerated truck in Bellamy, and your sister's the bride in need of a truckload of flowers."

"But what do we know about flowers?"

"Nothing. And nothing's what we need to know. Miss Louella and Mama said Maggie told you what flowers she wanted. All we have to do is order arrangements made with the stuff she asked for and pay with the check she gave you. That's it."

Lark crossed her arms over her chest and sank into the seat. "Rosebuds, carnations, and baby's breath seem like a total waste of time to me." Then she straightened, shot him a look.

Uh-oh, he thought.

"Unless . . . ," she drew out, "we can use the travel time to brainstorm our plan of attack . . . er . . . our investigation."

Rich clenched the steering wheel. "Look, Lark, I have Mama's matter under control. We don't need you sensationalizing her situation with your yellow journalism."

She jerked as if he'd stuck her with a hot cattle prod. "Take that back."

"What? The truth?"

"Your offensive insult, that's what."

"Can't face the truth, can you? You and your big city if-it-feels-good-do-it mentality. Here in Bellamy we have standards, and they usually start with the scriptural injunction to do to others as you want them to do to you."

"There you have it. I'd want my friends to help me if I were in your mother's shoes."

"The operative word there is *help,* not *interfere* or *generate publicity.*"

"I intend no interference, and there's been no publicity, has there? I'm sensitive to Mariah's plight, and I have no intention of hurting her. However, I can't control the actions of the Secret Service."

How was he going to get her off his and his mother's backs? The woman was more tenacious than a hungry leech.

"Look, Lark, for Mama's sake, let it be. I've already hired a new team of lawyers—" who were going to wind up wealthy beyond their wildest dreams at his expense—"and they're ready to do battle on her behalf. Sticking your nose into this will muck up everything."

"Get real, Rich. A large law firm is only interested in what they're going to get—exposure and dollars being foremost in their minds. Not your mother's innocence. They're probably figuring out how to finagle her into copping a plea."

Remembering his conversation with Mama's new lead counsel, Rich squirmed. Besides their per-hour rate, which was staggering, the man's hints about plea bargaining had bothered him in view of Mama's determined rejection of that option. But Rich refused to grant Lark even that. "I tell you, it's under control. Go back to doing whatever you came to town to do."

Then he realized what he'd just said. She'd returned to Bellamy to make a success of her magazine—by interviewing him. Well, his alter ego. *Quick! Think of something.* "Better yet. Go back to bossing your sisters. They've been on a Lark vacation for a number of years. Why don't you catch them up?"

When Lark failed to snap back with an argument, an uneasy feeling grew in his gut. He glanced her way and went cold. She'd fixed her speculative green gaze on his face. His imagination pictured sparks flying as gears sped thought after thought through her red head.

"I can't back down for you," she said, her serious tone a surprise. "I gave your mother my word. If nothing else, she wants my support, and I intend for her to have it. She's been there for me every time I've called on her. Don't ask me to fail her the one time she turns to me."

Unbidden admiration rose in him. She might be a thorn in his side, and she might be trouble, too, but Lark had just displayed a depth of integrity he couldn't challenge. Not to mention love and loyalty for his mother.

Despite his better judgment, he said, "I understand. I guess we're stuck with each other until this is cleared up."

"Looks that way."

"Then we'd better declare a truce and cooperate."

"No problem with me. I didn't come back to town aiming at you."

"I didn't welcome you with a loaded gun, either."

"You didn't need one. Your attitude said it all."

"You can't deny I have reason to mistrust you."

"I've never done anything to you."

"Maybe not to me, but your actions always backfired on me."

"You don't think your superior disdain hurt me?"

"Give me a break, Lark. I was a kid, and you were a little brat with a world-class crush on me. Your mooning around after me embarrassed me to death."

Her eyes developed a moist sheen. "Your reaction to me encouraged everyone to make a little girl's life a misery," she said in a quiet, earnest tone. "You have no idea what it was like to be laughed at by everyone in town—even by grown-ups who should have known better—and to eventually be labeled an oddity, crazy, and strange. Just because I thought you were . . . special."

Had it really been that way? Had he really caused her pain? He'd only wanted to discourage Lark's puppy love.

"I'm sorry if you suffered," he said, sincere in his regret. "But you made me miserable. You and Reenie pulled so many loony pranks on me. There were the phone calls with the disguised, pseudo-alluring voice suggesting that love lived just next door—the night of my birthday sleepover party. Then came your wacky support of my candidacy for student council president, and your outrageous 'kings are stronger than queens' campaign to crown me homecoming king. And need we mention my prom?"

Lark opened her mouth to speak. Rich beat her to it. "You

made me feel as though everyone saw me as the world's greatest fool. I was as embarrassed as you say you were."

"I was a pain, wasn't I?" she asked ruefully.

"What makes you think you're not now?" he asked with a smile to lighten the mood.

"Well, I'm not lobbying to have *People* magazine name you the sexiest man alive, am I?"

Now what did she mean by that? Did Lark see him as some exemplary specimen of manhood? He stole a look at her but saw only a satiny, cinnamon-dusted cheek and a riotous tumble of auburn curls.

She was beautiful, and he hated noticing it.

As he had the day the dog dragged her into the police department. And especially when the mutt lassoed them together on his living-room floor. To Rich's horror, he'd nearly kissed her that time. If his mother hadn't come into the room when she did, he would have covered Lark's lips with his own.

If they'd actually kissed, he feared he'd have had a hard time pulling away—no matter how unreasonable the attraction, no matter how frustrating the woman. Especially since he'd found more to admire in Lark than just her titian beauty. He would chew broken glass before admitting it, but her tenacity and drive impressed him. She'd accomplished more in a few years than most did in a lifetime. And she took risks he'd never even consider.

Now she'd revealed a fierce streak of loyalty for his mother. What would it be like to have someone stick to you like that? Someone who wasn't related to you by blood. Someone whose respect wasn't inspired by your accomplishments, great though they might be, or by your family's position in town, upstanding though it was. What would it be like to have Lark support him just for himself? As a man?

He'd known her infatuation. Rich shuddered. But what would the grown-up Lark's love be like? When he realized where his thoughts had strayed, he slammed on the brakes. Literally. The truck skidded sideways. Lark screamed.

Rich felt like screaming, too.

"What was that all about?" she asked as they rolled to a stop on a bumpy shoulder.

He jerked a hand through his hair. "I . . . thought I saw an . . . animal run out onto the road."

She looked at him as though he'd lost his mind. "Try again. I was watching, and nothing of the sort happened."

"Hey, I said I *thought* I saw something."

"Get some new thoughts, then, OK? I don't want to die just yet. My sister's flowers aren't that important."

New thoughts. A renewing of his mind.

OK, so that's where he'd gone wrong. He hadn't turned to God since he'd first learned of Mama's troubles. And he couldn't remember if he'd sought the heavenly Father's guidance in coping with Lark.

Rich silently confessed his mistake, then sent up a brief SOS and a promise—to come to the Almighty's throne in prayer once he returned home.

With a look at his passenger, he smiled wryly. This wasn't the moment for soul-searching. Right now, he had trouble on his hands. The unwanted attraction he felt for his former nemesis was mind-blowingly scary. It threatened not only his dignity but his peace of mind and heart, insane though that was.

"That's what Maggie wants?" Lark asked, her nose wrinkled in distaste.

"Hey," Rich answered, "you told me she said blue-tinted rosebuds and carnations, plus baby's breath. This lady—" Rich gestured toward the designer who'd offered help when they'd entered the wholesale florist's warehouse—"seems to know her business. I'm no expert, but these look like unopened roses, carnations, and these tiny puffs on slender stems look like something they might call baby's breath. I'd trust her."

"Sure," Lark said, studying an array of brilliant-hued flowers in glass-fronted refrigerators while ignoring the buckets of pastel blue blooms before her. "I trust her, but I can't trust Maggie. My sister hasn't a clue what she needs. She's too . . . sheltered and inexperienced to realize that these flowers are way boring. Besides, she's going to pay plenty for them. She may as well get the most bang for her bucks."

Her eyes donned a speculative gleam as she approached the coolers. Rich's stomach lurched. "Where are you going with this?"

Lark stared through the glass door and studied the floral bounty. A finger crept through her wealth of curls and twined one around its tip. "Give me a minute here."

Uh-oh. Giving the zany redhead a minute to concoct a plan could only mean grief—of the well-known Lark variety. Rich's thoughts swam with foreboding.

"You know," he said, determined to avoid a catastrophe, "we should just ask this lovely lady and her very able helpers to make us up an assortment of blue rosebud and carnation table decorations, corsages, and the other stuff Maggie needs for her rehearsal dinner and wedding while we go . . . get something to eat. I'm starved, aren't you?"

"Nope, it's not even eleven yet." She came nose-to-nose with one glass door. "What are those gorgeous orange flowers with the freckles on the petals?"

Rich peered at the blossoms. "Beats me."

"Those are tiger lilies, miss," said the patient floral arranger at their side. "They're the latest rage in weddings. Brides are crazy for the wildflower look."

"I can see why," Lark murmured, her attention on the

opulent flowers. "The attendants' dresses are long, ice blue satin. That sure isn't my style, and that washed-out color can't possibly do a thing for my hair and eyes. Give me a soft pair of jeans and a T-shirt any day."

Lark's words drew Rich's attention to her. Wearing her preferred faded jeans and a pale green pocket T-shirt, she stood against the backdrop of exotic flowers. The tall tiger lilies brought out the russet in her hair, while clusters of sensuously curved white calla lilies lent a freshness to her features.

Rich wished he could freeze the moment. Lark had never looked lovelier than she did right then, a faraway expression on her delicate face, framed by God's most exquisite jewels. The foliage scattered here and there among the masses of blooms heightened the deep tone of her eyes, making him again wonder about their hidden depths.

She'd given him a glimpse of the inner woman on the drive into town. Now he wanted more than that glimpse.

"So," she said, ripping into his reverie, "what do you think? Doesn't the wimpy ice blue satin just cry out for something to spice it up?"

The florist stepped forward. "Rosebuds and carnations are wonderful with blue satin, miss. Classic and traditional and always right."

At Lark's frown, she hurried on to say, "But on the other hand, a wildflower theme based on tiger lilies would be stunning against the cool tone of the blue. Exciting and unusual. Very unique and now."

"See?" Lark crowed, poking a finger at Rich's chest. Spinning toward the arranger, she added, "We'll take the wildflowers. Maggie can't spend all that money and wind up with a yawn of a wedding."

Queasiness hit Rich. "Lark, shouldn't you check this out with Maggie? Just give her a quick call."

"Why? She said she was too busy to do it, so she sent me. As her older sister, I have to watch out for her. Besides, she knows I'll do the right thing. Better than she, I might add."

"In your mind, maybe. But it's *Maggie's* wedding. I don't think it's smart to go with your taste rather than hers. Please call her."

"It's smart when I'm right and she's wrong." She donned her stubborn-mule, jutted-jaw, crossed-arms stance. If past experience proved anything, nothing would budge Lark.

Still, Rich felt the need to try. "I think you're making a terrible mistake. Think about it, please. Would you like Maggie to dump what you want in favor of what she wants? For your wedding?"

A chuckle made her wild auburn curls dance. "She'd never have to," Lark said. "I'd know from the start what works. I covered dozens of elaborate events at the beginning of my career in Baltimore. Ho-hum decorations make for snooze-fests. Besides, I'm not getting married. I've yet to meet the man I could stand for any length of time. And I assure you, should I find one, he won't be of questionable honesty like Maggie's ex-con, Clay."

Urgency filled Rich. He had to do something to prevent this misery in the making. "Remember what you said in the truck? How everyone in town laughed at you? Considered your schemes outrageous and crazy?"

"Yes . . . so?"

"So don't you think if you make a hash of your sister's wedding they'll think even less of you?"

She sucked in her breath. He'd struck a nerve.

Then she exhaled. "No, I don't think so. I think they'd look at me like more of a fool if I let Maggie ruin her wedding. I've always had to clean up my sisters' messes. This time I'm going to avoid one. Don't worry, Rich, I know what I'm doing. I know what's best."

To the saleswoman, she reiterated, "We'll take the wild-flowers."

As Lark ordered not only the arrangements for tonight's rehearsal dinner but also for tomorrow's wedding: church, reception, and even bouquet—which Clay was paying for but Maggie choosing—Rich felt helpless. How could he, so eloquent in his writing, have failed to persuade Lark of the enormity of her arrogance? the extent of her pride?

He'd tried, he really had. But in typical Lark fashion, she'd ignored him, forging forth to her waterloo.

He ached for Maggie. And for Lark. No wonder they squabbled so much.

"Ready?" Lark asked, temporarily done wreaking havoc. "Didn't you say something about food earlier?"

"Yeah, but you said you weren't hungry."

"Not then. I had more important things to think about. Maggie's wedding's going to be beautiful. Besides, my stomach's growling. Let's go eat."

With a shrug, Rich turned to the bemused saleswoman. "I know it's still early for lunch, but do you have any suggestions where we could go? I figure you'll need the truck for loading, so food has to be within walking distance."

"Yes, we need the truck. How about Rosarina's Little Italy? It's only four blocks away. They have the best pasta and pizza in town—in my opinion." She patted her robust middle and winked.

Rich grinned. "Sounds good to me."

"And too good for me," countered the lady, chuckling.

He asked Lark, "Is Italian OK with you?"

"Yum. Lead me there."

Following the simple directions the woman had given them, they reached the restaurant in less than ten minutes.

At the table with its red-and-white-checked cloth, Lark sniffed appreciatively. "Nothing smells better to a hungry woman than the perfume of oregano, onions, garlic, and olive oil. I'm glad that lady sent us here. I'm starved."

In contrast, foreboding had stolen Rich's appetite. "Order up, then. I have to call Mama's operations manager at the distribution center after we're done. Plus I'm expecting a shipment of poultry tomorrow, and I need to check on the delivery time. Seems I can't keep the store in boneless, skinless chicken breasts these days. Everyone's on a health kick, I guess."

Lark arched a graceful brow. "Smart folks want to live longer, and especially, a little better while they do so. Health matters, you know."

"I guess. There's nothing wrong with chicken."

"Oh, now, I didn't say that—"

"Have some fresh garlic bread." The black-haired waitress placed a basket of fragrant, golden chunks between them.

Lark pounced. "Thanks," she murmured right before her first bite. "Mmm . . . "

Rich smiled. He had to give her credit. Lark never did anything halfway. She lived life to the fullest, relishing every aspect of it. "Plenty more where that came from," he said. "Enjoy."

She said nothing more, just munched happily, savoring the bread, the olive-oil-and-red-wine-vinegared salad, and ultimately, her vegetable tortellini in marinara sauce.

After a short, private prayer, Rich picked at his veal parmigiana, his thoughts on impending doom—on various fronts. Not only was Lark going home to face Maggie's wrath while dragging him into it through his involuntary association, but they also had to deal with his mother's predicament. All while he kept Lark out of his personal business.

Which would likely prove the most difficult thing he ever did. He worked from home. He received calls there. And Lark would insist on sticking to him while Mama's misfortune continued.

He'd lived through that already. She'd always been underfoot, especially after his mother took the orphan under her wing following Mr. and Mrs. Bellamy's deaths. Matters grew worse when Reenie and Lark became inseparable. Best friends. Closest confidantes.

Rich's self-protective alarms went off. He had to do something to maintain his personal status quo. "You know," he said, "if you're going to stick your bloodhound nose into Mama's case—"

"What do you mean *if*? And Pooch-Face and I resent that bloodhound crack."

"OK. Since you're sticking your snoopy nose into Mama's case—"

"That's no better. I'm Scoop. With good reason and better track record."

Rich held up his hands in defeat. "Fine, fine. Since you're on the case, Scoop, there's one thing you have to keep in mind. Reenie."

Lark forked away the last bites of tortellini. "What's Reenie got to do with this?"

"Exactly. Nothing. She can only fuss and worry about Mama, and that's not good for her or the baby. Besides, you know Reenie's never been good at keeping secrets."

"I'll say. The minute I told her I thought you were cute, the whole rotten town knew. We can't let her know much, then, can we?"

"Right. And we have to keep Mama from telling Reenie any more than she already knows."

"That won't be easy."

"Crying defeat already?"

"Not on your life."

"Then are we agreed?"

"On this, yes."

"And you'll back me?"

"Totally."

He snorted. "This I need to see."

"I work very well with others toward a common goal."

"That remains to be seen," he said, skeptical.

She grinned. "You're on. I'm going to prove to you how well you and I can work together. You'll see."

What had he done? "I doubt that'll ever be the outcome of this wild-goose chase."

"Are we betting on it?"

"I don't bet. I'm a Christian."

She blinked. Paused. "OK," she said, unusually compliant. "We'll just see who's right at the end."

"Agreed."

After picking up the flowers late that afternoon, they drove home in silence; Lark closed her eyes and dozed. Once in town, they drove straight to the Bellamy Community Church's Fellowship Hall and turned over the truck plus contents to a contingent of Garden Club members led, as always, by Miss Louella.

Then, after saying something about Maggie and a silk sheath, Lark headed toward Main Street.

Rich went home, ready to put in a couple of hours on the play in progress before showering and shaving for tonight's event. He looked forward to talking more with Maggie's future husband. He'd heard good things about the man from Hobey, who was the best judge of character Rich knew. Lark's mistrust of her future brother-in-law notwithstanding.

Rich stopped by the mailbox and gathered up the day's offerings. Then he saw it: from the law offices of Chickering, Martindell, Ludwigs, and Benn—the firm that had handled the legalities regarding the consortium of investors in Mama's company.

The queasy feeling he'd harbored since Lark had done her thing at the floral warehouse congealed into raging nausea. This could mean only one thing. Word of Mama's woes had reached the investors.

What remained to be seen was how furious they were and how large a piece of Mariah Desmond they'd want.

NINE

WITHIN MINUTES AFTER CONFERRING WITH HIS MOTHER'S new counsel, Rich decided, against the lawyer's advice, to cover the investors' losses. He couldn't stand for those men to think Mariah a crook.

He emptied out his bank account. He'd used his longtime savings to bail Mama out of jail. Then he'd plunked down one CD of movie money as a retainer for the new attorneys, and today, he'd kissed the other one good-bye.

He doubted Desmond's Country Store could generate enough revenue to cover his and Mama's albeit modest needs. He needed a new contract. Soon. But not the one Storey kept pushing.

What was he going to do? He couldn't let Mama down. She'd stood by him during his early writing years, lean as they'd been. She'd covered his costs and helped him at the store until his writing began to pay. Rich couldn't fail the woman who'd believed in him even before he'd believed in himself. The woman who lived the human version of unconditional love. The woman who would never, ever cheat a soul.

Rich wanted nothing to do with a wedding rehearsal dinner. He wanted to stay home, think through Mama's and his plight, brainstorm his work-in-progress, and see if he could come up with a compromise the big guys would find palatable, one he could accept in good conscience.

After today's disturbing thoughts about Lark, he didn't want to see her decked out in that sheath she'd trudged off to find.

The last thing Rich needed was an attraction to a woman, much less an attraction to Lark. He didn't want to discover yet another appealing side of the maddening redhead. She already sparkled enough on many different facets.

"Fine," he grumbled as he knotted his classic, rep silk tie. "I'll just keep my distance. I'll concentrate on the bride and groom, and talk to Hobey the rest of the night."

When he spoke his determination, Rich realized how wise it truly was. If he avoided Lark, he'd also avoid Reenie. That would go a long way in preventing further grief.

Despite the tension in his muscles and the pounding in his temples, Rich was encouraged. He could do this. He could take care of Mama's dealings. Then he could go back to figuring out what to do with his career. He wouldn't write anything that would shame his God.

With a sure step, he decided to walk to the Bellamy Community Church's Fellowship Hall, making certain he concentrated on the balmy summer-evening breeze. The scent of roses, spicy geraniums, and sweet freesia wafted from gardens all around, and the velvet sounds of darkness descended on a town peacefully rolling up its streets for the night.

Everywhere but at the BCC grounds. As Rich approached—late, since he'd planned to miss the actual rehearsal, to which he'd been invited due to the families' long, close, friendship—the sound of cheer migrating from the sanctuary to the adjacent hall welcomed him before he reached the buildings.

"There you are, Richie," his mother called when she spotted him. "I thought you'd be here for the rehearsal. We had such fun. Why, I can't wait until the day you marry. Your sister's weddin' brought me such joy, I just want to watch you promise yourself to—"

When she brought herself up short, Rich winced. He knew what she'd been about to say. Mama had never made a secret of her hopes for him and Lark.

But he'd just made a commitment to himself to avoid that woman. Mama would have to survive the disappointment.

"I'm here in time for the dinner, aren't I?" he said with forced cheer. "I had . . . business to attend to back home. Couldn't be helped. Paperwork, you know."

His mother pursed her lips and said nothing as they entered the hall. The guests oohed and aahed over the creative use of wildflowers, especially the arrangement of deep apricot tiger lilies, bronzy red daisies, black-centered miniature sunflowers, ferns, long-leaved greens, and cascading ivy that adorned the center of the head table. The proud lilies soared over the verdant mass past the other blossoms, elegant and exotic, reminiscent of Lark.

Against his better judgment, Rich searched the gathering for the woman responsible for this unique and exquisite display of God's artistry.

He found Lark speaking with petite Sophie Hardesty. Lark's mahogany hair gleamed with the russet tones of the flowers. Her slender form, encased in a simple emerald sheath that enhanced the color of her eyes, resembled a flower's stem. Her fair skin glowed with health, and her cheekbones boasted a hint of the same shade of coral found at the edge of the lilies' petals.

Her family had had the right idea to name her after a

flower. But *Larkspur?* Weren't those purple? With her red hair and green eyes, purple didn't work for Lark.

They should have thought of *Lily;* it would have matched her as wonderfully as Magnolia matched the bride-to-be. The bride, who stepped into the arched doorway to the room, her hand clasped by the tall, dark-suited man at her side. The bride, whose delicate porcelain complexion turned waxy white, whose delft blue eyes opened to horrified proportions, whose normally smiling lips didn't smile.

As the guests became aware of the arrival of the fêted couple, a wave of clapping crested. The expression on Maggie's face, however, soon brought everyone to a standstill.

Her eyes darted from table to table, fixing finally on the dramatic elegance of the head table. She then shook herself, peered down at her powder blue suit, then stared at the ribbon bouquet in her hand, made by the guests at her bridal shower from the decorations on their gifts.

The satin streamers gleamed pastel; the flowers didn't.

Rich's earlier nausea returned with a vengeance, and he studied Lark. As he watched, the expectant smile on her mouth melted into something different altogether, until she caught her bottom lip in its descent. She stared at her sister, then at the flowers. A wary look bloomed in her eyes, and she unerringly found him in the crowd.

The color of the bronzy red daisies in the arrangements blazed across Lark's cheeks and made its way up to her hair-line. A tiny crease formed between her brows, and a flicker of what looked like fear darted across her features.

Then she straightened to her full height, drew her shoulders back and down, and held high her mass of dark red curls. She met her sister's gaze.

Rich caught his breath. He'd never seen a more magnificent woman: brave in the face of trouble, accountable despite her blunder, vulnerable in her courage.

He took a step toward Lark.

"How could you?" asked Maggie, her voice cracking. Her words, though whispered, were audible in every corner of the room. "I trusted you, Lark. And this—" she gestured toward the tables—"is what you bring back. I thought we were gettin' on better." With a sob, she turned and ran from the room, the frowning groom a step behind her.

The bridal couple's departure unleashed a flurry of murmurs. Every eye in the room flew to Lark, who now looked very alone despite Sophie's small, plump self at her side.

"Why would Magnolia trust that wacko, vegetarian Lark?" someone asked.

"D'you reckon she switched the food, too?"

"Girl's been strange all along."

"Tetched's what I say."

"Humph!" snorted Myrna Stafford. "That Lark's been odd from the cradle, an' then went an' got right citified. One can't rightly know what she is these days. Other than after Rich Desmond again for a ring on her finger, if you ask me. It's all she's wanted since she weren't but knee-high to a grasshopper."

All color leached from Lark's beautiful face. Willowy as she looked, Rich feared she'd collapse. But she proved him wrong.

Wrapping a mantle of dignity around herself, Lark took sure, slow steps to the open sliding doors at the west side of the hall, then vanished into the darkness outside.

That's when the talk roared, even though the guest list numbered only twenty-two.

Camellia Bellamy Sprague, who'd evidently followed the bride and groom from the sanctuary, stood in the spot from where Maggie had fled, looking first after Lark, then after Maggie, as though torn between her two older sisters.

With a quick prayer for help and wisdom, Rich ran to the youngest Bellamy Blossom. When he reached Cammie's side, relief eased her expression.

"I'm so glad to see you, Rich," said the gentle sister. "Could you go see after Maggie while I follow Lark? I don't think it'd be such a fine idea for you to see to her, with all your past and Myrna's awful reminder."

"Don't forget our present. I was with her when she did this." He nodded toward the troublesome decorations. "I warned her, tried to reason with her—"

"But she wouldn't listen," Cammie broke in, resignation in her voice. "I know my sisters . . . some. This is just like Lark, thinkin' she always knows best. But she doesn't. Only God does, and she hasn't checked with him in years."

"That about sums it up. Look, we can talk later. I'd better go tell Maggie what happened. She knew I was driving the truck, and I don't want her to blame me. Besides, tough though she tries to look, I think Lark's as upset as Maggie. She honestly thought she was helping. We'd better see what we can do."

Cammie gave a nod, her midlength, silky, brown bob falling into place with simplicity and grace, much as the woman herself did. Rich again felt the peaceful pleasure he always felt in Cammie's company and wished, irrationally, that Lark had somehow inherited that trait as well.

Then he shook his head. No time for whimsical and futile wishing. "Poor Maggie."

"Poor, proud Lark," Cammie responded and walked away.

Inwardly Rich agreed as he set off to find the bride and groom. Pride was an ugly sin. That was why he refused to take glory or acclaim for his writing, like many writers and artists did. "To God be the glory," the old hymn said, and Rich lived by that motto. He'd continue to do his best for Christ, refusing to become like the publicity seekers. He knew better than that.

Rounding the corner in the corridor, Rich found a sobbing Maggie and a bewildered Clay sitting on a cream-and-plum-colored, striped love seat.

"What was I thinkin' to trust hardheaded, hotshot Lark to bring home what I told her to get?" the bride moaned to her groom.

Rich felt even worse at his failure. "Maggie."

She lifted her blonde head, and her makeup-smeared, teary eyes met his. "Hi, Rich."

He knelt by the couple. Holding his hand out to the man at Maggie's side, he said to Clay, "It's too bad we're meeting again like this. I've heard good things about you and am looking forward to knowing you better."

The dark-haired groom shook Rich's hand and gave him a smile. "I don't understand all that's happened tonight, but I'm pleased to see you, too. Hobey speaks well of you."

Despite his friend's endorsement, embarrassment struck Rich. "I'm afraid I'm partly to blame for tonight's upset."

"What do you mean?" Maggie asked.

He hoped for a smile. "I drove the getaway truck from the scene of Lark's crime."

He got it—a ghost of one. "I should be used to my sister by now. But I never lose hope that someday we can . . . become friends maybe. I do love her, you know."

"I know, and Lark loves you, too," Rich said, even though Lark's actions were often impossible to comprehend.

"That seems hard to believe," Clay said, echoing Rich's thought. "Maggie spent weeks trying to think of a gift that would be meaningful to Lark. I thought that puppy was perfect."

"Oh, trust me," Rich said, "he is. Much more than you'll ever know."

Clay shook his head. "Then Lark turns around and does this. Why?"

Maggie blotted her eyes on a man's handkerchief—one Clay would never use again since streaks of black now smeared the white linen. "You have to know Lark, I guess."

"Maybe I don't want to." Releasing the petite hand he held, Clay wrapped his arm around Maggie's shoulders. "Not if she can hurt you on a day like today."

Rich winced. "There's more."

Knowledge dawned on Maggie's face. "She didn't."

"Oh, yes, she did."

"Everythin'?"

"Everything."

Clay T-ed his hands like a ref. "Time-out, guys. What are you talking about?"

Rich braced himself; the worst was yet to come. "Lark—"

"Let me tell him," Maggie said. "Clay, honey, I'd be willin' to bet anythin', were I a bettin' woman, and I'm not, that she changed my flowers. Do you understand? *All* my flowers."

Disbelieving, Clay asked, "You mean . . . for the wedding?"

Rich and Maggie gave matching nods.

"Oh, man." Clay ran a hand down the back of his neck. "Can you fix the order?"

"Not a chance," Rich said. "All the flowers are already done."

Clay sat back against the love seat. "At least Lark has excellent taste."

Maggie turned poisonous eyes toward her groom. "Now don't Benedict Arnold me, Clayton Marlowe. My very own baby sister, Cammie, made my Victorian-ball-gown-reproduction weddin' dress. It plain hollers for elegant flowers. Lark's weeds are not goin' to work. Besides, she, Cammie, and Miss Louella are wearin' ice blue. Those orange an' yellow things will look near as ugly against those dresses as the biggest toad rearin' up its homely head in a puddle of sin. An' sunflowers? Why? Did she think I wanted a bunch of blackbirds to come a-crowin' to my weddin' for seeds?"

Twin spots of pink splashed on Maggie's cheeks as her anger grew. "My goodness, Rich, now I truly understand what she put you through all those years."

You don't know the half of it—the current half, Rich was thinking.

In an effort to smooth matters between the sisters, Rich took his life in his hands. "I have to agree with Clay. The wildflower look may not be what you wanted, but it's stunning. The flowers look great against the tablecloths. The contrast makes the pale blue linen seem clearer, softer. It should do the same for the dresses."

"Lark does have good taste," Clay repeated, despite the danger of rousing his fiancée's ire again.

Maggie deflated. "Yes, she does. And I know the flowers are pretty. But Clay and I are marryin' at the Ashworth Mansion, Rich, remember? It's supposed to be a historical weddin'. Those flowers are too . . . too modern."

"Not exactly," Clay said, displaying yet more daring in the face of an emotional female. "Don't forget how much the Victorians appreciated nature, sweetheart. None of the flowers Lark chose are weeds. They're just not the formal, classic ones people—you—expect."

Instead of a flaring of Maggie's temper, as Rich had expected, a musing smile tilted the corners of her lips. "Y'know, I believe you may be right. Why, wasn't there some sort of naturalist movement back then? Wildflowers are natural, after all."

For several minutes she remained thoughtful. Then a radiant smile broke through her earlier gloom. "I know! The impressionists at the end of the nineteenth century. They were Victorians. And wasn't it Monet who painted those lovely *Water Lilies?* Yes, I think we can redeem Lark's latest display of pride."

The two men looked at each other and smiled. Weakly, but they smiled.

"Come along, now," Maggie said, standing. "Let's go greet our guests. Ooo-eee! I can imagine what they're thinkin' and sayin'." Her steps slowed. "Then I'll need to find Lark. I truly must apologize and ask her forgiveness for my reaction. Just because she did what she did doesn't mean a Christian woman can behave as I did. . . ."

Chuckling nervously, Clay and Rich followed the now cosmetic-free yet radiant Blossom back into the room.

"Thank you, Jesus," murmured the groom.

Rich gave Clay a sideways look, then smiled in earnest. "Welcome to town, brother."

Rich's chicken, rice pilaf, and just-ripened garden vegetables were delicious, his mocha mousse sumptuous, but one of the bridal attendants was missing.

Earlier, when the servers waved everyone to the buffet table, he'd caught a glimpse of red curls ahead of him in line. He'd assumed Cammie had managed to smooth Lark's ruffled feathers, but no sooner had he taken a bite of his dinner, than he noticed a conspicuous vacancy at the head table. *Had* Cammie found and spoken with Lark?

Where had she gone? An hour and a half had elapsed, and she hadn't returned.

When Miss Louella, Maggie's maid of honor, rose to congratulate the happy couple, Rich excused himself from his mother, sister, brother-in-law, and other tablemates, then took off in search of Trouble.

Why hadn't she listened to him? It turned out he'd been right. She should have just had the floral designer do up the decorations as Maggie had wanted them in the first place. Then no one would have had her feelings hurt.

After witnessing Lark's response to Maggie's discovery of

her actions, Rich felt certain that, despite her brash, bold exterior, there was much more to Lark Bellamy than most suspected. What lay behind those fabulous eyes ran deep.

She was hurting. And in spite of every bit of wisdom God had ever given him, Rich had to find her. The strangest urge to comfort Snoop-Scoop pushed him along.

He checked the entire Fellowship Hall, even calling into the ladies' room and raising twitters of alarm. "Sorry," he called as he beat a hasty retreat.

Had she gone home? he wondered, as he walked up and down the rows of parked cars outside. She must have. He couldn't imagine Lark hanging around the church parking lot this long. Bellamy was a quiet, peaceful town, but it had a handful of teen pranksters he didn't trust. Neither should any sensible woman.

Then again, he was looking for Lark.

Anxiety threatened, but he forced himself to focus on searching the darkness. He thanked God for the beautiful moon he'd provided. Rich visually scoured the yards along the street as he headed homeward, hoping Lark had long since made it back to safety and her dog.

As he approached the Bellamy home, he caught a glimpse of green on the white porch swing. "Thank you, Father," he murmured. "Lark?"

Silence.

"Are you all right?"

Nothing.

"Why did you leave?"

"Do you think I'm stupid, too?"

Again, he gave thanks. If Lark had it in her to be feisty, she had to be fine. As though approaching a wild creature, Rich ascended the porch steps. "I never thought you were stupid. In fact, I don't know anyone who does."

"Yeah, right."

"Impulsive? Oh, yes. Somewhat thoughtless? I think so. A tiny bit arrogant? proud? Definitely."

"I'm not proud or arrogant. I just have more experience than most around here."

Rich bit his tongue as objections erupted in him. Thanks to his career, he'd seen far more of the world than his hardheaded neighbor, but this wasn't the time to enlighten her. He doubted there would ever come a time. Not as long as she published her magazine.

"Look," he said, "you made a mistake in judgment. It's not the end of the world. Just apologize to Maggie. Ask her forgiveness. I know she'll give it. She said she felt badly about her reaction and wanted to speak to you."

"Mm-hmm. I'll just bet she does. Wants to chew me out. But the flowers I got her are a million times better than what she wanted. Can't she see I had it right?"

"It's not a matter of right or wrong, Lark."

"What is it then?"

Rich wondered how far he could push her before she'd run again. "It's a matter of having a servant's heart."

"You see me as Maggie's maid? You're nuts."

Help me, Lord! "No one sees you as anyone's maid, Lark. I'm talking about Christian servanthood. Remember back in Sunday school? They taught us about Jesus and his powerful humility. We're to grow more like him each day."

She waved. "Forget that, Rich. I gave up on God when he gave up on me."

"When did he do that?"

"When he let Mama and Daddy die. When he let me become the brunt of everyone's mockery. When he made my sisters turn on me. When he took Granny Iris, too. When he let me suffer all kinds of knocks as an adult. Believe me, lying down and letting everyone use me as a doormat is not the answer to anything."

"A servant is not a doormat," he argued. Seeing her arms cross over her chest and her chin jut forward, Rich realized he'd have to play tough to break through her defenses. "So tell me. Is clashing with and alienating your sisters on a regular basis the answer?"

She gasped.

"Is putting yourself right where everyone can think poorly of you the answer?"

Her breath came out in a sob. Rich sat by Lark on the swing and noticed her wet lashes, the tear tracks on her cheeks, the chin that still spelled out pride.

He went for another prod. "Is arrogant rebellion against the God who created you, gave his Son for you, loves you totally, the answer?"

Her shoulders heaved.

Knowing full well he was about to hurt her even more, Rich said what he had to say. "I don't think so. Putting yourself above everyone else is not going to prove a thing. You can't force respect, just as you can't force love. You have to first give love, as God did, to be loved in return."

Sobs ripped from Lark's throat, their sound one of anguish, of long-held bitterness, of disillusionment, of rage. Rich ached as he heard her misery, witnessed her pain. Again, everything urged him to offer comfort, and this time he didn't stop himself.

He wrapped his arms around the most unusual woman he'd ever met and shivered at how well she fit his embrace. Lark's slim figure molded itself to him, her scant weight warm against his chest, his shoulder. He ran tentative hands over her quaking back, amazed by the delicacy of her form. How marvelous a creation God made when he took that rib from Adam.

Such fragility, yet such steely strength. All in one beautiful package. Woman. Lark.

Rich kicked the swing into motion, seeking to simulate the rocking of an infant in its mother's arms. He wondered how long it had been since someone had held Lark. With her porcupine exterior, he suspected far too long. He ran a finger down her soft, tearstained cheek. She gave a hiccup but didn't pull away.

After a while, Lark's sobs ebbed in the soothing sounds of the night, the swing, the silence. Rich was glad he'd followed his impulse and gone after her, once it had occurred to him that Cammie most likely hadn't found Lark. He couldn't stand the thought of her crying all alone.

He tilted his head, trying to assess her condition. When he couldn't see due to the position of her head as it rested on his shoulder, he curved a finger under her chin and tipped it higher.

The shallow wells under her eyes looked bruised, her eyelashes spiked, her lips marked with teeth marks, her nose tinted pink. He suppressed a tender smile and again gave thanks for the moonlight. He would have hated to miss this heart-tugging sight: a soft, needy Lark.

Then she met his gaze. "I'm sorry I cried all over your nice suit—"

To Rich's surprise, his lips stopped the silly apology. The softness of her mouth stunned him.

A light sweetness scented his nostrils, sending his senses reeling. But what most affected him was the tremor of Lark's mouth beneath his.

He tightened his embrace.

She wrapped her arms around his neck.

The kiss deepened.

Emotion roared in his ears, and Rich lost track of time, of place, of reality.

Then the woman in his arms quivered. He tore himself away. This comforting business had gotten out of hand way too fast. What he felt for Lark was too much, too deep, too . . .

"Rich?" she asked, a bewildered look in her eyes. Her lips remained parted, as if waiting for another kiss. Rich fought the irrational urge to comply. He couldn't. The unexpected passion they'd generated was not something he could pursue. Not and face himself and God in the morning.

It was Lark, Lark Bellamy, he'd just kissed.

Whom he didn't even like—he thought.

Rich gently released her and stood. "I—" His voice cracked, forcing him to clear his throat. "I have to go."

He hurried toward the sidewalk, needing to seek the heavenly Father. Before he reached the hedge separating their homes, he heard Lark cry out like a wounded animal.

"So what was that?" she asked, her voice ragged. "The *pièce de résistance*? The total humiliation of Lark Bellamy? Wasn't it enough when everyone laughed at me during my sister's dinner? Did you have to prove how great you are by kissing me silly, then calmly walking away from crazy, odd, love-struck Lark?"

If she only knew how wrong she was . . . how much it took to leave her side.

When he didn't respond, she persisted. "What were you trying to prove? How great you are? How in control? How much better, higher, and mightier than I am? I never noticed your two faces before. Pride, thy name is Richard Desmond."

TEN

THE NEXT DAY CAME FAST. TOO FAST, IN LARK'S OPINION.
She didn't relish facing the guests who'd witnessed the
rehearsal dinner debacle, much less the crowd of a hundred
at the wedding.

True, Maggie had spoken with her last night, apologizing
for her reaction to Lark's floral changes. Although Lark felt
awful about the shock and misery Maggie experienced, something inside her resisted voicing those difficult words. *I was
wrong* had never been in Lark's vocabulary, and she wasn't
certain she even had been wrong this time.

Still, something else altogether kept making Lark question
her actions, her attitude. Could Rich have been right? Was
she arrogant? proud?

Lark didn't think so; she just felt she knew best. And that
knowledge was exactly what Rich had attacked with those
offensive words. Would pride and arrogance make her think
herself right?

And what about that servanthood deal? How did that
figure into her relationship with Maggie? with Cammie?

She had no idea, but she feared the questions wouldn't leave her for a long time. If ever.

Until she found some answers.

Since she didn't have any, where should she go? Who knew her that well? Who knew about arrogance? about pride? about the even more unpalatable servanthood? Did Rich?

Frustrated by the mental cartwheels that were getting her nowhere, Lark studied her half-ready image in the mirror. She still looked like the woman she knew so well, or had always thought she did.

She hadn't applied makeup to her freckles, hadn't yet tamed her curls. Was the real Lark, the oldest Bellamy Blossom, bridesmaid at Maggie's wedding, as unattractive and unappealing as the marring freckles on her skin and the rebellious curls on her head?

Was that ugliness what had always cast her as an oddity in people's eyes? The butt of everyone's mockery? Was there anything she could do to change the basic essence of who she was? Was there anyone who could do that for her?

A sound of despair ripped from her throat, and she grabbed her thick, concealing foundation. Time to cover the ugliness so as to face the world. Time to hide what Lark suspected everyone saw while she remained as blind as ever.

Was she really that flawed?

At the Ashworth Mansion fifteen minutes later, Lark dashed up the glorious curving staircase Clay had restored for Miss Louella. Every time she saw her future brother-in-law's work, she had no choice but to admire him and his talents. If Rich was right and she so wrong about herself, could she also be wrong about her sister's soon-to-be husband?

The rehearsal dinner and humiliating encounter with Rich

had shaken Lark to the core. She no longer felt certain of anything.

Stop! she ordered her rioting mind. *Time to think of happy wedding things. After tonight, you'll have all the time in the world to sort out your crazy thoughts.*

Somewhat out of breath, she knocked on the door to the master suite.

"Is that you, Lark?" called Maggie.

"It's me."

"Come on in, child," ordered Miss Louella. "Goodness knows you and your other sister are runnin' late enough as it is. I don't rightly know what's wrong with you young folks these days."

Lark closed the door behind her and came to a halt. Maggie looked . . . magnificent. Although she was on the phone right then, the glow on her delicate, classically beautiful face radiated a joy Lark couldn't help but envy.

How did one achieve that? And why hadn't she—capable, successful, professional Lark—been able to do so?

As Lark stared, Maggie pushed the white lace of her veil past her forehead. "When did you say you'd deliver my granite?" she asked.

Miss Louella batted the hand away. "Hang up that telephone, Magnolia. Just tell the man it's your weddin' day."

Covering the mouthpiece, Maggie hissed, "Shh! I can't hear him."

Miss Louella clucked her disapproval and continued fussing with the pearl-bedecked headpiece. "That's because you're not supposed to, child. You're supposed to let your sister and me button you up and fix that veil."

Looking over at Lark, Maggie's elderly maid of honor said, "Come over here, honey. I need young eyes to help me do up these teeny-tiny pearls all up Magnolia's back. Why, that wonderful Clayton is near dyin' of nerves, and here she's as cool as aspic, actin' like this was any ol' day."

"A week from Monday?" Maggie said, flipping through a weekly planner. "If you say it has to be then, why, I suppose we'll have to wait on you, now won't we?"

"Sit!" Miss Louella ordered the distracted bride, her frown formidable.

Maggie sat. "Fine," she said, her tone belying the word's meaning. "Deliver it directly to the site, and don't call us this comin' week. Mr. Marlowe is closin' the office. We're on . . . vacation."

Miss Louella reached for the receiver. "Tell the fool you're goin' on your honeymoon. You'll be done quicker."

Maggie angled away and brought a finger to her lips. "Very well, then. We'll see you the followin' Monday."

Hanging up, she faced Miss Louella, who did not look pleased. "I declare, Magnolia," the older woman said. "If your Granny Iris could see you now, she'd be after tyin' you down to that chair with rope."

Reaching up with a tender hand, Maggie patted her friend's cheek. "I had a few loose ends to tie up, is all. Now I can go to the altar without a worry in my head."

Lark swallowed hard. Maggie had handled that caller masterfully. She'd been serious, determined, and when matters had not been resolved her way, she'd made her displeasure clear. Lark's younger sister—the pretty, useless doll—had sounded incredibly professional. Capable.

As Lark's stomach dipped, she realized her foundation had just been rocked again. Could she have misjudged her sister all this time? Could Maggie not be the helpless ditz she'd often thought her to be?

Had arrogance—as Rich said—led Lark to aggravate the differences between them? Had her efforts to protect Maggie been unnecessary? intrusive? prideful?

As these tough thoughts clamored in Lark's mind, Maggie rose, hugged herself, then gave a twirl, her satin train swirling around her feet.

"This is so incredible!" she said, a rapturous note to her voice. "All day thrill after thrill has run clear through me. That same thrill I've been experiencin' ever since I met Clay." She closed her eyes momentarily, then met Lark's gaze. "Today, sissy, I'm goin' to become his wife before the Lord's eyes."

Uncertain how to respond and choking back a weird knot in her throat, Lark murmured, "That's nice."

"Well," Miss Louella said with a sniff, "I say it's a pure blessin' that boy offered you a job as well as marriage, Magnolia, dear. Otherwise, you were done for."

"I didn't mean quite that, but the job is great. I'll be working at my husband's side for the rest of our lives."

Lark wondered if any man alive would ever cause her to want to work at his side that long. To her dismay, the memory of Rich's kiss last night flew into her head, heating her cheeks. Not a business-related vision. Not even a particularly pleasant one, since it brought the heat of humiliation with it.

"So long as you two keep the snipin' down to a minimum," Miss Louella warned the bride, shaking a finger just below the edge of the short, lace-frothed veil over Maggie's face.

"We don't argue anymore, seein' as how I'm a Southern Yankee and all."

Skepticism marred Miss Louella's expression. "You sure you're workin' for Clayton Marlowe? The same Clayton Marlowe you kept fightin' with over this mansion?"

Maggie beamed. "The one and only."

Miss Louella gave her a hug. "Oh, child, I'm so happy you two came to your senses. I'm so glad you came to the Lord."

Maggie wrapped her arms around Miss Louella. "I am, too. And look at all he's given me: my lovin' Clay, a super job runnin' Marlowe Historical Restorations, and you, too. I'm glad you agreed to give me away. You're the closest I have to a parent."

Old eyes misted. "I'd never have believed it, but the Lord's given me a daughter—and at my age." Then Miss Louella turned Maggie to face Lark. "But you know, child, I'm not your only family."

Maggie sighed. "I know." She studied her twisting fingers. "Things aren't great between us, you know."

Lark stiffened. She knew.

Miss Louella's voice softened. "It's goin' to take time, patience, and prayer. From all three of you girls."

The sheer tulle length of her veil shielded Maggie's face as she said, "Amen."

As if on cue, the door opened. Cammie walked into the room. "Oh, Maggie," she said, "you look lovely. Isn't she a beautiful bride, Lark?"

Maggie smiled, a bit strained, true, but a smile nonetheless. "Thanks, Cammie. I'm almost ready."

Lark strode to the window, her usual energy and vitality gone. Everyone who knew her had always envied that zing, but now she missed its presence and wondered if it had been a part of the woman she'd believed herself to be. Was it something else she needed to question, come to grips with? Just like her looks, her discontent with her Southern roots, her situation with her sisters?

Looking over her shoulder, she watched Cammie take Miss Louella's place at the buttons on Maggie's gown. She turned, knowing she should help, and caught sight of their faces in the mirror. Studying her sisters, Lark wondered if the three of them would ever grow beyond their differences. And if she was to blame for many of them, as Rich's accusations seemed to imply.

"Cammie? Lark?" Maggie said hesitantly. "I have somethin' to say."

Both Blossoms turned curious eyes on her—Lark's suspicious, Cammie's expectant.

"Things have never been good among us, and I'm truly sorry," said the bride. "I've been guilty of snooty comments and unfriendliness, and God's called me to ask your forgiveness."

Cammie smiled. "So you really and truly have . . . ?"

"I should have made myself perfectly clear," Maggie said. "Yes, Cammie, I've come to Christ, and over the last month or two he's shown me I have some personal restorin' to do. So I want to promise you both, as I promised him, that I'm committed to buildin' somethin' wonderful among us. Sisterhood, friendship, love."

"Magnolia!" cried Miss Louella. "I'm so proud of you, child."

Maggie sent her friend a teary smile, then turned back to her sisters. "So what do you two Blossoms say? Can you forgive me? Will you try?"

Discomfort eating at her, Lark looked away. "There's nothing to forgive. You're just—"

"Stop, Lark," said Cammie. "That's just what Maggie's talkin' about. I agree. There's a lot wrong among us, and we need to look deep inside to find what's really right." She reached a hand out to Maggie; Maggie took it. "I can't promise things will be perfect, but I can promise to try. And pray."

Maggie's eyes glittered with tears. "That's a wonderful start."

Lark felt she should speak, voice a promise, but that wounded part of her kept her from figuring out how to respond. Instead, heading for the door, she said, "Speaking of starts, the wedding's about to start without the bride. Let's go."

Lark felt Maggie stare after her, obviously wanting more. A foreign sensation swam through her. It made her feel awful but didn't tell her what to do next. Wanting to rid herself of the negative feelings, knowing her sister sought something but not knowing what right then, she managed a weak, "I'll try, Mags."

"Thanks," answered Maggie, the word full of emotion. "Let's go marry me to my Clay."

As Lark descended the curved stairs, a baby grand's song soared through the Ashworth Mansion. Miss Louella had insisted the parlor at her old family home was the only place for Maggie to marry Clay. Bride and groom had agreed, since the old home had played such a major part in their romance.

When Maggie followed the sweetly pregnant Cammie down the stairs, a murmur rippled among the gathered guests.

"She looks like an angel. . . ."

". . . ethereal . . ."

"Who'd think she's as sassy . . ."

"That Yankee better do right by her. . . ."

Maggie reached the foyer and turned to the wet-eyed Miss Louella. "Are you ready?"

"Are you, honey child?"

A knot formed in Lark's throat. Something truly special was happening. She watched Maggie turn toward the vast parlor, seek her groom with avid eyes, and find him by the delft-tiled fireplace, love shining from his face.

Even Lark had to admit Clay looked handsome in his black tux, the white shirt showing off his tan to advantage. His hair was neatly combed, and his smile mirrored Maggie's.

"Yes, Miss Louella," Lark's younger sister said in a firm voice. "I'm more ready than I've ever been."

The familiar notes of Lohengrin began, and the bride took her elderly friend's arm. The attendant sisters, in their ice blue satin dresses, took their first steps toward the groom.

A ripple of laughter broke the solemnity. Lark looked at

Maggie, who looked at Miss Louella, who looked back at her. Both shrugged, trying to identify the source of the guests' mirth.

Lark craned her neck.

Then Maggie laughed, too.

Lark spotted the reason for the commotion and grinned along with everyone else. Next to Clay and before the pastor stood Horace Hobey, a leash in his huge hand. At his knee, Buford panted, his tongue lolling to one side. A white bow sat askew of his collar as he nuzzled Clay's hand.

Laughter exploded.

Myrna Stafford said, "Well, I never!"

"I'm sure you haven't," Clay answered, unperturbed. His gaze on Maggie, he winked. "What can I say? He's my best man."

"Now I really know," Maggie said, "deep in my heart, that God is smilin' down on us. Let's get married, Clayton Marlowe."

"All's I can say," added Myrna in her most reproving way, "is it's all gone straight to the dogs!"

Once the laughter over Myrna's comment died down, the guests took their seats and Lark took her place next to Cammie, at the bridal couple's left. At their right stood the two ushers, a friend of Clay's from Gettysburg and, of all people, Rich Desmond. Directly behind the bride and groom, the best man . . . er . . . man and pooch and the maid of honor poised to play their parts.

The fireplace mantel, before which Pastor Melbourne held court, wore a splendid array of tiger lilies and daisies, setting off the classic simplicity of white marble. And, as Lark had thought, the flowers' vivid colors enhanced the cool sleekness of the blue satin she and Cammie wore, even adding to the luster of the pearl beading on Maggie's exquisite gown.

143

The pastor's voice, a mellow baritone, rang through the reverent hush in the room. Lark could practically touch the uniqueness of the moment, the sense that something of great magnitude was happening here, something far more meaningful than a legal exchange of promises that could be broken by the mere signing of a document at a more unhappy future date.

If she believed in God, she would think he was present in this room. Looking at the faces of those gathered around her sister and Clay, Lark saw nothing but respect, admiration, and joy in their expressions. Even the glimpse she got of Rich revealed the same response.

Then he turned a fraction.

His eyes snagged her attention.

Lark found herself unable to look away from his silver eyes, even though the light within them brought to life those dangerous tingles she always experienced when around Rich. During that electric visual exchange, the scent of the wild-flowers grew more intense, the air around her more charged, the pastor's voice more meaning-filled.

"Do you, Clayton, take Magnolia as your lawful wedded wife, to love and to cherish, in good times and in bad, in sickness and in health, until death do you part?"

"I do."

"Do you, Magnolia, take Clayton as your lawful wedded husband, to love, honor, and respect, in good times and in bad, in sickness and in health, until death do you part?"

"I do."

"Then by the power vested in me by almighty God and man, I declare you man and wife. Clay, you may kiss your lovely bride."

At the organ, Rosemarie Melbourne, the reverend's wife, broke into the triumphant chords of "The Wedding March," Lark continued to stare at Rich. The longing she'd always felt for him increased inside her, expanding and magnifying until she remembered the joy she'd witnessed in Maggie just before they'd come downstairs.

If only she and Rich could find the happiness her sister and Clay had. . . .

If only . . .

As Lark swallowed the last of her angel hair pasta with its light cheese sauce, delicately seasoned baby vegetables, and her fresh, crusty roll, she heard the musicians Maggie and Clay had hired tune their instruments. She knew the plan; in a few minutes, Hobey would lead Maggie to the dance floor as the band played a sweet Strauss waltz. Clay would cut in and dance with his brand-new wife.

Then . . . well, the bridal party was supposed to dance, too. But since the two ushers upon whose services Clay had called were some guy from up North who walked with a horribly painful limp, and that miserable Rich, upon whom Clay had called at the last minute, Lark had no idea what would follow.

She would not waltz with Rich Desmond.

The waltz began, and the huge, grinning Hobey led the petite Maggie into the dance. The joy in her sister's expression again made Lark wonder how it had escaped her. Well, it would simply have to become one of her top priorities. After all, she always accomplished what she set out to do.

Miss Louella sat to her right. "Are you ready, honey?"

"Ready for what?"

"Why, the waltz, child. You're supposed to dance. You're a bridesmaid."

"Nope. Hobey's going to come for you as soon as Clay cuts in, and Cammie loves to dance. Rich can dance with her. As far as Clay's friend, I heard he's been in the hospital since a very serious car crash. He's not too steady on his feet, and I doubt anyone would suggest he risk another accident."

"Larkspur Bellamy! I can't believe you, child." Rising, Miss Louella leaned over the table. "Mariah! Mariah Desmond! Get up here right now. This girl has no sense at all."

As Rich's mother approached, Lark noticed that Clay cut in and took Maggie into his embrace. For a second, they stood still in each other's arms, their eyes locked. Lark caught her breath at the depth of feeling the bridal couple revealed in that unguarded moment.

"What's wrong, Lark, honey?" Mariah broke in.

"Nothing, Miss Mariah. Miss Louella's got some nutty idea I have to dance. She should take advantage of the beautiful music and Hobey's love of dancing. He's bound to come up here any minute now—"

Lark quit talking when Hobey led her pregnant sister to the dance floor. Oh, no. Absolutely, positively, no. No, no, no, no, no. She was *not* dancing with that arrogant kiss-'em-and-leave-'em Richard Desmond. There was no way she was letting herself be humiliated another time this week.

"If you'll excuse me," Lark said, pushing her chair back. "I must go to the ladies'—"

"Richie!" Miss Mariah called out. "Come on up here."

"Well done," said Miss Louella to her friend, her hand manacling Lark's. "Now you listen to me, young lady. Your Granny Iris is surely spinnin' in that grave right now. You already had your say in your sister's weddin' with those flowers of yours. You're not goin' to ruin her reception now, you hear? Maggie wanted her bridal party to dance, and you'll be dancin' if it's the last thing I do before the good Lord calls me home. You hear?"

The starch leaching from her, Lark collapsed onto her chair again. "I hear. But—"

"But nothin', missy. That little girl's finally havin' her

night. And the only decent thing for you to do is celebrate with her. Now me, I've never been one to dance. It's a matter between the Lord in heaven and me, so don't go askin'. And Horace knows it. So he was never goin' to ask me to dance. And neither will Richard."

As the song built to its exulting richness, Lark dreaded her first close encounter with Rich since last night. At the ceremony, she'd only caught fleeting glimpses of his dark suit, his sandy hair, his serious, reserved expression. And that long, unnerving exchange of looks.

She didn't know what she'd do if these two busybody matchmakers forced them to dance.

"Richard!" insisted Miss Mariah. "Get back here. Right now. You are not about to run out on your new friend, Clay. Besides, here's Lark all dressed up and no one to dance with. You're part of the bridal party. Dance with her."

Every word had Lark wishing to die. Especially since his mother's cry foiled Rich's escape at the door of the BCC Fellowship Hall, where the reception was being held.

When he turned, his features in a scowl, mortification made her long to burrow into the ground—under the table, at the very least. As he reluctantly approached, everything in Lark shrieked yet another No!

Rich had more sense than to force them to dance. Didn't he?

"Now both of you have to be on your best behavior, you hear?" Miss Louella asked. "You caused enough of a spectacle last night. I surely hope you learned a lesson."

"Hey, I'm innocent," Rich objected. "The whole mess with the flowers was her—" he pointed at Lark—"fault. I argued, knowing what she wanted to do was wrong. But she's too hardheaded and proud. I'd never do that to another person. It's hardly the Christian thing to do."

Lark ground her teeth. This whole "Christian thing" was

becoming more and more difficult to deal with. Did everyone in Bellamy break everything down to its Christian denominator? Did they view life through Christianity-tinted glasses? Wasn't that like escaping reality?

Then she thought of Cammie's reliance on her faith since as far back as Lark could remember. And Maggie's joy before the ceremony, her comments about her commitment to her Lord. There was also Miss Mariah's "All things" verse, and Miss Louella's and Granny Iris's devotion to Christ.

But Lark had never needed that kind of crutch. She was a capable woman. She always succeeded. Look at the flowers. Her choices were perfect.

Rich cleared his throat. She saw the outstretched hand. He'd evidently been waiting for her response. During a wild, insane moment, she thought of standing, turning tail, and running. But she didn't want to give him the satisfaction of knowing how badly his arrogance had hurt her last night.

In an icy voice she said, "If we must."

When he wrapped his arm around her, Lark trembled. The warmth of his touch affected her more than she wanted it to. Steeling herself against his nearness, she remained stiff and far from him.

"Lark," he said softly into her ear.

"Yes?"

"I . . . I wanted to apologize for last night."

"Stop!" Anger began its slow burn. "If you're going to give me that dumb I-never-should-have-kissed-you-it-was-all-a-mistake line, I'm going to sock you right here in front of everyone we know in town."

Watching him from under the cover of her lashes, Lark saw Rich clench his jaw. Then he said, "That wasn't what I was going to say. Will you keep your mouth shut long enough for me to say what I have to say?"

"This should be interesting."

For a few stiff, awkward steps, he held his peace. Then, "I was going to say that our kiss went too far too fast. It caught me by surprise, and I've never been a man who plays at romance. I wasn't about to begin with you. I had to pull back in good conscience."

She came to a standstill. "Come again?"

Rich tried to keep leading, but she refused to budge.

"Oh, Red, why can't you ever make anything easy on a guy?"

"I wasn't the one who decided to show who was superior to whom last night."

"That wasn't what I did, and you know it. That kiss about blew my head off. The last thing I expected to do was kiss you, much less find the kiss so . . . so . . . "

Lark shoved him away and smacked her fists on her hips. "Oh, so now I've left you speechless."

Rich crossed his arms. "Something like that."

"Good grief, you men are all alike. You never know what you want."

"All men? Alike? Just how many men did you come to know in Baltimore?"

"Enough to know that I'm not always thrilled by the actions of your species."

He placed his hands on her shoulders and pulled her close. "Poor Red. You got burned. I'm sorry."

His words were so sincere that Lark allowed his embrace. They began swaying with the music, oblivious to the world around them.

Rich took her right hand in his, wrapped his left arm across her waist, and Lark let the old-fashioned waltz soothe her injured senses. After the waltz ended, she glanced up. Met Rich's silver gaze. Shivered at the tenderness she saw there.

She smiled tentatively.

Rich responded likewise. New music started, its tempo

brighter than that of the one before. Eyes fixed on Rich's, Lark felt a flicker of happiness enter her heart.

Everything felt very right just then. Could this be . . . joy?

Maybe Rich wasn't an ogre after all.

🌿

When Lark excused herself to go to the ladies' room, Rich watched her disappear down the hall. She was something else. Especially when she stopped being so mouthy, so tough. He smiled, remembering her akimbo stance in the middle of the dance floor.

Oh, yes. Red Bellamy was something; he didn't quite know what, but she was something else, all right.

"Rich," Maggie said at his elbow. "Clay and I are about to leave, but before we do, I need to talk to you."

He turned to the beautiful bride. "Sounds too serious for such a joyous night."

Maggie bit her lower lip. "You're right. It's very serious, and I wish I wasn't the one to tell you, but Ruby at the Bellamy Fiduciary Trust called me this mornin'. It seemed you were having a problem with your phone, and she couldn't reach you. She said I had to make sure you knew before Clay and I left for our honeymoon."

"Knew what?" he asked, dread joining his guilt over the Storey-avoiding unplugged phone.

"What your mama just did."

Uh-oh. "And what was that?"

Maggie put a gentle hand on his forearm. "She just mortgaged your house and the store. I don't know what she needs that much money for, but I sure am concerned."

Shock made a response impossible. A mortgage? His interest-hating mother? The house *and* the store?

It couldn't be.

Could it?

Forcing the words, he asked, "Are you sure?"

"As sure as I am that I just became Mrs. Clayton Marlowe."

Maggie's integrity and years of experience at the bank were unquestionable. Rich smiled despite his fear. "Thanks for telling me. Don't worry another minute. This is your night, your time. I'll look into Mama's latest antics. I'm sure it's nothing."

But he didn't believe a word he said. Mama had mortgaged everything they had left.

Why?

ELEVEN

His mind in a frenzy of thought, Rich returned to the head table, knowing Hobey wished to offer the newly-weds words of wisdom earned during his forty years of marriage.

He found his mother surrounded by her Garden Club cronies. Well aware he couldn't discuss anything with that gaggle around, he touched her shoulder and said, "Could you please excuse yourself for a moment, Mother? We need to speak."

"Mother?" Mariah asked, her expression troubled. "Dear me, it must be serious for you to call me that, Richard."

"Just something we need to discuss right away."

Although Mariah separated herself from the group, every eye followed mother and son out the doorway and into the hall. Rich glanced over his shoulder and saw the cluster of gray-haired ladies—plus one purple-haired one—craning their necks in their direction.

"I guess their curiosity can't be helped," he said quietly. "Please, Mama, keep your voice down. This is private."

His mother gave him another quizzical look. "Son, I have no idea what you're up to. I haven't a thing to discuss.

Perhaps you should just start speakin' clear, and if you need secrecy, why, by all means, keep your voice low."

"Fine." He shot a brief prayer heavenward. "I spoke with Maggie—"

"Isn't she the most gorgeous bride?" his mother rhapsodized. "Well, maybe not *the* most gorgeous. Reenie was lovely, if you'll recall, and I imagine Larkspur will look spectacular the day she marries—"

"Mother, Maggie's not the issue."

"Oh, dear. That 'mother' again. And that awful scowl. What is it, Richie? You know you can tell me anythin'."

"Mama, Maggie said you'd mortgaged the house and the store. Why did you do that?"

Mariah sighed. "I had no choice. The department stores I recently contracted are clamorin' for their Dream Squeezes, and Frank keeps callin' for funds. You know we can't buy more Squeezes from the manufacturer to distribute without money. So I did what I had to do."

"But we may lose the house. And the store."

"So be it. I can't default on my commitments, Richie. That would be wrong before God."

"So is risking our home and livelihood. Then there's the issue of interest. Aren't you the one who insists 'neither a borrower nor a lender be'? Don't you always quote those Scriptures about usury? Why would you do this?"

Mama stood taller. "I've been called to help women, and I've made a commitment to my customers. I won't let them down. Besides, God will provide for us."

Realizing he wouldn't get anywhere down this path, Rich tried another approach. "Just what did Frank say when he last called?"

"What I told you. The stores want their merchandise. I must provide it."

Rich rubbed his throbbing temples. "The first thing to do

is meet with him. Why don't you give him a call tomorrow morning—"

"On a Sunday?"

"On a Sunday. We can go to early service before he comes or the noon one after he leaves. This is serious, Mother. Very serious." How could he make her understand? "Anyway, have him bring the books. You know, since you can't leave Bellamy. Then we can see where we stand."

His mother's soft hand patted Rich's cheek. "See, son? I knew you'd understand why I had to do what I had to do. And you'd help me work through it." She gestured toward the Fellowship Hall. "Come, now. Hobey's about to speak. He's such a wise man; it should be good."

Having learned pitifully little but having cobbled a plan of action, Rich followed Mama back into the room. Hobey was a simple, godly man, and whatever he told the gathering would indeed be worth hearing.

"Hey, all," said the mason as he wrapped one massive arm around Clay's shoulders and one around delicate Maggie's. "I just want to send these two off with a mite of what I learned to avoid since I been hitched to my Ellamae all these forty years. An' I can say it in one puny little word. That word's *pride*."

Rich jerked upright. He'd never forget Lark's words: *"Pride, thy name is Richard Desmond."* He wasn't a proud man. He couldn't be. He was a Christian, committed to glorifying the Savior, not himself.

"That ol' sin pride comes in many colors and fancy getups," Hobey continued. "An' we cain't recognize it when its roots dig into our hearts. But our actions sure do show us up as prideful. An' pride's the first and worst enemy of marriage. When one or both of you decide you gotta get your own way all the time, well, then, you're good'n sunk."

The room had fallen silent, the gentle giant's words the only sound to be heard.

155

Hobey went on. "Don't never forget Paul's words to the Ephesians. He told 'em to be humble and gentle, to be patient with each other, an' especially said they'd better be makin' allowances for each other's faults on account of their love. That love is the love Jesus brings every believer. Like the both of you."

The bride and groom smiled at each other, then nodded to Hobey, who continued.

"Plus the apostle Paul said for you to always give thanks for everything to God the Father in the name of his Son. He also ordered us, 'specially married folks, to submit to each other from reverence to Christ."

Grinning, the mason clapped Clay's shoulder, patted Maggie's. "Boy, an' ain't that a mouthful of truth there? Remember to be humble, son. Stiff-necked pride ain't never gonna do you one bit of good. An' Maggie, honey, be patient with this boy. You both submit to one another 'cause you love Jesus. Am I clear 'nuff?"

Maggie rose on tiptoe and kissed Hobey's clean-shaven cheek. "As a bell, Hobey. And thanks. We love you, too."

Clay reached out a hand, shook his best man's firmly, then gave him a one-armed hug. "Keep building your solid walls, and Maggie and I will build our marriage on the Rock."

"Amen and amen," chimed Miss Louella.

Rich, however, had lost all trace of cheer. Could Lark have been right? Was he arrogant? proud? stiff-necked? Was his impatience with her zany nature a sign of his reluctance to make allowances for her faults? Did he display, as she'd said, a superior attitude?

Where was he going wrong?

After a mostly sleepless night, the phone's merciless ringing in the early morning did not ensure a good mood on Rich's part. "Hullo."

"We've got to talk," Lark said with no preliminaries. Not that a "good morning" would do any good after the awful thoughts her accusation had engendered in him.

When he didn't respond, she added, "Right now."

"What's wrong now?"

"Before she left on her honeymoon last night, Maggie told me your mother had mortgaged—"

"AAARRRGGGHHH!"

"Rich? Are you all right?"

"As right as I can be when I'm wishing I could throttle your little sister's pretty neck. Why'd she tell you our family's financial business?"

"Probably because she knew I could get you out of the corner you're in."

Her smart mouth was going to get Lark in trouble some day. And Rich wasn't going to be able to get her out of it. "I don't care if you think you can raise the Empire State Building single-handedly. You have no right snooping into our business. This conversation's over."

He hung up and crawled back into bed, despite knowing sleep was not a commodity he'd soon acquire.

The doorbell rang. A fist pounded the door.

Great. No sleep. Lark's wake-up call. Now a visitor. Today had all the earmarks of a lousy day. *Help me, Lord.*

Donning his cotton pajama shirt, since he wore only the bottoms during warm weather, Rich trotted down the stairs.

The pounding continued.

"Hang on. I'm coming." He opened the door and heard the yowl before he saw her. Collapsing against the doorjamb, he said, "I should have known it'd be you."

Lark yanked on her bloodhound's leash. "Of course. I'm determined to get your mother out of trouble."

"So am I."

"So let me in, and we can decide what to do next."

Rich crossed his arms over his chest. "We can talk here on the porch. Mama's already taking the next step. She's asking her manager to meet us this morning. As I've told you many times, I have things covered."

Those green eyes narrowed. "Interesting concept," Lark said, "since things seem to have gone from bad to worse. Kind of like what happened to Maggie over at the Ashworth Mansion. Every time I tried to help, she told me she had everything under control. But things kept getting worse."

"I'm not Maggie—"

"I know. And I expected better from you. I'd hoped you'd show more common sense. But I can't see how letting your mother mortgage everything she owns demonstrates your great and admirable control of things." She shook her auburn curls. "I'd have thought she'd be the kind to know how bad interest can be. She must have listened to your bad advice."

Rich pushed closer to his nemesis. "I gave her no such thing. I only learned last night at the reception what she'd done, without my knowledge. Now I have to straighten out her affairs."

Heedless of the fact that he was still in his pj's, Lark pressed her shoulder against his chest and invaded his house. Her dog licked Rich's bare toes on his way indoors.

"Looks like you need an expert, Rich." She perched on the sofa, Pooch-Face at her feet. "I've been cleaning up after my sisters' messes forever. I'll investigate the entire situation, solve your mother's case, and get her back on track before you can even blink."

The thought of Lark investigating the entire situation made Rich's stomach drop. He had too much at stake to give Snoop-Scoop free rein. "Oh, no. You're too busy with your sisters' lives. Get back to them, and leave my mother's business to me—"

"Are you two back to arguin' again?" his mother asked from the front doorway. "Why, you looked so happy last night, we all thought the troubles between you were over."

"Trouble between us?" Rich asked. "The only trouble is her. She's never been anything but."

And never such dangerous trouble as after that kiss.

Lark winked mischievously and went to his mother's side, snuffly dog at her heels. "Miss Mariah, can you believe your big, strapping son here is scared of what lil ol' me can do? I bet he's afraid I'm about to show him up."

"Larkspur Bellamy," Miss Mariah chided, "I told you to drop that Miss, and I fully expect you to do so. Then, child, I want you and Richie to remember what Hobey said last night. I know he meant it for Maggie and Clay, but I'm thinkin' the good Lord meant it even more for both of you. Why, if you haven't been displayin' the most prideful attitudes I've seen in longer'n the Israelites wandered the desert."

Tension swamped the room. Rich again felt the sting of Lark's words, the disturbing thoughts that had kept him awake. Even his mother had accused him of a terrible sin. Had her words affected Lark as well?

He took in the paleness of her cheeks, the contrast of her freckles, the tight whiteness of her compressed lips. Oh, yes, Mama's words had hit Snoop-Scoop, too.

But was Mama right? Was he proud? He knew Lark was—

"Now that I have your attention," Mama said, "I'll tell you both that Frank Vallore is due any minute now. I called him at seven this morning, and he assured me he'd be here no later than nine-thirty. I'd suggest, Richie, that you change from those pajamas into somethin' a mite more businesslike. Before my operations manager arrives, you understand."

As if Rich were five years old and Mama had just caught him dipping into the cookie jar, he turned without another word and ran upstairs.

Trouble. Lark was trouble. No matter what he did, she seemed to follow, sticking to him like a burr. How did a man get out of trouble? Especially when his own mother welcomed her presence at every turn.

He didn't know. But he would—before Lark figured out how much she could really "scoop" about him.

Lark watched Rich vanish upstairs, his mother's words echoing in her thoughts. First Rich had accused her of prideful acts; now his mother did the same. Did she really have a problem?

Lost in her own questions, Lark didn't notice the new arrival until Miss . . . er . . . Mariah called her name—evidently not for the first time, either. "Yes?"

"I'd like you to meet my right-hand man at the warehouse," Mariah said. "Frank Vallore, Larkspur Bellamy."

The most that could be said for the thirty-something man before Lark was that he was . . . there. Average height. Average weight. Average brown hair. Average brown eyes. Average men's clothes.

She smiled, despite her disappointment. She'd hoped to finally meet the guy with the Jag and pricey wardrobe, thinking the fashion plate might be Mariah's manager.

She shook this man's hand. "Pleasure."

"Oh, no," he said in the best baritone she'd ever heard. "The pleasure's absolutely all mine."

The rich notes of his words flowed over her, wrapping her in a cocoon of male admiration. Wow! Who woulda thunk?

"Larkspur?" he said, his eyes fixed on her face. "What a gorgeous, unique name for a beautiful woman."

Frank's undivided attention and unmasked appreciation did something to Lark's brain—like scramble it.

"Oh, well," she began, "the way I figure, my mama and daddy just couldn't think of a good flower name when I was born, so I got stuck with Larkspur. But they improved with time. When they got to the younger two, they came up with Magnolia and Camellia. I mean . . . what about Petunia or Lobelia? Even Begonia would have worked. They could have gone real creative and used Robinia, Aralia, Kalmia, or Lyonia. And how about Achillea, Artemisia, Centaurea, Rudbeckia, Vernonia, or Utricularia? I'd almost rather have one of them that match my sisters' names than run around named after a tall, loud, purple, weedy plant. . . ."

The hush in the room smothered Lark's drivel. Frank had backed away from her, eyes colored with concern. Miss Mariah appeared horrified, and on the stairs, Rich looked ready to bust a gusset laughing.

Lark wanted to dive under the couch cushions and never come out again. Her inexperience with admiration had leaped up and walloped her in the face. "Sorry about the floral disquisition," she said lamely.

"Fascinating," said Rich, trotting down the stairs. "You must continue the commentary later, Lark. I never knew such a botanical expert lived right next door."

Swallow me, Earth. "Well, floral names are just a personal quirk I took up while wondering about our family—"

Lark clamped her mouth shut, noting she'd done it again. Babbled—and in the presence of two males. True, one was the boy next door—not much of a boy these days—but still, she hated making such a lousy impression on the man who'd treated her with approval.

Unlike the other.

She tipped up her chin and gave Frank a dazzling smile. Or what she figured might be a dazzling smile, considering her inexperience with dazzle. "Pleased you could join us this morning, Frank, as we consider Mrs. Desmond's circumstances."

"Again," that double-fudge voice said, "the pleasure's all mine." His brown eyes didn't look quite that sure.

Oh, well. The guy hadn't come to romance her, after all. They had more important matters to attend to if they were going to keep Rich's mother out of jail.

But oh, if only Rich looked at her like that. More than once. That kiss once. She'd be a goner for sure.

"Grrrrrrrrr." Red. Brilliant, gaudy, shrieking scarlet. That's how mad Lark was.

"The nerve of the man," she said to her as-yet nameless dog. "Miss Mariah—Mariah—invited me to join them for the brainstorming session. And then that horrid son of hers chases me out as if I were a kid. 'Go on home, now, Lark,' he says to me. 'We can handle things from here.'"

The dog sneezed, shaking his long-eared head and sending drool flying. "I feel exactly the same way," she commiserated, opening her front door.

The house seemed strangely empty now that Maggie had gone on her honeymoon. Not that the two older Blossoms had spent much time together before the wedding. Still, knowing she was now alone again left Lark with a sense of melancholy.

She unclipped the dog's leash, hung the gadget on its hook in the hall, then headed for the kitchen. A glass of water might cool off her anger.

Yeah, right.

As she passed the small TV on the kitchen counter, she automatically turned it on to the twenty-four-hour news channel. She reached for a glass and headed for her watercooler.

". . . And now for today's entertainment news. This reporter has been able to ascertain that negotiations for drama and screenplay sensation Des Richter's next script have come to a halt. . . ."

Clutching the glass to her chest, Lark spun, gluing her eyes to the screen. A picture of the promo poster for Richter's recent blockbusting movie *vavoomed* out at her, enhancing her commitment to interview the guy. Her magazine needed Des Richter.

"According to our sources," the slick-smiling male reporter continued, "the hitch comes from Mr. Richter himself. Fundamental differences have been cited by the studio seeking the rights to the unfinished property. . . ."

A knock at her kitchen door sent Lark backing to it. Eyes on clips from Richter's previous work, she said, "Who is it?"

"Hobey, Miss Lark."

"Let yourself in. It's not locked."

"Now, Miss Lark," the mason scolded as he stepped into the cheery kitchen, closing the door behind him, "you know it ain't safe for a right pretty young woman to be leavin' her doors unlocked like that. Who knows who's out there up to no good?"

Lark groaned inwardly. She loved Hobey, but this wasn't the time for a lecture on personal safety. The news program had gone on commercial break, and she didn't want to miss one second of their report on the elusive playwright when they came back.

"Hobey," she said, tamping her urge to find Richter, "I'm listening to a very important newscast. Would you like to take a seat, have a glass of juice—wheat grass or carrot, fresh from this morning—or maybe water, until it's over? Then we can discuss my back door, and whatever else you came to see me for."

The tall, burly man shook his head. "You girls are all the same, ain'tcha? Your sister went an' got herself in all kinds of trouble with them Garden Club ladies by not usin' common sense."

"Well, that was Maggie, and this is me. There's a world of difference between us. I'm perfectly capable of handling myself, but she's not quite—"

Lark caught herself, remembering Maggie's handling of the recalcitrant supplier yesterday afternoon. "Anyway, I'm sure that's not what you came for. What's up?"

"Ain'tcha watchin' your news?" the mason asked.

Lark spun to face the TV. An ad for diet aids assured her she'd lose sixty pounds in thirty days if she just popped one of their pills while eating anything and everything she wanted. "Still on break. Besides, I don't think I need the stuff they're hawking, do you?"

"No, ma'am," Hobey said, chuckling. "Any thinner'n y'already are, an' you'd just plain vanish."

"So why'd you come visit me?"

"It's like this," the gentle giant began, blushing furiously. "I need some help, an' I figger you're the plumb best to help me."

"What kind of help?" Lark asked, touched by his willingness to turn to her, the town's oddball.

"I . . . well, I never learned me to talk as nice as you. An' seein' as you don't talk so country an' all anymore, well, I figgered you could teach me."

Lark didn't know what to say. True, she'd always worked to leave behind the small-town Southernisms she'd acquired while growing up, but she'd never have thought Hobey dissatisfied with himself. "Why?"

"Well, now, there's the trouble," he answered, refusing to

meet her gaze. "I cain't rightly tell you why. You just hafta trust me. Take my word. As a Christian man."

Lark had no doubt that Hobey's reason would cause her no harm—or him. A more decent, honest man she'd yet to meet. "You got it. I'm very busy with my magazine but—"

"Real nice one, too."

"You've read *Critic's Choice?*"

"Tried to. Every issue you put out, Miss Lark."

Again, his interest touched her heart. "OK, Hobey. I'm going to help you, but you have to stop calling me Miss Lark. I'm young enough to be your daughter, and I feel strange having you call me Miss. Lark's fine."

"Oh, yes, you're right fine," he answered, winking and smiling. "Hey, will you look at that guy on the Tee-Vee? I seen 'im around town. Haven't you?"

Lark pivoted toward the screen but saw only the reporter.

". . . Mr. Richter's agent assured us that as soon as the parties come to terms, he'll give us details of his client's exciting new work. Until then, Mr. Richter's fans will have to wait patiently. Of course, as always, Mr. Richter could not be reached for comment. This is . . ."

Rats! She'd been so busy with Hobey's warming the cockles of her heart that she'd missed the most important part of the newscast. Literary agent, Storey Newburn. A high-flying New Yorker, from what she'd heard, but practically impossible to corner.

Why? Why were agent and author so secretive? What did they have to hide? And why would a New York agent ever come to Bellamy?

As always, the puzzle dug at Lark like an unreachable itch in the middle of her back. She had to get to it, scratch it until she satisfied her need to know. She had to find Des Richter. Before anyone else did.

"So we have us a deal, then?" Hobey asked.

"Oh, I've got deals, all right," she answered, thinking of her promise to work things out with her sisters, her agreement to help Mariah, her determination to sniff out the real Des Richter, her pact with Hobey. "And Scoop Bellamy never fails to come through."

TWELVE

Tuesday morning, while riding in Rich's plush Toyota Avalon, Lark alternated between suspicious curiosity about the existence and financing of the vehicle and satisfaction over her recent vindication.

She knew Desmond's Country Store did not bring in the kind of revenue needed to pay for this nice a car. Not without substantial supplementation from some other source. Therefore, Rich was hiding something. Like that source. Not to mention the car itself, which evidently resided in the garage, since she hadn't seen it until today.

So on Sunday, when Mariah had dragged her son to the Bellamy front door shortly after he'd banished Lark from the discussions with Frank Vallore, Lark had relished Rich's capitulation.

"Lark's an experienced investigative reporter," a determined Mariah had said. "You, son, are not. If the Secret Service has me on tape breakin' the law, why then, we need to see it. And discuss with them the evidence piled up against me. But since I can't leave Bellamy, and they're none too crazy about cooperatin' with me, I need you two to act on my behalf."

"Your attorney's already acting on your behalf, Mama—"

"So he says," Mariah retorted. "I think he's actin' on his own pocket's behalf. Go see him. See the tape. Check out the evidence against me. I don't trust a man who only does business over the phone. And take Larkspur along with you. Without another argument, do you hear?"

Rich had nodded once. "Loud and clear, Mama."

So now, on their way to the lawyer's office two days later, Lark had to choose between questioning Rich about his finances or keeping quiet and alert, waiting until he slipped and revealed something. Would he? Or had he perfected this newly devious persona?

Maybe she meant criminal persona.

Could the Rich she'd known and loved as a child and teen have turned out that bad? Could he be framing his mother to keep on living the good life?

Could a crook kiss the way Rich did?

Lark realized where her thoughts had strayed. She had to forget that horrible, humiliating night.

"So, we're going to visit this guy who's handling your mother's case. What's he like?"

"I'm not sure. I'll be meeting him today."

"You mean you turned over your mother's future to a complete stranger? How could you, Rich?"

"Hey, wait a minute. Edgar Neville came recommended by a number of my business contacts. Don't forget, as a local merchant I can tap into sources that are both reputable and reliable."

"Still, how do you know he'll do a good job for Mariah?"

"I have to go on trust, Lark. And on our contract. I insisted on one before I forked over his retainer."

"Well, that's a start. Still, I'm glad I'll have a chance to check out this guy before we go any further." She'd dealt with enough lawyers over the length of her career to view the profession with somewhat jaundiced eyes. "So, what's he done up to now?"

"He's obtained copies of the evidence against Mama. That's what we're going to review today."

"Why didn't he bring it to her? After all, she's the one most affected in this case."

Rich shrugged. "He's busy. I imagine he can't just drop his other cases to spend the day in Bellamy. I understand that."

"For what your mother said this guy's charging, you'd think he'd go to the ends of the earth to justify that kind of money. Which leads me to my next question."

Rich sucked in his breath, shot her a brief look laden with . . . could that be fear? He clenched the steering wheel, his knuckles reddening, then blanching. "Don't."

"Don't what?" she asked, finding his reaction more than suspicious, maybe even nudging guilty.

"Don't stick your nose in my personal business."

"Why? Are you scared I might find something to sully your perfect reputation? To bring the mighty Rich Desmond to the level of us other imperfect humans? What are you hiding, Rich? Don't think I forgot how you chased me out of your house yesterday morning."

His face turned the same ghastly white as his knuckles. "Nothing," he snapped, eyes glued to the road ahead. "I'm hiding nothing, but I also don't want my life spread out in front of you for the future delectation of your readers. I'm a private man."

"So, private man, where are you getting the money to fund your mother's very public defense? You know and I know it isn't coming out of the proceeds from Desmond's Country Store. What did you get into? And why are you dragging your mother along with you?"

Silence.

"While we're at it," she continued, knowing she'd struck

dead center with her questions, "who's the rumpled guy with the white Jag? Where does he get his money? And is he the one who's going to make your knees bend the other way if you don't do as his higher-ups say?"

Rich went a sick shade of green.

Aha! She'd known all along the affluent stranger held the key to everything. Now all she had to do was get Rich to confess to his crimes. And if she couldn't, then she'd have to concentrate on digging up the identity of the mystery man.

Although the probability of success gave her a rush, Lark felt a deeper measure of disappointment. She hadn't really wanted Rich to be guilty of harming his mother, especially for nothing more than fancy shoes and cars. And him so quick to call himself a Christian, too.

Disillusionment tasted awful. Bitter. Empty.

"You know I'll find out what you're up to," she said softly. "So why don't you just save us both the time and agony, and confess right now? I'm sure if you turn state's evidence, they'll go easy on you."

Rich's only response was the car's increased speed.

"Are you that afraid of what your associates will do to you?" A hideous thought occurred to her. "Have they threatened Mariah? Reenie? Oh, Rich, how could you do something like this? What would your father say if he knew? I never would have believed it of you."

"Then don't. And put your insane imagination to bed. There's a criminal involved in Mama's situation, but it's not me. I'd never harm my mother or sister in any way. I resent your accusation," he said tight-lipped. "I've done nothing— nothing, you understand?—to be ashamed of, much less to endanger anyone."

"Then where'd you get the money for this car? your fancy shoes? the sprinkler system? And why do you refuse to tell?"

"Because it's none of your business, Snoop. And it's legal.

Totally and completely aboveboard. So drop the issue."
Streaks of scarlet painted his cheekbones. "Why don't you
take that wild imagination and use it wisely? Write a book.
Paint a picture. Carve a statue. Do something constructive
with it, instead of accusing people of ludicrous things. No
wonder everyone in Bellamy has always found you strange."

Despite the slap of his words, Lark refused to capitulate.
"Not nearly as strange as a man who refuses to let light shine
on his affairs, even to the point of casting suspicion on his
own mother."

"I refuse to continue this conversation. We're nearly to the
law offices, and I suggest you clear your mind of all that
garbage."

"Have it your way—but only for the moment. You know
me better than to think your wimpy privacy argument is
going to stop me from finding out the truth. Especially since
it affects Mariah."

As she savagely clicked on the radio, she thought she heard
him say, "That's what I'm afraid of."

She let his comment pass. She'd get to the bottom of this.
For Mariah's sake. For Reenie's.

And for her own. Especially since the memory of Rich's lips
against hers, his arms around her, continued to haunt her.
She feared it always would.

"There she is," said Mr. Neville, a fifty-something gentleman
with jet black hair and distinguished demeanor. "Watch
now."

On the TV screen, Rich saw his mother jot down a series of
numbers, punch them into her computer keyboard, wait,
then nod at the young, brown-suited man on the other side of
the counter. When her printer spit out a sheet of paper, she

handed it to her customer. Minutes later, a khaki-uniformed man appeared from her left, pushing a steel cart piled with boxes. The customer and his mother's warehouse employee left.

"The credit-card number your mother wrote down," Mr. Neville said, "was stolen. The man came to the store, gave it to her without showing a card—possibly telling her he'd left it at his office—and she approved the transaction."

"How does that make her a criminal?" Rich asked.

"The guy's one of the more important members of the ring the Secret Service is investigating. The girdles he picked up were traced to a number of professional shoplifters up and down the Eastern seaboard."

"I don't yet understand how my mother can be accused of fraud or theft as a result of what I just saw. It would seem to me she's the victim of the scam."

"She approved a sale on a stolen number. It's now her word against his that she didn't know it was stolen. She's on shaky ground."

It still seemed unfair. "How was the number stolen?"

Mr. Neville used the remote control to turn off the TV. "Probably someone charged something—a dinner, a purchase at a store—and the carbon was not destroyed. Or the number might have been scoped by the criminal as the rightful owner used it."

"So what can we do to prove her innocence?" Lark asked, piping up for the first time since introductions were made.

Neville came out from behind his desk and propped a hip on its corner. "It's going to be difficult. The man in the video has known mob ties. But knowing about them doesn't mean the connection can be proved. All the authorities have right now is proof that he supplies the shoplifters with girdles. The Secret Service hopes to use him to get to his bosses."

"How does that affect Mariah?"

Waving toward the television set, the lawyer continued. "The Secret Service will argue that Mrs. Desmond knew what she was doing when she charged purchases to stolen numbers. They'll insist she's part of the crime ring."

"Then it's up to us to prove she's not," Lark said. "And the way to do it is to bust open the ring."

"Miss Bellamy," Neville said, "that's best left up to professionals. You don't have to do a thing."

"What have the authorities done so far?" she countered. "On Mrs. Desmond's behalf, I mean. How about you? Have you infiltrated the ring? Have you tailed the guy in the video? Have you followed his mob associates? Why can't you find out who gives him his orders? What are you doing to earn the obscene sum of money the Desmonds are paying you?"

Rich could have killed her. Again. It hadn't been enough for Lark to accuse him of having mob ties, not to mention framing his mother for his nonexistent crimes, but now she'd attacked Mama's pricey new lawyer. Rich wouldn't be surprised if Edgar Neville followed in Percy Baker's footsteps and quit on the spot.

But Neville was a different sort of man—or perhaps a greedier one.

"Miss Bellamy," the attorney said with patience, "we have scarcely received this evidence. Give us the chance to do our job before you question our competence. I do admit, however, that I expected as much from you. Your reputation precedes you, Scoop."

"Good," she came back. "Then I guess you'll understand when I tell you I have no intention of returning home and sitting around waiting until Mrs. Desmond's fitted for an orange jumpsuit."

"That won't happen," Mr. Neville stated.

"Of course not," Lark said. "I'll make sure it doesn't."

Rich groaned. Mama was doomed. "Lark—"

"Whatever you do, Miss Bellamy, don't forget how high the stakes are in this case. Organized crime does not play nice. If you stick your nose where they don't want it, you could lose more than that appendage. To protect my clients, I prefer to use professional investigators and add their results to what the authorities find. Crime is ugly, and you're just one person."

"An experienced investigative reporter kind of person," she fired off, again reviving Rich's reluctant admiration. "One who has learned to handle herself in all sorts of situations. Don't worry about me, Mr. Neville. I'll get you the information to prove Mariah Desmond's innocence. I know what I'm doing."

Rich didn't know whether to laugh or cry. Lark had courage and tenacity, but he wondered if she wasn't as foolish as he'd always thought. She couldn't think she could take on the mob—single-handedly—and bring them down. Could she?

The government had tried to do that for decades, and they had all the manpower, resources, and money imaginable. They hadn't succeeded. How could Lark be so arrogant as to suggest she could succeed where they couldn't?

"Scoop Bellamy never fails," she said, standing. She held out her hand to Mama's lead counsel. "You'll see. I won't need the Secret Service's help, either. I always work alone."

Rich gagged at her gall. What had Mama gotten them into when she'd insisted on making use of Lark's talents? Could Lark really be that blind? that proud?

He'd have to do something about Lark, especially since he was the only one who seemed so inclined. He'd have to pray that Lark would return to Christ—the only one who could take on the mob and win. The one on whom she'd turned her back years ago.

And as for Lark uncovering his secret, Rich knew he'd have

to stick to Snoop-Scoop like the burr she was. He couldn't let her out of his sight for a second.

"Do you recognize the man, Mariah?" Lark asked that afternoon as she, Rich, and his mother watched the tape on Lark's kitchen TV.

"Why, of course I do. That's Tony Alberti. He supplies small boutiques in the Carolinas with all sorts of lingerie."

"So he's a regular customer."

"That's right."

"Then why doesn't he carry a running account with you?"

"I reckon that's just how he prefers to do business. He charges the merchandise, and I give it to him. I've never had any trouble with him. He's one of my steadiest and most reliable clients."

"I'll say," Lark muttered. "If he's supplying shoplifters with the girdles, as the Secret Service says, then of course he's going to keep coming back for more. There's always a crook looking to make an easy buck. He must have new recruits all the time."

Distress furrowed Mariah's forehead. "Oh, I can't believe Tony's a crook. I keep tellin' you, this is all a big misunderstandin'. It must be. Tony's a dear boy. He even reminds me a little of you, Richie."

Lark noticed Rich's blush. Yeah, well, if her suspicions about Mariah's son proved correct, there might be plenty in Tony to remind anyone of Rich.

"It's clear we're getting nowhere fast," Rich said as he rose to his feet. "Let me call Frank and have him run out here this evening. He should see this video."

Mariah reached for his hand as he went toward the telephone on the kitchen counter. "Excellent idea."

To Lark she explained, "Tony and Frank get on very well. They go to lunch whenever Tony comes to pick up a new order."

"Not bad," Lark said, grinning at Rich. "For a newbie, that is. Maybe Frank's noticed something about Tony your mother hasn't. Call him, and see when he can come over— wait! Better yet, ask Frank to meet us at the distribution center. You and I should look through all of Alberti's trans- actions. Maybe we can find a pattern or something."

"We don't keep charge slip copies since we do everythin' by computer," Mariah said. "We're a modern business, you know. But records of Tony's transactions are there in the computer."

Rich nodded. "I'll call Frank."

"Make it quick," Lark suggested. "I'm anxious to get started on this. We wasted too much time after your mother's arrest with you trying to get rid of me. I hope you've figured out by now you can't do it."

Rich didn't answer but picked up the cordless phone on the blue counter, shaking his head.

"You'll be careful, won't you, honey?" Mariah asked Lark.

This time Lark did the hand-patting. "Of course I will. I've investigated a zillion crimes." The rush of a new project sizzled through her veins. "Trust me, I know what I'm doing. Even though this time, I'm saddled with a rookie."

"A rookie?"

"Yeah, Rich's never done anything undercover, has he? He may have to do that before this is over."

Mariah paled. "Under . . . cover."

"You know, pretending to be someone he's not to get what he wants."

"I . . . see."

"It might be the only way to get to the bottom of what's going on at your company. And we must look at every last detail, every piece of paper, every investment and transaction, not to mention past and present employees and clients."

Mariah's hand shook. "Oh, dear. I had no idea. . . ."

Lark felt a swell of sympathy. Clearly that kind of deception was foreign to Mariah and added to her worries. "Don't fret. We'll reveal every secret and prove your innocence. They don't call me Snoop—er, Scoop—" she shot a glare at the chuckling man with the phone in his hand—"for nothing."

"OK," Rich said to Frank, "we'll be there shortly—give us time for supper, though." To Lark, he added, "Come on, Snoop. Seems as though you had a good idea for once."

She followed him to the front of the house. "Give me a break, Rich. I have great ideas all the time. And I'm going to show you . . ."

"Lord Jesus," Mariah prayed out loud as Lark reached the doorway, "watch out for those two. They're so busy one-uppin' each other, I'm afraid they'll be trippin' on their pride before too long."

Lark stumbled. There was that word again. Was she guilty as charged? Or simply self-sufficient, self-reliant, self-contained?

Who knew?

Louella Ashworth wielded her gavel with her usual zest. *Bang, bang, bang!* "This week's meeting of the Bellamy Garden Club will now come to order."

Mariah sat quietly, a soft smile on her lips. If she didn't have the trials at her company and Lark's and Richie's safety on her mind, today would be a happy day.

"We have the honor of installing our newest member tonight," Louella proclaimed. "Reenie Ainsley, come up front, dear."

The Garden Club meant more to Mariah than just a group of women with green thumbs. These were her friends, the women she'd grown up with, who'd prayed with her over her troubles and rejoiced over her blessings. Now her daughter would also be part of the group.

Reenie signed the membership book, having already completed her application, been interviewed by the Acceptance Committee, and paid her dues. Then, with a flourish, Louella took the lapel of Reenie's bright red camp shirt and attached the club's golden bouquet pin. "A full member, with all voting rights," the president declared. "How's that feel?"

Reenie chuckled. "I'm not sure. I haven't had the pin on long enough yet."

The other members tittered, and Reenie headed away from the podium toward her chair at Mariah's side.

"Not so fast there," cried Myrna from the far side of the library's meeting room. "Now that you're a member, we expect you to work with us. An' Louella here's made your brother an' your bosom buddy our most urgent project."

Still standing, Reenie looked at Mariah, a question in her eyes. Mariah blushed but said nothing. She didn't have to. Myrna did it for her.

"What's happenin' between them two these days?" asked the town's premier gossip, her purple hair rolls quivering with intensity.

Reenie looked confused. "Happenin' between them?"

"Oh, for goodness sake, Myrna," chided Louella. "You can't even wait long enough for the ink in the girl's signature to dry, can you?"

Myrna subsided with a *humph.*

"Miss Louella?" Reenie appealed.

"We've decided your brother and Lark were made for each other."

"Oh," Reenie said, "I figured that out years and years ago. What's so new about it?"

"Nothin's new, and that's what's wrong," Louella answered. "We're hopin' romance is what's up with them—before Lark hares off after another story or somethin'."

Reenie grimaced. "Romance? Not so long as they keep on arguin' all the time."

"That's exactly what we mean. We've got to do somethin' before those two mess up their lives."

Mariah stood, feeling a twinge of guilt as she prepared to discuss her son and Lark in public. But the ladies did, after all, mean well. "You can all settle down. Lark and Richie are on their way to Leesburg even as we speak."

Delighted gasps burst from every corner of the room.

"Do tell," urged Louella.

Mariah squared her shoulders. "I have . . . business concerns they've agreed to help with, and they're workin' together this very moment."

Reenie grinned from ear to ear. "Really, Mama? I didn't know. Why, that's great. I figure they'll stop somewhere for supper. Maybe a place with soft music, candles . . ."

Ooohs and aaahs echoed her sentiment.

"Wouldn't that be grand?" Reenie marveled. "An' you-all are tryin' to help them get together?"

Miss Louella nodded.

"Well, happy day!" Reenie cried. "I've joined the fun at just the right time. I want nothin' more'n Lark for a sister. The sooner we get those two together, the better."

"I'm not setting foot in a steak house," Lark declared, fists on her hips, fire in her eyes.

"What's the matter this time?" Rich asked, his patience

thinner than the sliver of moon illuminating the restaurant parking lot.

"Nothing's the matter with me. Not now, not ever."

As she tugged on Pooch-Face's leash, Rich's irritation grew. He still disagreed with her contention that the animal would aid their search. He knew the creature could only be a hindrance.

"Then why won't you leave your dog in the car and come inside for supper? We'll bring him scraps so he doesn't go hungry."

"My dog would rather starve than eat his own."

"Huh?"

"You heard me. Pooch-Face is not a cannibal."

"You've lost it this time, Red," Rich said, utterly puzzled.

"Don't call me that, and I haven't lost a thing."

"Then lock up the dog and let's go eat. We're keeping Frank waiting."

Lark spread her feet apart, shoulder width, clearly digging in her sneaker heels. "I'm not entering that kind of establishment. I couldn't carry that on my conscience."

"Carry what?"

"Patronizing a place that adds to the martyrdom of myriad helpless beings every hour of every day."

An uneasy niggle started up in the back of Rich's head. "Are you telling me . . . ?"

Out came the jaw, up went the nose. "What? You can't even ask the question? Well, I won't answer until you do."

"Fine. Are you a vegetarian, Larkspur Bellamy?"

"As are all the wisest, healthiest folks. Like Mr. Rogers . . ."

He should have known. Contrary as a mule. How were they ever going to solve his mother's problems if they couldn't even agree on food?

"OK," he said in the interest of compromise. "You're a vegetarian, and I want a steak. We can find middle ground.

I'll get my steak, and you can order a baked potato and salad. How's that for being accommodating on my part?"

"Couldn't we do Italian again? Please?"

Rich sighed. Deeply. "I suppose. As Shakespeare said, 'Lay on, Macduff.'"

THIRTEEN

AFTER A MEAL CONSUMED TO THE TUNE OF A FERVENT
aria on the merits of vegetarianism, Rich drove them to the
Dream Squeeze Distribution Center on the outskirts of
Leesburg. As they approached, his every nerve tightened, and
he sensed the tension build in Lark as well.

Upon their arrival, the meager moon slipped behind a cloud,
turning the night stygian. Vehicles on the road just beyond the
vacant parking lot rushed by, their engines and tires providing a
backdrop of speeding whines, whooshes, and crunches.

What would the records reveal?

"Ready?" Lark asked, nervous energy thrumming in her
single word.

"As can be."

Pooch-Face wailed in accord.

They walked to the steel door, and he took out the key
Mama had given him and inserted it in the dead-bolt lock.
The tumblers within clicked; Rich pressed down on the latch
and held the door open for Lark and the dog. As she stepped
into the entrance, he heard approaching footsteps—running
footsteps.

Lark crashed back into him, knocking both of them down onto the cement landing outside the door. Pooch-Face sprawled across them, howling eerily. A pair of ski-masked figures jumped over them, dashed down the steps, and disappeared around the corner of the building.

"Stay right where you are," he told Lark, then scrambled after the intruders.

"Yeah, right," Lark muttered as she jumped to her feet and dashed after Rich.

Rich's heart pounded as hard as his feet. His legs ate up the distance the men covered seconds ahead of him. But when he rounded the building, there was no one in sight.

Turning to Lark, he said between pants, "I told you . . . to stay put. Don't . . . follow. This could . . . be dangerous."

Lark shoved him forward. "Go."

Concerned for her safety yet determined to find the pair, Rich went on, not particularly reassured by the sound of her only a step behind him, her dog snuffling apace.

On the road out front, an eighteen-wheeler clanked and rumbled by, drowning out any sound the prowlers might have made. Still, Rich sprinted ahead.

He—with Lark and dog in his wake—checked the circumference of the gray cinder-block warehouse but found no evidence of the men who'd rushed them at the door. "I have to call the police," he said, breathing easier.

"Let's check the building first. That way we can tell them if there's been a burglary or something."

"What's this *let's* and *we? I'll* check the building; *you'll* stay out of trouble. Stick the dog in the car, and wait for me there."

"Aren't you the one who's always calling me trouble?" she quipped. "How can I stay out of trouble if you say that's who I *am?*"

"Look, I don't have time for your convoluted and creative but flawed logic right now. So just do what I tell you, for once."

"I'll have you know my logic's not flawed, and I have a brain, thank you very much. I will decide on my own what I'll do. But I'll take care of Pooch-Face first."

Rich stepped inside and flicked on the overhead light, searching his mind for an argument that would make Lark listen to reason. His mind froze when he saw what the prowlers had done.

Just outside Mama's office, Frank Vallore lay facedown, motionless, blood seeping from a wound to his temple and spreading in a dark puddle beneath his head.

Rich's stomach clenched, then plunged. He sucked in sips of air, fearing he'd lose the dinner he'd just had. He had never seen anything so sickening in his life. A man he knew had been beaten—perhaps killed. Only minutes ago.

Was there anything he could do?

Running to Frank's side, he prayed for the man's life.

When he heard Lark enter the room, Rich asked, "Will you listen to me now?"

Since she didn't answer, he glanced over his shoulder. The normally bold redhead stood still, her face a mask of horror, her eyes huge and dark.

"Lark? Are you OK?"

Without a sound, she shook her head, nodded, then shook her head again. She gulped but said nothing.

Dear God, what do you want me to do? he begged. *Frank needs me, but so does Lark. I can't expose her to any more danger than I already have. Please, please, Father, show me what I should do next.*

From the uncharacteristic lack of movement on Lark's part, Rich assumed she was in too much shock to do herself immediate harm. So he turned to Frank.

Fighting his natural revulsion to gore, he reached for the man's wrist. He prayed, but when he failed to find a pulse, panic rose. Persisting, however, he was eventually rewarded with a weak cadence beneath his fingers. "He's alive."

Lark moaned. Rich turned his head and saw a tremor rack her. "Stay right there," he said, and thanked God when she nodded in agreement. He'd take care of her as soon as he got through to 911.

But first, Frank. Tearing off his shirt, Rich wadded the cotton and pressed it gently but firmly to the wound, hoping the pressure would help stanch the steady flow of blood.

As time ticked by and the impromptu bandage did its job, he remembered he had to call for help if Frank was to have a chance to survive the attack. He stood and ran to the office.

It took only seconds to alert the authorities. As soon as he was assured help was on its way, he hung up the phone and went to Lark. He took her in his arms and was stunned to feel how cold she'd become.

"Hey, we're going to be all right," he crooned. "So's Frank."

Guilt bit at him, since he couldn't really know Frank's condition, but he had to do something for Lark—at the very least, reassure her. She looked fragile, frightened, weak. Utterly unlike her vibrant self.

A well of emotion opened inside him. He knew he should check out the building, make sure no trespasser remained, but his arms refused to release Lark. Not when she needed him.

"Hush, honey," he whispered when she moaned again. "I'm here. You're OK. Nothing's going to happen to you."

She sobbed, then finally said, "Let's go see what else they did."

Rich drew back as though she'd slapped him. "What are you, nuts?"

"No." She shivered. "For all we know, they may have an accomplice. If we don't check things out, they'll get away with—" she gestured toward Frank—"what they've done."

Lord, is this a test? If it is, I think I'm failing it. How can I let this woman barge headfirst into danger? It's Lark, Father. I can't let anything happen to her.

But he knew she was right. There could be another intruder in the building. If Rich didn't search the place, the guy could get away with the attack. He had to go look.

But he couldn't let Lark go along. Yet he couldn't leave her here without protection either. Who was to say the perpetrators wouldn't come back and do to her what they'd done to Frank?

The thought had Rich drawing her closer to his chest again. No, he couldn't let anything happen to her. As a Christian and as a man, he had to do the right thing.

Help me, Lord. Guide me. Show me what to do.

From the second floor, he heard a skittering sound. Lark stiffened in his arms.

Someone was in the building.

So was Lark. And the injured Frank. How could he protect them? Both of them.

"Heavenly Father," he prayed, "I don't know in my own mind what to do. Only you know what's in store for us. I trust you. . . ."

He paused, fighting the urge to rush forward and control the situation. "I will trust you to lead us through this. Your knowledge is so much greater than mine and your vision so much broader than mine. I will trust you to bring those men to justice. I will rest in the confidence you give us through your blessed son, Jesus."

When Lark pushed against his chest, Rich realized he had prayed out loud. And he acknowledged that, even though he'd promised he would, he really hadn't turned to God in any kind of serious way since the trouble with Mama had started.

Dread gave him pause. Had he been acting out of pride? Relying on his own strength and wisdom instead of seeking the ultimate Source? Had he pushed God away?

As if blinders were falling from his eyes, Rich got a glimpse into himself and saw much he didn't like. "Forgive me, Father."

"If you're counting on him to save us," Lark said, wrenching out of his clasp, "you're out of luck. Come on, before whoever's up there comes down to finish the job on Frank and adds us to the body count."

Before he could catch her, she hurried toward the rear of the vestibule. Rich's heart quaked.

Another set of scales dropped away. He cared about her. Really cared. About Lark Bellamy. The thought of anyone harming even one red hair on her head was enough to curdle his blood.

How could that be?

Lark was the one who'd made his life a misery as far back as he could remember. She'd ruined his prom. Cost him Mercy's friendship. Given him the runs with her love potion, plus headaches galore. Her return to town had made him the brunt of the town's gossip—again.

But she also consumed his thoughts. She awoke his protective instincts, not to mention the most consuming need to hold her, kiss her.

It couldn't be. She was trouble. She was after him.

She'd turned her back on God years ago.

Oh, Father, help. I'm losing my mind.

A nervy voice in the back of his head taunted, "That's not all you're losing. Check out that fickle internal organ that gets every man alive in trouble."

Thump, thump, thump beat his heart, propelling him after Lark even though his common sense set off warning sirens. He'd have to think about all this: his feelings for Lark, his failure to seek God, the mess he'd made of things. Later.

Right now he had to make sure the daring redhead didn't get hurt. He'd never be able to live with his guilt if he failed Lark.

Heaven help him, for Rich was pretty sure he was far beyond helping himself.

"I have no idea how the mutt got out of the car," Lark insisted for the jillionth time since they'd climbed back into said vehicle. "What's your problem? You don't speak English anymore?"

"Of course I do," Rich answered. "It's just highly suspicious how the critter turned up on the second floor. You sure you didn't send him snooping ahead of us while I tended to Frank?"

"Yeah, I'm sure. It's not as if I can make animals disappear. Besides, you'd have seen him if he'd run past you. I left him in the car, and he can't open car doors. At least, I don't think he can."

"Did you leave a window open?"

"Only partway. He needed to breathe, you know."

"There you go. He squeezed his way out the opening. Now, how'd he get inside the building?"

"Any broken windows?" Lark queried.

"I didn't notice any when we looked for those men."

"Well, there you go. You didn't notice."

Lark studied the irritating man at the wheel. Faint moonglow and shadows outlined his face, revealing only the impression of strength and earnestness. Intelligence. The essence of masculinity and power.

Oh, brother. Rich was still the most attractive, fascinating man she'd ever met. And the worst man for her to find appealing.

When he'd held her close back in the warehouse, her heart had taken flight. She'd wanted nothing more than to stay in the shelter of those sturdy arms and be comforted by the words he'd whispered into her ear. Longing for more had overwhelmed her, and his prayer for their protection had moved her.

Despite her broken relationship with God. Despite knowing her feelings for Rich could again make her the brunt of town gossip and mockery. Despite her need to prove herself more than a lovelorn female; her need to clear Mariah of all charges; her need to ensure her magazine's success; her need to find Des Richter to do so.

Lark's feelings for Rich were a distraction she could ill afford. But there they were, strong and deep as ever, as she feared they always would be.

That prayer. She shivered. Did Rich care enough about her to pray for her?

She shot him another look.

"You really should have left the dog at home as I said," he murmured.

"Not hardly. Pooch-Face was the one who found the smashed-in file cabinet and the running computer upstairs. Led the cops straight to that ransacked room."

"Do you mean to tell me the police are so incompetent they wouldn't have found that on their own?"

"No, of course not. But who knows how long it would have taken them? With Pooch-Face, it was a done deal."

"I guess you've decided to call him Pooch-Face, after all."

"No. I just haven't found a name yet."

"How about Sherlock?"

"Too obvious."

"Well, then, Holmes."

She considered his suggestion. "Nah. It doesn't feel right."

Lark turned to the backseat. What *was* she going to name the furry, funny creature? She really didn't like the idea of calling him Pooch-Face for life.

"I've got it," Rich said, then chuckled. "The perfect name for your bloodhound."

"OK. So what is it?"

"Mycroft."

"My what?"

"Not your anything. Mycroft. As in Sherlock Holmes's older, smarter brother."

"Hmm . . . " Lark studied the animal some more. "Mycroft," she said, testing the name.

The dog lifted his head, a quizzical look in his expressive eyes.

"Mycroft," she repeated.

A doggy snuffle, sneeze, and head shake—replete with drool—followed.

She grinned, then giggled. Finally, she laughed out loud, full peals that dispelled the anxiety and some of the fear she'd felt since they'd arrived at the Dream Squeeze Distribution Center.

"Mycroft." She reached back and scratched one of the dog's ears. "So that's who you are."

"Sure looks like a Mycroft to me."

Lark laughed again. "Hey, didn't I tell you awhile back that I'd prove we could work together? Well, here's proof. We stopped those thugs before they killed Frank. My dog led the cops to more evidence. And we've given the authorities something to think about besides your mom."

"Looks that way, doesn't it?"

"Does to me." She got quiet, then smiled again. "Hey, I gotta give you credit. You sure do have a way with words. And names."

Rich's humor vanished. His hands tightened on the steering wheel so much that, even by the faint light trickling into the car, Lark noticed his blanched knuckles.

What was his problem? What had she said wrong? Lark thought over her every word. Nothing. Absolutely nothing. She'd actually complimented the guy.

Sadness swept over her. It seemed that no matter what she said or did around Rich, it always turned out wrong. A terrible state of affairs, especially when her heart had taken another momentary flight when they'd named the dog and shared a laugh in the quiet night.

Why did she have to feel this way about him? And why did her feelings have to be so hopeless? Rich would never see her as anything more than trouble. He'd never see her as a woman worthy of standing at his side, supporting him, sharing his life, helping him solve its mysteries and complications.

The thought wrung her heart, and the satisfaction she'd fleetingly felt disappeared.

Why? Why, why, why?

They arrived home at a little past one. Rich pulled up in front of Lark's home. "We're here," he said to wake her.

She blinked. "Oh, sorry. I didn't realize I'd fallen asleep."

By the light of the gas lamp next to the Bellamy picket fence, Rich saw Lark's sleepy eyes, her slumber-puffed lips, her creased cheek, her tousled curls. She looked so soft and feminine.

Utterly appealing and desirable.

Utterly wrong and dangerous.

But even that knowledge didn't dent the need to touch her face. So he did. Running a knuckle tenderly across her jawline, Rich marveled at the soft satin of Lark's skin. He already knew the silk of her hair, the warmth of her body in his arms. The firm ripeness of her lips under his. Her rejection of his Lord and Savior.

At that thought, he pulled back abruptly and cleared his throat of the thickness there. "See you."

"But not too soon, right?" she asked, bitterness in her voice.

"I didn't say—"

She got out of the car and slammed the door, cutting him off.

Lark Bellamy was the most exasperating creature he'd ever met. Knowing how wrong she was for him did nothing to stop him from wanting to call her back, reach out for her, hold her, kiss her . . . and never stop.

Regretting his weakness, he changed gears and headed the few yards to his driveway. What he found waiting there made him want to howl like the newly named Mycroft.

Storey Newburn sat in his Jaguar, his frizzled noggin against the headrest, his mouth gaping wide. Rich turned off his car, got out, and approached his agent.

Before he reached the car door, he heard what sounded like an oncoming semi—Storey's snoring. Rich rapped on the window.

"Go home," he said firmly as Storey bolted upright, smacked his head against the low-slung roof of the car, then swore. "It's late, you're cursing, and I'm going to bed."

"Not until you see reason," the New Yorker said, his voice rough with sleep.

"I've seen reason, and you're not promoting it. We have nothing more to discuss. Not in the middle of this grim night. Go."

Storey opened the door to his car and ran after Rich. "Wait a minute, there, Des—"

"Rich!" he yelped, praying that Lark had gone inside already, or at the very least, hadn't heard Storey use the dangerous name.

"Yeah, yeah, Rich. I can't help it, you know. Sorry. But we gotta talk; we got things to discuss, straighten out. A contract to sign."

"Is it any different than the last time I saw it?" Rich asked, slipping his key into the front-door lock.

"No. And there's nothing wrong with that contract."

"Maybe not for you, but there is for me. Good night, Storey. I'm going to sleep."

Rich closed the door and leaned against it. Storey pummeled the wood, refusing to give up. That stubbornness made him a fabulous agent; right now, though, it just made him a problem. Another problem. And Rich couldn't handle any of them right then. He was shot. Discouraged by what God had showed him about himself. Irritated by his unwanted . . . affection for the wrong woman.

"Lord," he said out loud, "help Storey accept my position. And get him to go home. I need to sleep so I can figure out where you're leading me, so I can follow you better, especially with all that's going on."

He dragged himself up the stairs, his feet heavier than anvils probably felt. He was glad they'd arrived at the warehouse when they did, or Frank might have died. He had no doubt the intruders had intended just that. And he knew they hadn't been run-of-the-mill burglars.

Lark had been right. Mama *was* in danger—from organized crime.

Rich couldn't get his mother out of this kind of ordeal. Not on his own. And not with Lark's help. He didn't even know if the authorities could help Mariah a whole lot.

But he knew who could. He had some praying to do. As soon as he was lucid enough to beg forgiveness and restore the relationship that should never have become strained.

Then he'd beg for help.

As she climbed the steps to her porch, Lark heard her impossible next-door neighbor cry out his own name. She craned her neck to see what he was up to, and instead spotted the now-familiar, sleek Jaguar napping in the drive.

It couldn't be coincidence. No way. Frank Vallore, Mariah's operations manager, had been nearly beaten to death. Then, hours later, the New Yorker in the Jag had turned up in Rich's drive—again.

Nausea rocked her. She'd been right to suspect Rich all along. There had to be a connection. She didn't believe in coincidence.

It was yet another reason to fight her feelings for Rich. She couldn't let herself fall in love with a mobster, and she had to protect Mariah Desmond from her own son.

But, oh, how she wished she didn't, not after that comforting embrace. Not after he'd called her "honey."

Emotions notwithstanding, and with the trusty bloodhound at her heel, Lark crept around the hedge separating the two homes to take down the license plate number on the white car. Tears bathed her cheeks.

Why did Rich have to be a crook?

Well, it couldn't matter, could it?

Tomorrow she'd learn who Jag-guy was. Tomorrow she'd put together the exposé that would blow Rich's scheme wide open. Tomorrow she'd kill every last bit of leftover childhood love she still harbored for the man who'd framed his own mother.

Richard Desmond had broken her heart for the last time.

This time, Lark was going to break him.

FOURTEEN

He'd slept, but not well.

Every so often he'd awakened, anguished. One time—the last time—tears had wet his lashes, and salt tracks down his cheeks told him he'd wept during this latest dream—one he couldn't remember, no matter how hard he tried.

He'd gone downstairs, brewed a pot of coffee. Then, steaming cup in hand, he'd headed right to where he'd known he'd end up.

Rich placed the coffee on the table next to the overstuffed armchair in his bedroom, sat, and took his worn leather Bible in his hands.

The tactile sensation sent a thrill of recognition through Rich, yet it did nothing to abate the discomfort in his heart. Only the Father could do that, the God he'd pretty much ignored as he'd acted on his own strength for so long now.

He winced. He'd talked a good line; he was a Christian and thought himself faithful and committed to God. Yet, in truth, he'd marched to the beat of his own drummer instead of that of his maker. What did that say about him? about his submission?

Not much.

"Forgive me, Father," he murmured, shame burning in him. "Your Word speaks against leaning on our own understanding, but that's what I did. No wonder I haven't a clue how to help Mama. I don't know what the future holds. You do."

As Rich remembered every hideous moment of the previous night, he couldn't help but think of Lark. Bold, brash, proud Lark. Even while in shock, frightened, she'd pushed forward, certain of her ability to succeed.

Another set of scales fell from his eyes. Although he thought of Lark, Rich saw himself instead. Her actions mirrored his own.

He didn't like what he saw in that reflection.

Perhaps he wasn't quite as blatant as she. And he certainly didn't reject God, at least not overtly. Yet he'd turned away from the greatest source of wisdom, just as Lark had done earlier.

His actions revealed a shunning of the God who'd made him, who'd given his only Son for Rich's sake. The God Rich had promised to follow and serve for the rest of his life. He'd turned his back on the one who'd given him eternal life. How could he have done that?

Misery tightened his throat. He'd done it by viewing himself as high and wise as God. By making his choices and taking his actions without regard to God's leading. He'd given in to the same temptation that had damned Adam and Eve in the Garden.

Pride.

Mama had been right.

Worse, Lark had been right. Despite her unbelief, she'd seen right through Rich's thin veneer of faith to the sinner within. She'd called him proud and arrogant—what he'd been.

He'd been so blinded by her return, by his fear of what she might do to him and his well-guarded secret, the embarrassing gossip she might re-ignite, that he'd closed his ears—his heart—to everything she'd said.

And she'd been right.

He had been proud.

"Oh, Father," he cried out, his voice rough, "I don't deserve your love and forgiveness and all the gifts you've given me. But I do love you, and I want to serve you, even though I've put up a lousy showing lately. Forgive me, Lord. Take my pride, my arrogance, my self-reliance and self-involvement. Heal my heart. I can't do it—only you can work this miracle, and I thank you for not giving up on me."

Tears again dampened Rich's eyes, this time leaving no doubt as to their cause. His guilt. His rebellion. His weakness of faith.

Rich recognized where he'd gone wrong, turning to God only in brief, panicked prayers rather than seeking godly wisdom regularly and nourishing his spirit with his maker's words. He opened his Bible. The translucent pages parted in the book of Psalms.

How appropriate. David, sinful as he'd been, had known to call out to God in times of trouble. Yet in that trouble, he'd also had the sense to praise God for his never-failing goodness.

Rich could do that. And he could trust the Almighty to work out the intricacies of his situation. His mother's predicament. Lark's desire to uncover his secret. Even her unbelief.

A thought flew through his mind. Could God have brought her back to town for Rich's sake? To be the mirror that would show him how far he'd strayed from his walk of faith?

Could Rich be more like Lark than he thought?

He had pushed her away out of fear. She'd found out his adolescent secrets, prom night included, and he knew that, given time, she'd reveal his latest one. He hated the spotlight of gossip.

But he'd also acted out of pride. He'd thought he could handle Mama's business by himself. Just as Lark had insisted she could solve the fraud case all on her own.

Was that what God had in mind when he'd thrown them together again and again? Was there more to come?

Rich shuddered at the thought.

Did he really want the answer to his questions?

No, not really.

But he suspected his wants in this case wouldn't matter one bit. God seemed to be leading him straight to those answers anyway.

Answers Lark held.

Lark hung up the phone and stared at the contraption, wondering if she'd heard wrong. Rich had asked her out to dinner. Voluntarily. As far as she could tell, no one had held a gun to his head.

She grimaced at her attempt at humor. Guns and bullets had become far too real to her after last night. True, she'd covered all kinds of crimes, including murders, during her career, but she'd never seen the victims before they'd been treated for their wounds. Never mind the corpses.

It was a sight she hoped never to witness again.

She marveled at Rich's presence of mind. He'd thought of checking for Frank's pulse when it had been all Lark could do to keep from vomiting at the stench of rubber girdles sweetened with blood. He'd ripped off his shirt and tended to

Frank's wound when she'd hugged herself and fought just to retain consciousness. He'd thought to comfort her when all she'd registered was the horror.

It had to have affected him, too, yet he'd held her, insisted on protecting her—not that she'd needed the protection, of course. She could take care of herself. But he'd cared enough to look after her in the face of danger.

He'd called her "honey."

Had he done it unwittingly, as a mere Southernism? Or had the endearment meant something more? Enough to have him ask her to dinner the next night? Or was it part of his criminal master plan?

Pooch—Mycroft—nuzzled her hand. "Only one way to know, right?" she asked, rubbing a long, soft ear. Mycroft snuffled his agreement, then collapsed by her kitchen chair. She propped her chin on her fist and let her imagination soar.

It would be lovely if they dined at an out-of-the-way place, be serenaded by violins, their faces illuminated by flickering candlelight. They wouldn't notice the food they ate, gazing into each other's eyes, communicating rich feelings of love, admiration, respect.

Then they'd leave, walk in the moonlight. They'd kiss under a tree, secluded by its leaves, a cluster of shrubs, enveloped in the perfume of summer blossoms. . . .

Footsteps on the back steps burst Lark's dreamy bubble. "Who's there?"

"Hobey, Miss Lark. We agreed I'd come over today to work on my talkin' an' stuff."

"Come on in. I . . . it sort of slipped my mind." After last night, it was a minor miracle she still had a mind, as her sophomoric fantasy proved.

Good grief. She couldn't be falling back in love with Rich, could she? Not now that she had reason to suspect him, even fear him.

"No way," she told Mycroft, who'd greeted Hobey and returned to plop down at Lark's side.

For the next hour, she concentrated on language arts, teaching Hobey what she'd found useful in losing her countrified sound. Yet all along the thought of a date with Rich—their first—teased her, defying common sense.

As Hobey was about to leave, he turned to her. "I know I need to talk better so's to serve God as he's called me to, but I cain't rightly figger why you went an' changed yourself into someone else, Miss—Lark, Lark."

Lark's cheeks warmed. How was she going to tell this generous, decent man that the thought of revealing her roots—his roots—by her speech had shamed her?

She couldn't. She couldn't hurt him that way.

"It was just something I had to do," she said, "to accomplish what I wanted to accomplish."

"An' you did it at that, didn't you? We're right proud of you here in Bellamy, you know. One Pew-litzer Prize, an' now a magazine all your own. Awful proud of you, we are."

"Thanks, Hobey, but the magazine's far from a success yet."

"Not from what I hear. But I figger you must know best. If you say it ain't what it should be, then I reckon you must be right." He donned his navy blue Hobey's Masonry cap and took the doorknob in his massive hand. "Ain't seen ya at church since you been back. Did you leave the Lord behind with your talk when you left town?"

The candid voice landed a solid punch in Lark's middle. Hobey's question expressed what Granny Iris would have thought. She'd have been disappointed in Lark.

"Yes, well, something like that," she said, her innate honesty winning over the urge to equivocate. Just as it kept her from pretending a faith she'd long ago lost, just to be seen in church on a regular basis.

He removed his cap again, rubbed his head. "Tell you what, Lark. You go find yourself a Bible an' read all them verses you learned yourself all those years ago. They ain't changed a lick since then. An' God's the same's he's always been. Don't you go turnin' blind to your need for 'im."

She turned away. "He wasn't there when I needed him, so if what you say is true, that he never changes, he won't be there for me now."

"Ah, Lark, I'm right sorry you feel that way. God was always there. You just weren't lookin' for 'im rightly. You were lookin' for the God you wanted him to be, 'stead of the God he is."

She shrugged but said nothing more.

A heavy hand fell on her shoulder. "Ah, Father," Hobey said, "this little girl of yours is hurtin', been hurtin', I reckon, for a lot of years. Come hug her with your love, Daddy God, send her your peace, an' use me however's your will. Let her see how much you love her, an' how much you want to help her. Heal her of her pride. In the name of our Lord Jesus, Amen."

The tears that had formed in Lark's eyes at the beginning of Hobey's prayer vanished at that hated word. She yanked away from his grasp.

Hobey couldn't possibly think her a proud woman, could he? Would a proud person spend time helping him overcome a personal flaw, like she was doing?

"I'm—"

"I ain't finished yet, Lark. Just hear me out."

She nodded courteously, if reluctant.

"Don't you go thinkin' on pride as folks do. Think on pride as God does. It's a sin that separates his children from 'im. Makes 'em forget all he's done for 'em in the past. An' lets 'em think they know better'n he does what's right for them. But we don't know, an' we more'n more mess up when we turn hard against 'im. Loneliness an' troubles are sure to follow a hardened heart. I don't rightly think Sister Iris woulda wanted that for you. I know I don't."

Hobey's sincerity tightened the knot in Lark's throat. She didn't agree with his sentiment but felt his affection. "Thanks for caring, Hobey. I'll think on what you said."

"You do that, now, you hear? An' I'll be goin' back to work. See you at church?"

Again, Lark couldn't lie. "I . . . don't know. Maybe after I think."

And she would think about what he'd said. She just didn't believe any amount of thinking would change her mind about God. He'd let her down too often in her past.

Lark was going to kill a man. One particular man.

Here she'd torn apart her closet, looking for just the right thing to wear on their first "date," finally settling on a jade silk blouse and slim black linen trousers, and Rich had the audacity of running them by the drive-through at Taco Bell.

"It's the only place I knew that would carry meat-free food," he said, taking the cardboard tray from the teenager in the window and handing it to Lark. "Besides, we have to talk. We don't have time for ordering and waiting to be served at a restaurant."

Definitely death. And she'd make sure it was a painful one. Slow. Agonizing. Torturous.

Then Lark remembered poor Frank Vallore. She shuddered. She was mad at Rich, all right, but she, who'd never been violent before, knew she'd never tolerate violence again. Not after seeing its effects.

"Fine," she ground out as she held the steamy, spicy meal

well away from her nice clothes. "Are we in a hurry to go somewhere?"

"Not exactly."

When he didn't elaborate, she waited.

And waited some more.

Finally, she lost patience. "What do you have planned that can't wait for us to eat while sitting rather than in motion?"

"Oh, we're not going to eat in the car," he said, never taking his eyes off the road. "We're going to Hollings' Memorial Park to eat. It's just that we have to talk, and I don't want interruptions. You know, by a waitress. Oh, and I'd rather not have anyone eavesdrop on us."

One thing was for sure. Bellamy's most eligible bachelor didn't have romance on the mind. So it could only mean one thing. "You've finally decided to see reason and work with me to help your mother."

"Could you please wait until I no longer hold our lives in my hands?"

"I guess."

Curiosity surged in her, belying her benign acceptance to his request. What was Rich up to? Why had he asked her out to . . . run for the border, as the Taco Bell commercials once said? What was so important he had to discuss it in the park down by Langhorn Creek? In the dark? With no one around?

Uh-oh. He wouldn't.

Would he?

Well, maybe. After all, he'd implicated his mother in his dirty dealings. Maybe he'd decided Lark knew too much—not that she did. She didn't have a clue what he was up to. True, she had her suspicions, but she really didn't know.

Could she argue her way out of his trap?

At least he wouldn't be fitting her for cement shoes. Only an undernourished mouse could drown in shallow Langhorn

Creek. Then again, the mob was even better known for well-placed bullets to rid themselves of obstacles in their path.

Poor Maggie. She'd have to come home from her honeymoon to bury her sister. And Cammie. What would Lark's brutal death do to her pregnancy? to Reenie's? How would Mariah cope with Lark's death at her son's hand?

"We're here," her future murderer said as he parked in the small lot near the picnic tables. "I'll carry the food."

Scared, Lark got out of the shiny Avalon and followed Rich to one of the tables. Why she didn't make a run for it, she didn't know. Unless it was her eternal curiosity. She really wanted to know what he had to say.

"So," she said as she took a bean burrito out of its wrapper, "what's so important you had to discuss it tonight? Out here?"

He closed his eyes. When he opened them again, he shook his head. "This isn't easy for me, you understand."

Lark's blood ran cold. Was this it? Was he about to pull out a gun? Or would an accomplice run out of the trees to her left and do the deed?

"You see," he went on, oblivious to her fear. The last thing she wanted was to die a coward. Especially not in front of him.

"You see, Lark, I realized last night that I . . . owed you an apology."

"A what?" she asked, not trusting her ears. Had he really said—

"An apology, OK? I'm sorry."

Confused, Lark went on the offensive. "For which of your zillion offenses?"

Rich glared, the moon giving enough light for her to register his impatience. "For . . . well, for being proud. And stiff-necked, as Hobey said at your sister's wedding."

"Run this by me again? I don't want to miss one bit."

He stood and began pacing just on the other side of the table's attached bench. "Last night, God made it very clear to me that I'd become a proud man—"

"Become?" she asked archly, latching onto something other than his faith.

"Give a guy a break and listen. I acted out of pride. I decided I was responsible for my mother's protection, and I barged ahead. I refused to consider what you had to offer in the way of help and experience, and I never stopped to think of the danger I could lead you into by letting you tag along."

"Tag along!"

He gave her another quelling look. She quelled.

"What I meant was that I thought I had everything under control. But I didn't. I led you right into that warehouse where you could have been hurt. Or worse."

Both shuddered. Exchanged a meaningful look.

Rich continued, his voice rough. "I took my eyes off the Cross and placed them on me. I leaned on my understanding of the situation rather than seeking God's wisdom in the matter. And you might have suffered because of my pride. I asked the Father's forgiveness for my rebellion against him, but now I need to ask yours. Will you forgive me, Lark?"

Uncomfortable with the conversation, she tried to make light of the matter. "Oh, you did nothing wrong. I went with you, and I knew what I was getting into. I've experienced the dangerous side of crime in my work."

Well, she'd often seen the results of that danger. Experienced it . . . ? If she continued stretching facts this way, she'd soon need a nose job and a name change. Pinocchio hardly made for a good byline.

"Anyway," she said, "you don't need to ask my forgiveness—"

"But I do. I haven't given the kind of testimony to my faith that I should have, and I might have obstructed your view of God. I should have remembered that too often I'm the closest to Jesus others may come. If I don't reflect his humility and submission to the Father, I become an obstacle in the walk of another instead of a fellow traveler."

Again, Lark tried to shrug off his efforts. "I'm fine. You haven't obstructed anything."

"Oh, but I might have. Who's to say God didn't bring you home for me to offer you an example of the life of faith? Who's to say he isn't calling you to him and wants to use me to lead you back to his side?"

Rich's words reminded Lark of the many lessons at the Bellamy Community Church's Sunday school years ago. Mama's and Daddy's prayers. Granny Iris's stories of Jesus' unfailing love.

Why had he failed her?

"I don't think so," Lark murmured. "He's never done much for me, so I can't imagine he'd want to do anything now."

"He never fails us, stops loving us, or gives up on us. Just remember that. We give up on him when things aren't going our way. Pride takes over and says we know better than he does."

Rich thought she had abandoned God. "You're wrong," she said. "I didn't take everyone who mattered from him. I didn't make a laughingstock of him. I didn't let him get pushed and shoved and used. So let's just talk about something else."

He looked sad in the soft silver light of the summer night. "As soon as I have your forgiveness. For real."

Self-consciously she said, "Of course I forgive you. I don't think you did anything that warrants your asking forgiveness, but since you asked, I forgive you."

"Thank you." Rich sat again, closed his eyes in apparent prayer, opened up his beef enchilada, then smothered it with hot sauce.

They ate and talked about the night before. They shared their revulsion, their fear, their relief that Frank would live.

But in the back of Lark's mind remained thoughts of the man who'd humbled himself to ask forgiveness because God called him to humility. And he'd instead been proud.

He'd accused her of the same thing. Was she proud? And if so, was that pride responsible for her alienation from God? Even as far back as when Mama and Daddy died?

Lark didn't know. But Rich had awakened in her a need to know.

Could pride separate someone from God?

FIFTEEN

At the same time but at the other end of town, Reenie ran into the Bellamy Public Library's meeting room. "Oh, Miss Louella!" she cried. "It's plain awful. Even worse'n I imagined. We have to do somethin' about it, too. Straight-away."

Miss Louella raised a chestnut eyebrow. "Awful? And we need to do something?" Her eyes danced with excitement. "Why, of course, honey. Soon's you tell me what the 'awful' is, and what you want done about it. I'm always ready to help."

"It's Mama. She's really, really in trouble."

A couple of gardeners entered and took chairs. Miss Louella nodded a greeting, but followed Reenie. "Well, sugar, I heard all about the silly misunderstanding with her getting herself arrested and all, but Richie took care of that."

Reenie shook her head, tears squeezing past her shut lids. "You mean . . . he didn't?"

"No, ma'am. An' I just found out what the charges against her are. She's charged with credit-card fraud and racketeerin'.

Somethin' about theft by girdle? Have you ever heard anythin' sillier in all your born days? I hear tell even the Secret Service is involved. They're sayin' Mama's a . . . a . . . mobster."

"Humph!" Myrna Stafford had arrived. "I knew it. Couldn't fool me none. That business of hers always seemed a mite shady."

"Distributing girdles, Myrna?" asked Sophie Hardesty, popping up from her chair. She shook her snow white, Gibson girl topknot. "Why on this green earth would you think that?"

"It ain't the girdles that seemed so shady—until now," Myrna argued. "It's the too much money she's been rakin' in that's questionable. An' now it looks like she's been caught." She dipped her purpled head as if to say, "So there."

"You listen here, Myrna Stafford. That's my mama you're malignin'. I won't stand for it. I came here, to her dearest an' oldest friends, for help. An' if you can't find it in your heart to help a longtime friend, why, then . . . you can . . . you can just . . . "

"You can just drop out of our efforts," Miss Louella said. "Like you did when we worked to take care of matters at the Ashworth Mansion this past spring."

Myrna hugged her circa 1950, black patent-leather pocketbook. "An' plum sensible I was about that, too. I didn't wind up in trouble, did I?"

"No," Sophie said, "but you weren't particularly friendly to Louella."

"Or Christian about things," susurrated Philadelphia, taking a seat in the front row.

Tipping up her bony chin, Myrna glared at Miss Louella. "Well, I ain't gonna be a fool this time, neither. I'm goin' home." She stalked toward the door. "I ain't fixin' to get into another of your fusses, Lou. Call me to meetin' oncet you're done messin' in Mariah's life."

Reenie stared after the elderly curmudgeon. "My goodness. Is Mrs. Stafford always like that?"

"'Fraid so," Savannah Hollings, the bank president's wife, answered. "She's the pruniest woman I've ever met."

"Oh, Vannie," chided Florinda Sumner, one of Sophie Hardesty's dearest cronies and a frequent victim of Myrna's snide comments, "she's lonesome since her Hugh passed on."

"But that's going on twenty-five years now, Florinda," reasoned Mrs. Hollings.

"Why, Vannie," said Sophie, "you still have your dear Mitch with you. Unlike some of us widowed ladies. It's God's pure blessin' not to experience our kind of loss. I know that for some, time doesn't do the job it's said to. And I'm guessin' Myrna's one of them. Unlike me. We need to keep on keepin' her in our prayers."

"Fine," Reenie said, panicking again. "We'll pray for Myrna, but what about Mama?"

"What's wrong with your mama?" Mrs. Hollings asked.

"Do tell," Sarah Langhorn asked as she set a small green-and-gold Blissful Bookworm bag next to the podium. "Here's your latest Pinkney title, Lou. And Reenie? What's wrong with our dear Mariah?"

"Yes, child," added Sophie. "What's wrong with my housemate? I left her on the telephone this mornin' when I went to work. She looked right fine to me."

"But she's home waitin' on a call 'bout this mess right now. Couldn't come because of it," Reenie said on a gusty sob. "See, the Secret Service is after her."

"Come again?"

"You're pullin' my leg. . . ."

"Surely not Mariah Desmond . . ."

"You quit your funnin' with us, Maureen Desmond Ainsley. . . ."

Miss Louella smacked her gavel against the podium.

"Order, ladies, come to order. I call this meeting of the Garden Club to order. Now it seems one of our fine members finds herself in a fix, and we've always come to one another's rescue. Let's hear from Mariah's girl just what the problem is, shall we? Then we can decide what to do."

Reenie presented an outline of what she knew—brief, since she knew little about her mother's situation. She'd have known less if she weren't friends with Jill Wiggon, whose Bellamy-cop husband had come home fretting over Mama's situation the night before. Like a good friend, Jill had told Reenie what she knew the moment Wiggon had left for work today.

"You can see how bad it looks for Mama," she said to sum things up. "And I can't just let my baby's granny go to jail. Especially since I know my mama didn't do any of those things they're accusin' her of."

When Reenie finished speaking, Miss Louella's eyes roamed over the gathered women. "Now I know we got ourselves in a mite of trouble last spring while we were concentrating on the restoration of the Ashworth Mansion. But we learned our lesson, didn't we?"

Every head nodded.

"Still and all, we can't let our sister be jailed for something she plain didn't do, can we?"

Side-to-side shakes took over.

"So we have to do something, don't we?"

Nodding resumed.

Turning to Reenie, Miss Louella smiled. "Honey, you were right to come to us. You can trust us to help your mama. With our expertise—"

"Just not the latest Marvin Pinkney, Lou," begged the bookstore owner.

"Indeedy, no. Why, he got us into the worst kind of skimble-skambled trouble that last time." Thoughtfully, Miss

Louella went on, "To be perfectly truthful, sisters, I got us into trouble by reading too much into his books. So this time we're just going to keep our eyes and ears open for anything that might could help Mariah."

A heartfelt sigh of relief rustled through the room.

"Don't you worry, Reenie," the group's chastened leader said. "We would never just sit idly by, doing nothing while your mama's in danger of getting herself convicted. We'll never let that happen to her. One of our own is much more important than any ol' bulbs. We'll clear Mariah's name, won't we, ladies? One for all and all for one, like the Mouseketeers."

"Musketeers, Louella," corrected the very literate Sarah.

"No, dear. Mouseketeers. Do you see any gentlemen in this room? Those Frenchmen were men, you know. But Annette Funicello, she was a Mouseketeer."

Reenie stared at Miss Louella. How had they leapfrogged from Mama's predicament to swashbuckling swordsmen, then on to vintage Disney shows? Well, it didn't really matter, did it? What mattered was that Mama's friends were coming to her rescue.

Right?

Still reeling from her conversations with Hobey and Rich, Lark rose on Thursday morning feeling restless. After Rich had accepted her forgiveness, he'd told her he intended to return to the warehouse to check the documents they'd never looked for once they'd found Frank. As soon as the police gave the OK, of course.

As she cupped her hands around her morning mug of Red Zinger tea, she decided she didn't feel like working on the next issue of her magazine—it was almost ready for the printer anyway.

She had yet to hear back from the friend in Baltimore who'd agreed to ask a friend of his in that city's police force to run a national check on the white Jag's plates.

She felt antsy, out of sorts, and sheepish for having feared for her life last night when all Rich had wanted to do was apologize. But he was up to something with the New Yorker, and she was determined to figure out what. Especially since she suspected it could ultimately hurt Mariah—if it hadn't already.

Sipping the snappy brew, she mulled over what to do today. Then she had an idea.

She hadn't seen much of Cammie since returning to Bellamy. A few times she'd driven her youngest sister to her prenatal appointments; together they'd tried to warn Maggie when the middle Blossom had charged headlong into trouble; they'd crossed paths a number of times during preparations for the wedding and the celebration itself. But nothing more.

Knowing too well Cammie's gentle nature and suspecting her boarders might be taking advantage of that nurturing kindness, Lark decided the time had come to check up on things at her sister's boardinghouse.

"Hey, Mycroft, we're going for a walk," she called, bracing herself. Her pup had quickly learned the meaning of that crucial word and, as expected, came careening through the kitchen doorway, ready to go.

She clicked on his leash, turned off the warmer under her teakettle, and closed the back door behind them. Rejoicing in the summer morning sunshine, she noted no sign of activity at Rich's house.

Good. She wasn't ready to face him yet.

Her walk to Cammie's proved uneventful and pleasant as she waited for Mycroft to sniff along the sidewalk while he followed who knew what tantalizing trail. She greeted a few neighbors and made herself think of nothing more serious than summertime.

Certainly not of yesterday's disturbing conversations. Much less, of her broken relationship with God.

At Cammie's, she whacked the brass knocker. The door flew open and a blonde, teenage tornado whizzed out. "Miss Cammie's in the kitchen, Miss Lark. Just go straight on in."

Lark knew the teen's parents had agreed to leave her behind when they were transferred to North Dakota so she could finish her upcoming senior year with her lifelong classmates. The separation had been difficult for parents and daughter, but Cammie had taken the girl under her wing.

Case in point. Cammie was about to have a child of her own. She didn't need to take over mothering someone else's half-grown kid.

Lark led Mycroft into the parlor of the well-kept Sprague home. "Cam? It's me. Are you too busy?"

"Never, Lark," Cammie sang out from the rear of the house. "Come on back. I'm bakin' some bread."

Another point. Who in her right mind would bother to knead and bake her own bread when health-food stores replete with handmade loaves could be found in Leesburg? Especially since Cammie looked so worn out these days.

As Lark stepped into the kitchen, an elderly man in a dark green suit opened the back door. "Cammie, my darling girl, are you making those marvelous caramel rolls of yours?"

Cammie beamed. "No, I wasn't, Willie, but now that you bring it up, why, I think I will. Thanks for remindin' me how good they are."

"Anytime, my dear girl. Anytime."

Lark's temper heated to a simmer. The nerve of the guy, to ask Cammie to bake special treats for him.

When Lark set off after the offending gent, ready to give

the character a piece of her mind, she had to plaster herself against a wall to avoid the pair of college-age males barreling down the lovely stairway of the home.

"Hey, Mrs. Sprague," called out the Asian boy, heading for the kitchen. "We're going to need some laundry done before the game on Saturday. And that washer-and-dryer schedule you set up for everyone isn't working out too well."

"I'll say," chimed in the African-American at his heel. "Too many folks wantin' to use it at the same time, you know?"

Lark heard Cammie sigh. "Yes, I know, Stu. But the deliverymen haven't come to install the set I bought. I'm sure the new equipment will be ready before your game. I reckon it's a big one for your summer league this week."

"Well, ma'am," Stu said, grinning, "with lacrosse, every game's a big one. That's what makes it the coolest game."

"I'll be there cheerin' for you two," Cammie chirped.

"That's what you said," piped in the Asian, who grabbed a banana from the kitchen counter and headed for the door.

"Later, Miss Cammie," added Stu, taking an apple and following his friend.

Lark exploded. "Camellia Bellamy, do you have—"

"Sprague, Lark, honey. My name's Camellia Sprague."

"Oh, I know you married what's-his-face—"

"David, dear. David Allen Sprague."

"Yeah, OK. But you're still a Bellamy and my sister, and that's what's driving me crazy right now. You're letting these people trample all over you. While you're pregnant, no less."

Cammie chuckled. "You never change, do you, Lark?"

"What do you mean?"

"I know you mean well, but you barge in here, accuse my friends of all kinds of meanness, and finish off by tellin' me you don't think I can even run my home. Are you tryin' to tell me how to do a better job? When was the last time you cooked, cleaned, and kept house?"

When Lark, struck speechless, failed to answer, Cammie went on. "I can see you don't think very highly of me. So there's not much I can do other than tell you I'm happy doin' what I'm doin'. These folks have become my family, and I love takin' care of their needs. Someone has to look after them, and I really *like* keepin' a home. It's too bad you can't see my work as worthwhile, but I'm not changin' my life to suit you."

Gentle though Cammie's voice was and as nonbiting as her words were, Lark realized her sister wasn't open to the help Lark was equipped to offer. Even if it came only through sage advice.

Lark took off toward the front door. "Time to go home, then. Come on, Mycroft. I've overstayed my welcome."

"You never have," Cammie said.

Lark paused.

The youngest Blossom continued. "You just haven't made your peace with God, is all. Once you do, you'll lose your restlessness, your need to control things, your—" Cammie took a deep breath—"your arrogance and pride."

"That's it!" Lark said, tugging on Mycroft's leash. "We're outta here. See ya." *Not soon, either.*

Just when she'd gone out of her way to avoid unpleasant thoughts and the memory of those two tough conversations, Cammie had gone and thrown that word in Lark's face again. If she still believed in God, she'd be tempted to think he was trying to tell her something.

That afternoon Hobey's second session went off without a hitch until he donned his trademark cap and stood. That's when he said, "You done any thinkin' on what I said last time?"

Lark's stomach dove for her toes. "Ah . . . some."

"Think on it some more. An' keep an open mind to what Jesus might could be sayin' to you."

Lark swallowed hard. Cammie's parting words, not to mention her own fleeting notion that God might be trying to speak to her, returned with a vengeance. "What do you mean, 'saying to me'?"

Hobey removed his cap and ran the bill back and forth through his thick fingers. "Well, Lark, it's like this. God spends his time raisin' his children—us, you know. Learnin' us—"

"Teaching us," she corrected automatically.

"Yes, ma'am," Hobey said. "Teachin' us what's what. An' you know? Straight up from the start, there ain't nothin' so natural to folks, so sly an' deceitful an' hidden in our hearts, nothin' so dangerous as pride."

When she went to object, Hobey held out a vast palm. "Hang on to your britches, there, girl. I ain't done just yet. When I talk 'bout pride, I'm talkin' 'bout that ol' original sin. You remember the snake in Eden, don'tcha?"

"Mm-hmm." She'd attended lots of Sunday school classes featuring that episode.

"Well, Lark girl, that rattler got to Eve by tellin' her she'd become like God if she ate them apples—"

"Those apples."

"Fine," Hobey agreed. "Those apples. It was that wantin' to know everythin', be everythin' on her own, that got her into all manner of trouble. That's the kind of pride I'm talkin' about."

"But I don't think I know everything—"

"You think you know better'n God what's right and what ain't for you. An' sometimes for others, too, like for your sisters, an' all."

Lark bit back her automatic objection.

Hobey just kept on speaking. "Well, it's like this. That kinda pride is what got Lucifer kicked out of heaven. An' it's the poison that leads to all what's wrong with this world. Think on wars an' selfishness an' cravings for more, broken lives an' broken hearts. I'm here to tell you, all them things come out the other end of pride. Worse, that there pride builds walls between them what's proud an' God."

Lark gasped. Just last night she'd wondered if pride could separate one from God. Thoughtfully, she said, "You know, I prayed and prayed, but he didn't answer my prayers for Mama and Daddy."

"He didn't take 'em from you, neither," Hobey said quickly. "The drunk driver what chose to give control to the bottle instead of God did the takin'. It don't mean the Father don't love us if we have our troubles or sickness, go hungry or cold, face dangers an' scares."

"I didn't think that—"

"Hush, now. Don't go arguin', 'cause you do that right well, too. Better'n me. Just listen and think on it some more. Let God talk to your heart. Open yourself to 'im, an' he'll reach in to heal that hurt you been nursin' so well."

Again, Lark bit her tongue. "I'll think about it." How could she not? Hobey's words had hit pretty hard.

"So I'll be seein' you day after tomorrow, then?"

"Unless something unexpected comes up for you or me."

Hobey again donned his cap and went to the back door. "God bless you, Lark girl. Just remember how much he loves you. Even when you think you cain't feel his love, it's right there all the time for you. He told us nothin'—not death, not fears, not demons, not even them powers of hell—can keep God's love from us. We're the ones what choose not to take it."

The knot tightened in Lark's throat. As Hobey closed the door in his wake, she couldn't help but wonder if she'd done as he'd suggested. Had she decided God no longer loved her when she couldn't feel his love through her pain?

Was all that powerful love just waiting there for her?

On Saturday, four days after the attack on Frank Vallore, Rich got the OK from the police to go back to the warehouse. Tamping down his natural reluctance to take her along, he called Lark. "Hey, it's Rich."

Her momentary silence threw him. "What's up?"

"I just heard from the police. We can go to the warehouse. Are you free this afternoon?"

"After three works for me."

"I'll pick you up then."

As he went to hang up, she said, "Hey, Rich?"

"Yes?"

"How come you always have to drive?"

What was that all about? "I don't. You want to drive?"

"Yeah. I'd like that."

"Fine. I'll meet you in your driveway at three."

"Great," she said in her usual bright tone.

He said good-bye, then hung up, puzzled by the conversation. What had gotten into her now? Did she not trust his driving? She had no reason not to. He had a perfect record; he'd never even had a parking ticket.

Weird. Nutty.

Lark.

He found himself checking the clock throughout the day, however, anticipation bubbling in him. He didn't want to believe that the thought of meeting Lark could energize him, but it did. She was great to look at, exciting to be with—you could never accuse her of being boring—intelligent, challenging. Everything a man could ever want in a female.

To Rich's amazement, with every day that had gone by, he'd experienced a greater desire to have Lark at his side. He must have lost his marbles. Anyone would think he, rather than Frank, had had the close brush with death after a knock upside the head.

He was falling for troublesome, meddlesome, Larkspur Bellamy. And she could bring down his carefully established, well-ordered life with her nose for news.

"Lord," he prayed aloud, remembering his promise to turn to God for guidance rather than relying on his own strength, "you know I treasure my anonymity. Lark is determined to crack it. And I'm losing more than my head over that zany redhead. Help me here, for I know she's not a Christian. Show me what you want me to do, protect me, and help me bring glory to you. Especially with my work."

He thanked God for saving Frank's life, for keeping Lark safe, for protecting him, too. A well of pure praise burst in him, and Rich worshiped God's majesty.

Feeling somewhat better for having prayed, Rich spent the last few hours before his meeting with Lark working on his current play. At 2:45 P.M., he saved his day's production, backed it up, and turned off the computer.

As he closed the house and loped around the hedge between the two houses, his heart began a brighter beat. He wanted to see Lark again. He wanted the challenge of talking with her, sparring with her, laughing with her. Solving Mama's case with her.

"Hey, there!" she called, coming out the side door of the Bellamy home. "Looks like we're both ready to go."

"Rarin'," he answered.

"All right, then. Get in."

He did. And lived every second of the way to Leesburg regretting his earlier acquiescence.

Lark drove the way she did everything else. Full throttle, all-out, challenging the curves in the hilly road, in a hurry to reach her goal. Rich's heart lodged in his throat and didn't budge until they screeched into the parking lot at the Dream Squeeze Distribution Center.

"You know what?" he said when he'd leaped out of the rattly death trap she called her car. "I'm driving on the way back."

She gave him a sassy grin and a knowing look. "Can't take my kind of excitement, can you?"

"No comment."

Lark laughed and ran up the steps to the door. When Rich reached the steel-bound entrance, he gestured for her to precede him.

"Hey, Rich," greeted a familiar but unexpected voice. "And Lark. Larkspur. What a pleasure to see you again."

Glancing sideways, Rich caught Lark's simpering smile and blush. Women.

"What are you doing here, Frank?" Rich asked. "Are you crazy? That bump to the head is nothing to mess around with. You should be in bed recovering."

Frank's handshake was firm, his hand naturally warm, but the large bandage over his wound did nothing to reassure Rich.

"I can't afford to stay in bed," the manager answered. "With Mariah not allowed to leave Bellamy, I need to be here. This place doesn't run itself, you know. I owe your mother at least that much."

"You don't owe Mama your life," Rich countered.

"I'm not about to die, if that's what you're afraid of. I have too much going on in my life to check out right now. Besides, if it weren't for your mother taking a chance on me when she did . . . well, let's just say my family had just given me an ultimatum, and she had the right job at the right time."

Rich marveled at the man's loyalty. "Well, so long as you don't overdo it, I suppose office work isn't too bad."

"You're right. Especially now that we pacified the investors with the money you—"

"Yes, yes," Rich rushed to say before Lark heard anything incriminating. "Ah . . . we came to check sales records for your regular accounts. I know the police, and probably the Secret Service, have looked them over a bunch of times, but I'm curious about some things, and Lark's willing to help me look them over."

Frank shifted on his feet. "Are you sure you want to do that? The police have studied them thoroughly, and the Secret Service made copies. It's a lot of paperwork to go through."

"We want the records," Rich insisted.

"Well, since you feel that way, I suppose you can use one of the computers in Accounts Receivable."

"That'll work."

As his mother's operations manager strode toward the rear of the building, Rich cupped Lark's elbow and led her after Frank. In minutes, they sat before a screen, staring at the list of Alberti's transactions.

Rich scrolled down the screen, his eyes following each entry. He whistled long and high. "Will you look at that?" he finally murmured.

"I'm looking, I'm looking," Lark answered, awed astonishment in her voice. "I can't believe nobody noticed it until the Secret Service came in."

"What's it look like to you?"

"You know what it means, don't you?"

"Tell me what you think."

Lark twisted her fingers. "It's an inside job. No wonder the authorities are after Miss Mariah. Oh, Rich, this looks bad for your mama!"

SIXTEEN

THE DISCOVERY OF THE MANY DIFFERENT CREDIT-CARD
numbers Tony Alberti had used not only shocked but ener-
gized Lark and Rich. They gathered up the company's business records: accounts receivable, payable bank statements,
ledgers, tax forms—in a word, everything pertaining to
Dream Squeeze Girdles for the last year.

Since someone on the inside was running the scam, Rich
and Lark couldn't review the material on location, despite
their sympathy for Frank, who obviously feared for his job
and felt they didn't trust him—which of course, wasn't the
case. But Lark and Rich couldn't let the culprit—whoever
that might be—know their intentions. So they boxed up the
paperwork and, with Rich at the wheel, returned to Bellamy.

Because Rich had the store to run while Lark could call her
own work hours, they decided she should start the monumental job of scouring the records for clues. Years of unearthing
newsworthy tidbits from masses of nothing also weighed in
her favor.

That was why, early on Monday morning, Lark parked

herself with the papers in the kitchen, set her kettle a-singing, armed herself with a fistful of fine-point, red-ink pens, and began the tedious task of reading every word they'd hauled home.

By one o'clock her eyes ached, her spine felt permanently warped, and she'd guzzled more tea than it would take to float Noah's ark. Unfortunately, she'd found nothing unusual in all that time. That is, nothing unusual beyond the Alberti purchases.

Mycroft gave a mournful wail at her feet. He lifted his head, turned toward the back door, and yowled again.

"OK, OK," she said, "just let me finish this last bank statement. I'm almost done. Then I'll take you for your w-a-l-k." As far as she knew, her undeniably brilliant pooch hadn't learned to spell. Yet.

Lark nearly croaked when, as she ran a finger down a column of transactions, she spotted one deposit with more zeros than it took to choke a giraffe.

"Good gravy and biscuits," she exclaimed, wondering where the money'd come from. Especially since after its appearance on the statement, a flurry of payments had gone out.

"Somethin' smells of week-old catfish here," she told her dog, who, evidently recognizing he'd have to wait awhile, collapsed on the floor like a deflating bellows.

Where had the money come from? Mariah had said some of her investors had demanded money back, while others were waiting until the case was solved before putting additional funds into the Dream Squeeze venture. She'd also mentioned her department-store clients' clamor for more stock. Stock she couldn't buy without an influx of dollars.

Here was the influx of dollars.

There was the payment for more girdles.

How?

"Only one way to figure this all out," she informed Mycroft, shoving away from the paper-laden table. "I'm callin' the bank."

Her call got her nowhere. She needed the account's password, and she didn't have it. But Mariah did, and Lark knew her friend would provide it to help the investigation.

She dialed Mariah's number, and in a handful of words, told Rich's mother what she was up to.

"Why, of course, honey," Mariah said. "If you need to verify transactions to trace our moneys, by all means, go ahead and do it. I'll call the bank in Leesburg, notify Charlie Walker of what you're up to, and make sure he gives you names and dates and . . . oh, I guess you have dates. Never mind. I'll have him call you and tell you all you need to know. I'm so thankful you agreed to help me, dear."

After shortening the thank-yous and good-byes, Lark topped off the kettle again and set it to boil. She took from the fridge a bowl of tofu-based, no-egg-salad sandwich filling and stuffed a whole-wheat pita with the savory mix. Munching and sipping from her fresh mug of peppermint tea, she waited for the call from the banker in Leesburg.

Finally her waiting was rewarded with a *briiiing!* She gulped down her mouthful of lunch. "Hello?"

"Miss Bellamy?"

"Yes. May I ask who's callin'?"

"This is Charles Walker, from the—"

"Yes, Mariah's bank in Leesburg. I'm so glad you called so promptly."

"Anything to help one of our better customers," he answered, his words lubricated with PR grease.

"Let's get right to the point," she said. "In lookin' over the most recent statement for Dream Squeeze, we noticed a large deposit to the account. I need to know everything pertainin' to that transaction."

"Is that all you wanted?" A hint of irritation diluted the oil.

"Well . . . yeah. That's what I want."

"Then why didn't you ask Mariah about it?"

"Does she know every detail about every deposit or with-drawal from the business account?" Lark asked, wondering if the oily banker's brains had skidded out during one of his excesses of politeness.

"No." This response was even less slick. "Of course not. But this deposit . . . well, let me assure you Mariah knows all about it. It's not a run-of-the-mill small amount, you under-stand."

Wasn't that what she'd said at the beginning of the conver-sation? Lark was so anxious to get on with the investigation, that the circular conversation was making her crazy. Patience.

"That's why I called about it," she enunciated slowly. "Now that we have that detail out of the way, why don't you tell me what you know about it? If I have further questions, then I'll call Mariah again."

A quiet, fat-free *humph* thrummed in Lark's ear. "Fine, Miss Bellamy. Not that I know why you're nosing in Mariah's business in the first place, but I can tell you about the large deposit. Her son came into my office to make another generous investment in his mother's business."

Lark spewed peppermint. Then her jaw slacked open. She closed her mouth. For a few seconds, she repeated the motions, feeling like the fish she'd smelled right before she'd called the mother of that scheming, duplicitous—

"Mariah's . . . son," she finally sputtered.

"Yes," the banker answered. "Richard. Do you know him? A fine young man, I'll have you know."

"Oh, yeah." She gritted her teeth. "Very fine."

"It's not often a man his age cares that much about his mother," continued the lubricious Mr. Walker. "And to help her with her new business—"

"You did say *another* generous investment, didn't you?" she asked—in the interest of getting things right, of course.

"Why, yes, Miss Bellamy." The oil spill receded again. "That's precisely what I said."

"So you're tellin' me Rich has been giving his mother huge lumps of cash on a regular basis."

"Well, no. I never said giving, nor did I refer to these transactions as occurring on a regular basis. But, yes, Rich has made available some very sizable sums for Mariah since the start of the business."

"To the tune of . . . ?"

The sum Walker mentioned sent Lark's thoughts reeling. And her stomach diving. She became distinctly dizzy. For the first time in her life, Lark hated having her suspicions proven true. Rich was up to something crooked. And he was more than likely using Mariah's Dream Squeeze Girdle Distribution Center for money-laundering purposes, too.

She'd known the New Yorker in the Jag was bad news. And she'd known Rich was part of that bad news. Still, she'd let Rich hold her, kiss her. Charm her.

Cutting off Charles Walker's effusions about Rich's character—none of which were true, as she'd just learned—Lark said, "Thank you for your time, sir. I know you're a busy man, and I have to return to my own work here. It's been a . . . an illuminating conversation."

As soon as she hung up, the phone rang again. "Yes?"

"Hey, Lark bird. How'ya doing?"

Only one person called her that. "Tim, you big galoot. You know I'm not a birdbrain. I'm flower power."

"You mean flaky like a petal?"

"Nah. Determined like a dandelion."

Her former coworker let out his rich belly laugh. Lark had often thought his mirth and joy were the main reasons his poor wife put up with the crazy cartoonist. The jokester's wife agreed.

"So," she said, "what do you have for me?"

"Not much, kiddo. Marina just called and gave me the name and address for the license you asked about."

"I figured that was why you'd called. Why don't you give them to me?"

"Got a pencil and paper?"

"I'm armed."

"OK. The owner's name is S. N. Martel. His address is 433 E. Park Ave., Suite YY-7, New York, NY. Know what that means, don'tcha?"

By this time, nothing much Tim Riley said could surprise her. "Money. Lots of it."

"You got it. What kind of knot are you in this time?"

"Oh, someone's in trouble, all right, but it sure isn't me. Hey, this is just what I was lookin' for. Now I gotta go. Thanks a million. Take care of yourself, give Sarah a hug, and kiss your little girls for me."

"Oooh! My favorite stuff. Love ya, kid. And whatever you do, be careful with that gorgeous head of red hair. Don't go sticking it where it might be harmed."

With this spate of mind-boggling revelations, it wasn't her head Lark worried about right then. "Don't worry, Tim. I always take care of myself."

When she hung up, her energy leached out. She slumped into her chair, held her head in her hands. She couldn't believe half of her had bought into Rich's charade of helping his mother clear her name.

"What a fool I am," she told Mycroft. "But no more."

She turned off the warmer under the teakettle and headed to the hall for the dog's leash. Hooking the metal clasp onto his collar, Lark tried to turn the mud in her mind into coherent thought.

"One thing's for sure, Mr. Mycroft Holmes. It's just you and me—and Miss Mariah—now. We can't trust that snake of a son of hers."

She swooped up the bank statement, kicked the chair back in under the table—wishing it were her own backside she'd kicked—and opened the door.

"I can't believe how stupid a rational, intelligent woman can get when it comes to a good-lookin' wretch," she grumbled as she waited for Mycroft to do his business. "Especially when that rational, intelligent woman has been makin' a fool of herself over the same ol' wretch for all her born days."

Lark slammed the door with relish. "I'm tellin' you, boy, you'd better be countin' your lucky stars you're not a girl. Why, we get the short end of the stick when it comes to menfolk."

Then Lark realized what she'd just done. She'd reverted to the Southern speech patterns she'd worked so hard to eradicate. Her heart quaked, torn in two.

No matter how she tried to make light of what she'd just learned, it had hit her hard. Learning how crooked Rich was had shaken her. If he wasn't what he seemed, then what was as it seemed?

Evidently, nothing.

A sob choked out of Lark's throat, but she forced it back down. "I really didn't want him to be guilty. Here I was worried about Maggie's Clay and didn't pay enough attention to Rich. And I've always thought myself such a good judge of character. How can this be? How can Rich be a mobster? A money-launderer? How can he do this to his sweet mama?"

Mycroft gave off a howling lament. The lump in Lark's throat grew as she identified with the dog's cry. Why couldn't she get Rich Desmond out of her thoughts? her life? her heart?

Was she doomed to repeat the same mistakes over this guy for the rest of her life? Why couldn't she fall in love with a decent, moral, upright man? One who wouldn't lie, cheat, steal, frame his mother, kiss the stuffing out of her, then break her heart. For the umpteenth time in her life.

She'd thought the guys she dated in Baltimore, especially the one she'd given much more to than she should have, had stolen a chunk of her heart, making her all the wiser for it. But it turned out that all they'd done was use her.

Rich was the one who'd done the thieving. He'd stolen her trust.

Why couldn't he have been just as he presented himself to the world? A small-town merchant with a wonderful mother, a sweet, pregnant sister, and a girl-next-door crazy about him? Why had he hidden such a dirty dark side behind the squeaky-clean facade?

And how was Lark going to get beyond him? Over the years, she'd tried everything she could think of, but none of it had worked. The minute she came back to town, there he was, and her heart did the same, silly flip as when she'd met him way back when.

You'd think she might have learned something during those intervening years. There had to be someone somewhere who could teach her how to stop making ridiculous mistakes. Someone who cared how badly she hurt. Someone who wished her joy and contentment. Someone who'd reach out a hand and save her from herself.

Lark hadn't realized how fast she'd walked. Now she found herself before Desmond's Country Store, bank statement in hand, knowing a confrontation was inevitable but wishing she could avoid it.

Then she saw it—the white Jag—and saw red.

Yanking open the store's door, she stormed the center aisle. She spotted Rich's head as it towered over display shelves to her right. Scant steps behind him bobbed a familiar gray, steel-wired head.

Debating whether to leap at the two monsters to confront them at the same time or to call Wiggon to do the nasty deed, Lark opted for a third choice. She backed out the door and tied Mycroft to the bike rack outside. Back inside and treading gingerly on the worn oak floorboards, she approached her prey while keeping a span of Pepto-Bismol, Metamucil, and Maalox between them. She strained to hear.

"I wish you'd listened and stayed away," Rich said to his shadow.

"And I wish you'd listen and sign the contract," the New Yorker countered.

Rich continued walking down the aisle. Lark followed, now crouching behind an assortment of pantyhose.

"Why are we doing the same dance all over again?" Rich asked.

The Jag's owner threw his pudgy, silk-suited arms up in the air. "We're dancing like my Aunt Eulalia's pet pink poodles because you're so stubborn. If you'd sign the contract, I could get you your advance, you could go back to writing like you're supposed to, and I could stay in civilization."

"Any changes to the contract?" Rich asked.

"What are you—thick? Uncle Carmen's niece's husband's brother can see this is as good as it gets—and good for you, Des, is pretty—"

"Watch it."

The Jag owner patted Rich's shoulder in conciliation. "Yeah, yeah. Rich. Cousin Louie's the one who got his head kicked in by a Central Park cop's horse. No one knows what kinda mess that hoof made of what brain he might have had, but all we know now is he doesn't have a drop of common sense."

"Fine. You can compare me to that poor kid—"

"Louie's no kid. He's forty-five, but I tell you, you'd have a tough time believing it."

The men rounded another end-cap display, then headed

toward the rear of the store. Lark waited, then darted into the aisle they'd just vacated. Nuts and bolts stared her in the eye.

Rich turned around. "Listen, Storey . . ."

Lark's heart stopped. She gasped for air. *Storey. Des.*

The guy with the Jag, S. N. Martel, had called Rich "Des." And Rich had just called him "Storey."

S. N. Martel. Storey Newburn Martel?

Des Richter. Richard Desmond?

Lark again fought for breath, and this time it jerked in, stinging her throat.

Could Rich be Des Richter? The elusive playwright he knew she needed to interview for her new magazine? Could that be what lay behind the gobs of money he'd poured into Mariah's account?

Then Storey. It was such a weird name that Lark couldn't imagine too many men went around with it.

But there was also that Martel.

Italian? With an Aunt Eulalia, Uncle Carmen, and a Cousin Louie. Maybe. Mob connected? Who knew?

Was organized crime behind Des Richter's astronomical success? Had mob pressure assured the playwright's meteoric rise on Broadway and in Hollywood? Was Storey Newburn, the driver of the ubiquitous white Jag, as she thought, the key to solving Mariah's case?

Sitting on her haunches, Lark listened some more, despite the pain jabbing at her heart. The pain of betrayal. On too many levels.

"Listen, Des—"

"You know better than to call me that. Especially here. I don't want these people—my neighbors, my friends—to change the way they see me. We've discussed this more times than necessary. Now, please, stop."

"Sorry. Is it my fault I think of my most successful client by his famous pseudonym?"

"No. But you're smart enough to know the difference between reality and fantasy. Please show some of your savvy in this regard."

"OK, OK. So will you sign?"

"Not unless the changes I asked for were made."

The short man then stormed away from Rich, chattering under his breath. Lark didn't catch a word he said, but from the tone of his voice and the expression on his face when he neared her spot by the cat food, she knew not a syllable could be repeated in polite company.

Storey finally quieted and returned to Rich. "Then there's nothing more to say, is there?" he asked.

"There hasn't been for a while."

The wire-haired head shook from side to side. "It's a shame, I tellya. But if you won't sign, you won't sign. I did my best, gave you my best advice."

"I know, Storey. It's not a matter of what you didn't do. It's a matter of where my heart is. Whom I serve. And God's made it clear I can't write what they want me to write."

Storey nodded. "That's what you've said all along. I can't say I understand you, but I do admire your conviction."

"It's a matter of obeying the God I serve. The God I want to glorify. If my work doesn't please him, then it means nothing. If I reject him and his leading, then that sin separates me from him. That's not something I want to do."

Storey swabbed his age-spotted brow with a large white handkerchief. "Do you want me to keep representing you?"

"I don't know if I have anything for you—or anyone—to represent. Clearly, the script I'm writing isn't going anywhere. I think it's time for me to reassess the direction God wants me to take with my work."

"Then, kid, you take your time doing that. And if there's anything I can do for you, don't hesitate to call."

"Thanks. For everything."

Storey waved with forced cheer, walking toward the front of the store. "Hey, but that last movie was good, wasn't it? Big bucks, big kudos."

Rich chuckled without humor. "Bucks that are all gone now."

Storey stopped in his tracks. Lark dodged behind bags of weed-killer-plus-fertilizer to avoid being seen.

"What did you just say?" the agent asked. "You couldn't have gone through all that dough this fast."

"You're right," Rich replied. "I didn't go through all that dough this fast. My mother's attorneys ate up a chunk of it, and when her coffers were empty and her customers clamoring, I had to use the rest to help her out."

"You're too soft, Rich—"

"Have you forgotten how she supported me while we shopped those first scripts all over New York and L.A.? You didn't think her soft back then, did you?"

"No. I guess you're right. She helped you and you do owe her—"

"I don't owe her anything except the love and respect of a son. What I did for her was something I wanted—needed— to do for someone I love."

"There you go again, kid, shaming me. You're right. I guess it was good you had the bucks, then, wasn't it?"

"God's ways are mysterious, all right," Rich said. "He provides for his children's every need. And that's why I'm not going to worry over my future. If he wants me to write again, he'll give me the stories and lead me to the right market. If he doesn't . . . well, then I guess I'll be a small-town grocer for the rest of my life. I can serve him here just as I can serve him writing."

"The best writing, at that." Storey resumed his trek to the door.

Lark darted into a celestial-hued bunker of windshield-washer fluid.

Storey went on. "Now, about this mess with your mother. You know I'm set up, and I can loan you some to float you two through the worst of it. Of course, I can't just give you the money outright, you know. But there are ways you can pay me back—"

Lark gasped. There he was! The mobster behind Rich's success and Mariah's troubles. She hid behind a pyramid of toilet tissue to catch Storey's next words.

"You can always return the favor by—"

"Larkspur Bellamy!" Reenie cried out directly behind her. "What are you doin' with the TP?"

Lark lost her footing, stumbled, and fell headfirst into the tissue rolls. The earth seemed to shake as the mountain crumbled. She floundered around, trying to regain her footing but, round rolls being . . . well, round, her efforts were to no avail. She eventually flopped to a beached-whale stop.

"Oh, Richie," Reenie cried out. "Thank God you're here. You have to come. I can't find Mama anywhere. She's gone. But on her kitchen table, I found this."

Lark's best friend handed a piece of paper to Rich directly over her. He unfolded the sheet, peered at the writing she couldn't read from her prone position, then paled.

"You're sure she's not off somewhere with Miss Louella?" he asked Reenie.

"Sure as sure can be, Richie. I found Miss Louella at the Blissful Bookworm buyin' up a stack of books. That lady sure does have the most amazin' readin' appetite."

Rich's jaw squared. "Then Mama's gone."

"That's what I've been tellin' you," said Reenie. "What are you goin' to do about it?"

"Call Wiggon, of course."

Lark struggled to rise but failed. So she brought the index and middle fingers of both hands to her mouth and gave a sharp shrill. "Help me up, will you?"

Rich darted his eyes from Lark to Storey to Lark again. Still on her back with the tissue, she gave him an accusatory glower.

He scowled in response. "You know?"

"You're busted!" she barked, staring at him in what she hoped was a menacing way. "What do you have to say for yourself?"

Rich stared, bewilderment in his silver eyes. He glanced over his shoulder at Storey again, then at Reenie, finally studying the sea of toilet paper at his feet. He met Lark's gaze and said, "Please, don't squeeze the Charmin."

SEVENTEEN

Rich couldn't believe he'd just quoted one of Madison Avenue's most inane efforts to Lark, who'd finally found him out.

Worse yet, his mother was missing, and he didn't know who had her. He only knew her disappearance proved things were getting hot for the perpetrators.

Snatching his mother right out from her own kitchen smacked of desperation. He prayed the desperate mobsters didn't think that offing her would help them.

He offered Lark his hand. "Come on. We've got a lot more to deal with than my pseudonym."

"I'll say," she crowed. "Like where the money for the mammoth deposit came from. And how about the earlier investments? Not to mention, Des Richter's mad rise to the top. Who paved your way? The ones who made sure you got the bucks you then laundered through your mama's girdle business?"

She rounded on the up-to-now astounded Storey. "How about you, Mr. Storey Newburn Martel? What kind of mafiosi connections are we dealing with here? And how about those

241

favors you told Rich he could do to pay you back for your 'generosity'? What have your goons done to Mariah? Have they broken her kneecaps? Gifted her with cement shoes?"

Storey paled. "Lady, that's a crock. I'm no mobster. Tell her, Des . . . er . . . Rich . . . you!"

Ignoring the agent, Lark turned on Rich again. "You're despicable. I can't believe you'd set up your mother—dear, sweet Miss Mariah—for the sake of filthy lucre."

"That's it!" he bellowed in a most un-Rich-like way. "I've always known you're crazy, but this time you've totally flipped your red-haired lid. I haven't done a thing to my mother, you madwoman. How could you even think that of me? Haven't you known me long enough?"

"Yeah, but look at all the secrets you've been keepin'. You face facts. You and your sidekick over there have been found out. Reenie heard all the evidence, and she can be my witness. You two are as crooked as reject pretzels."

"Richie . . . ?" asked Reenie, obviously bewildered. "What's Lark talkin' about?"

Rich wanted to scream. He wanted to yell. He wanted to punch a hole through the nearest wall. Lark should be hanged—for yet another attack on him. Not to mention how she'd gotten under his skin.

Forget the prom; she'd outdone herself this time. Reenie was pregnant. She didn't need her best friend accusing her older brother of unspeakable sins.

Rich forced a smile. "Nothing, Reenie. Your buddy's gone raving bonkers on us, and I'm going to have to take her back to her house to shut her up . . . er, calm her down. Just go home. I'll make sure nothing happens to Mama."

Reenie's gray eyes glittered. "You really expect me to go home like a good little girl?"

"It would be very helpful," he answered, knowing he'd goofed up but good.

A sniff reaffirmed his assessment. "Forget it, big brother. She's my mama, too, and I'm fetchin' Wiggon." Stomping out of the store, she headed toward the PD.

Before Rich, Lark's green eyes still spit fire. "So now that you got rid of your sister, will you at least admit to your crimes? We know the credit-card fraud was an inside job, and you and your money are about as inside at Dream Squeeze as it gets."

Rich looked around the store, thankful it had no other traffic. "Keep your voice down, Lark. Please. I don't want the world to know I've been investing in girdles. Not exactly the most masculine image, you understand."

"Hah! I know better. You've kept your involvement silent to take advantage of the money-launderin' opportunities in your mother's business."

Rich grabbed a pillow and smacked it against the floor. Feathers flew, but he'd needed to do something—or else he'd throttle her.

"You've always had a wild imagination, Red, but this time you've outdone yourself. You're not making sense."

"Of course I am. It's simple, actually. You sold out to the devil in the form of this sleazy, New York mobster paradin' as an entertainment agent. He got you the success you craved, and in turn, you sold out your mother to him, settin' up her warehouse as a mob front."

"Hey, Red," Storey said with a laugh, "you're so far off, you aren't even in the same universe." He patted Rich's back and said, "You got your hands full with this one, so I'm heading back to civilization. You take care of her—and yourself. If I can help you with your mother's situation, just give me a call." Storey exited the store.

"Mama!" Rich exclaimed, glaring at his albatross. "You're a menace, Lark. I can't believe you're talking garbage instead of focusing on what really matters right now. We should be discussing Mama, her safety, and getting her back. Not following your arrogance and insanity down this goofy yellow brick road to nowhere."

His words must have made an impact, since Lark didn't respond right away. Rich took advantage of her silence to tell Sophie he was going to find Mariah.

Since his store manager had heard Lark's outburst, she shooed him on. "Just bring Mariah home safe and sound, you hear? And don't you go worryin' none about Lark. She'll figure out what's what soon enough."

"You got it, Miss Sophie," Rich answered, then ran toward the door. But before he reached it, Lark darted into his path.

"Hold on," she said, smacking a palm on his chest.

The contact sent electric shocks through him, and Rich ground his teeth, irritated with himself. He really had to build better defenses against this woman, only not right then. "What do you want this time?"

"Did you—and your henchman—just deny any involvement in your mother's case?"

Dredging up all his patience, Rich said, "Yes. We denied all your loony suggestions."

When Lark opened her mouth to argue, Rich clamped his hand over her lips. She wriggled like a worm on a hook.

"We had nothing to do with the fraud," he insisted, "much less Mama's disappearance. I'm a playwright; Storey's an agent. Nothing more. Besides, if I were planning to do something terrible to her—which even you must know I never would—I'd just invite Mama on a trip. And I wouldn't leave my calling card—" he released his prey and patted his khakis' side pocket—"on the kitchen table. Why would I write myself a ransom note?"

Lark swiped her mouth with the back of her hand. "Is that what the paper is?"

"What'd you think it was, a love note?"

"Then let me see it."

Rich dug in his pocket and gave her the paper. "Here. And be careful with it. Even though it's got to be covered in Reenie's and my fingerprints already, the cops may find something on it. Read it quickly so we can get it to Wiggon. I know I'll never forget a word it says."

Seconds later, she met his gaze. "This is nuts. All they want in exchange for Mariah is the records we took from the warehouse. They don't threaten to harm her. It sounds as though they actually want her runnin' the business—oh, I get it. They need a patsy."

"Looks that way," he said. "And it's about time you called one right. Every other time you've nosed into this matter, you've put my mother at greater risk. You and your big-city pride and arrogance. You think you know more than anyone else, especially we hicks here in Bellamy."

"Look who's callin' the kettle black!" she cried. "You're the one who went out of your way to create a mystery out of nothin'. Des Richter, my eye. If that isn't pride and arrogance, then I don't know what is."

Rich's slow-to-rise temper began to simmer before he remembered the scriptural admonitions against acting in anger. "Your accusations show how far you've run from the Lord," he said. "I chose anonymity so I wouldn't get the glory for the gift God gave me. Not because I craved more attention."

"Well, it didn't work, did it? The only one who got the glory in your stunt was the nonexistent Des Richter. Not you, not God."

A heavy arm dropped onto Rich's shoulders. "Sounds about right to me," offered Hobey, who'd evidently walked into the store unheard during Rich and Lark's heated exchange. Hobey placed his other arm around Lark. "The both of you are 'bout as prideful as they come. Neither of you is willin' to give an inch. She's better'n he is, an' he's better'n she is. Ain't that about right?"

Rich darted a look at Lark. Her cheeks blazed a dark apricot, and she stared at her shoes. He couldn't meet Hobey's eyes.

That didn't deter the wise mason one bit. "Have either of you taken your eyes off yourselves long enough to check out what God's been tryin' to tell you?"

"Hey, wait a minute, Hobey," Rich said. "I saw where I'd been having a problem with pride—you know, refusing Lark's help on behalf of Mama—and I confessed. I asked the Lord's forgiveness; then I even went and asked Lark's. I'm not guilty this time."

"Hmm . . ." Hobey murmured. "'Bout you, Lark girl? Have you done as ol' Hobey told you an' opened your heart to God? Have you thought on all them things we talked about?"

"Some," she answered, her voice unusually meek.

"Well, I'm here to tell the both of you, you ain't done your spiritual work just yet. So long's you're so all-fired-up busy lookin' out for yourself, you ain't gonna see what God's puttin' right before your noses. An' so long's you're so self-centered, ain't no way you're gonna grow a servant's heart."

At that, Rich turned toward Hobey. Simultaneously, Lark did the same. Their gazes met. They then looked at the large, simple man between them.

"A . . . servant's heart?" Lark said.

"How could you say that about me, Hobey?" Rich asked. "I do all in service to Christ."

"See, Lark girl, a servant's heart's what we're all a-needin'. An' Rich, you ain't servin' Jesus when you're makin' sure he don't get no glory from the gifts he's given you."

"But Hobey, I made sure I didn't claim any glory for my success—" Rich stopped to stare at his friend—"you know."

Hobey shrugged. "Always did. Your mama was so proud—the right kinda proud—of you that she went an' told my

Ellamae all 'bout you an' your plays an' movies. But you didn't come out an' tell none of them folks who saw them shows that you belonged to Christ. You just went an' played hide-'n'-seek behind that Des Richter name. It woulda been right godly to take the praise in Jesus' name, son. Sayin' straight-out, 'Not that I, but my God, be glorified.'"

Rich couldn't counter Hobey's claim. He hadn't taken any praise—not for himself, not for God. *Was* he guilty of some weird kind of pride?

Hobey had no lack of words. "'Pears to me, son, you got yourself a bad case of spiritual pride. Goes somethin' like, 'Oh, I'm a better Christian'n the other guy who wants to be praised, so I'm gonna keep God my secret to myself.'"

At that, Rich noted the smirk blooming on Lark's face.

So did Hobey. "Don't go lookin' like the cat who had Miss Sophie's canary for supper, there, Lark girl. Ain't you the one who's been so busy sayin', 'I'm as good as God for knowin' what's what'? You ain't figgered out yet how many mistakes you've made or how many hurts you got you needn't have."

She started.

Hobey was on a roll. "You got the regular kinda pride, girl. An' you've run so far from God, you gotta far way to go to find 'im again. But he's there, all right. Awaitin' on you."

"But . . . what about that servant stuff?" she sputtered out.

"Aha!" Hobey cheered. "Thank you, Jesus for openin' her ears. Now please give me the right words to show these two what you want 'em to know."

He patted her shoulder. "Lark girl, a servant's heart works like Jesus'. You know, when he said, 'I do nothin' on my own,' an' 'I have no wish to glorify myself.'"

Lark's cheeks paled.

Rich's stomach dropped. "But—"

"Listen me out," Hobey said. "We're talkin' growin' more'n'more like Jesus, the holiest of holies, who served his friends by washin' their dirty feet. Not like that there Pharisee who said, 'I thank you, God, that I'm not a sinner like everyone else, especially like that tax collector over there.'"

"But I wasn't doin' that," Lark argued, albeit weakly.

"I'm not at all like that," Rich insisted, not quite vigorously.

Hobey shook his bald head. "You two are starin' straight at yourselves. Didn't I hear somethin' 'bout Mariah turnin' up lost? If you're servin' God and have pure servants' hearts, then why are you arguin' over who's smarter'n who, an' who's more to blame'n who?"

Lark and Rich gasped.

"Get on with you!" Hobey urged, giving each a gentle shove. "Go serve God in love. For the glory of the Almighty, find Mariah. An' while you're at it, why not both seek his wisdom? ask his forgiveness?"

Turning to Lark, he curved a thick finger under her chin. "Lark girl, come home to your heavenly Father. He's been waitin' on you for years, arms right wide open. Reach out to 'im, and you'll find 'im. Right there, lovin' you just as much as he did when he gave up his Son for you."

Tears dulled her eyes. "I'll try."

"An' I'll pray for you. Now go do somethin' 'bout Mariah, or my Ellamae won't never let me in my house again."

Awkwardly, Rich held the door open for Lark. Both descended the stairs and turned toward the police station. Neither spoke. Two hearts felt heavy. Two minds swam.

One point was clear: Mariah was missing. Her safety came before their concerns.

Rich opened his front door, his steps ponderous, his thoughts dark. He and Lark had spent the rest of the day with the police and the Secret Service, answering more questions than even Lark could spit out on her best day. Not a clue had surfaced to shed light on Mama's whereabouts.

During the interrogation, one thing had plagued him: the effect of Hobey's words on his heart.

Troubled, Rich fell on the sofa and reached over his head to turn on the lamp on the side table. As he settled deeper into the cushions, he felt a solid rectangle where only squishy foam should have been. Reaching under his back, he realized he'd left his Bible on the couch that morning after his devotions.

He sat up and clasped the dear, worn book in his hands between his knees. "Father? I guess you sent Hobey to us this afternoon. And he hit me hard. What he said rang true—unfortunately. Where did I go wrong? When did I take my eyes off you?"

Rich thought back over the years, remembering his need to write, to tell the tales that lived in his heart and soul and mind. He'd always known God placed them there, just as he'd also known God had given him the talent to bring them forth in a way that reached others. He'd thought he was serving the Lord with his gift.

When had he started focusing on himself? on protecting his privacy? on his dread of becoming the center of everyone's attention, as he had been while growing up? Between being the son of one of the town's most respected families and the object of Lark's loony affection, he'd always been cast into the limelight—an uncomfortable place for a reserved boy. The adult Rich could now see how his earlier experiences had affected his recent years.

"I guess it's true, Lord. I did become self-centered instead of God-centered." He closed his eyes, feeling the sting of shame. "And I'm sorry, so sorry. Forgive me, Father, for the pain I've caused you." Pain that went beyond disobedience and inattention. "I haven't been much of a witness for you, have I? I worried more about myself and my fears than about impacting others for you."

A raw breath escaped his tight throat. "Dear God . . . it took not just another fight with Lark or a reaming-out by Hobey, but my mother's kidnapping for me to wake up."

Truth hurt. "Oh, Lord, how I've offended you. . . ."

Tears burned Rich's eyes as he absorbed the full impact of his actions. His selfishness. His failure to serve his God as he should. And his pride when danger struck close.

It was his fault his mother had been taken. His fault. His stupid, sinful pride had delayed the discovery that it was an inside job. Although the authorities hadn't, he and Lark had known from the start that Mariah was innocent. Had he worked with Lark instead of clinging to his pride, they might have realized that someone posed a risk to Mariah. They could have taken the evidence to the authorities that much sooner. Mariah's disappearance might have been prevented.

Rich fell to his knees, still clasping his Bible. "Father God, please, please do whatever it takes to rid me of this pride."

The image of his mother swam before his closed eyes. "OK, I guess you're doing that, aren't you? You're letting me suffer the consequences of my sin. But I can't stand the thought of Mama's fear or of anything happening to her. All because I was afraid of what Lark could do to me."

True, Lark bore some responsibility in this tragedy. She was just as proud as he'd been. But she'd strayed far from Christ years ago. He couldn't hold her up to the same standards to which he held himself.

Unlike him, she'd rejected God.

As the thought crossed his mind, he groaned. "Right after I confess and ask forgiveness, I'm at it again. Hobey's right. I *am* spiritually proud. No better than Lark. I strayed from you, too. There's no such thing as a little sin versus a big one. Sin is sin, and I sinned against you. Just as much as she did."

He squeezed his eyes shut, rubbed the dampness from his lashes. "You can also add a judgmental attitude to my list of offenses. I've sure spent a lot of time judging her. What was I thinking? What was I seeking?"

A much-loved hymn entered his mind. *"Seek ye first the kingdom of God and its righteousness, and all these things shall be added unto you; Allelu, alleluia!"*

"Oh, yes. I was seeking my own comfort first rather than your kingdom, Father. And let's not talk about your righteousness. I sure blew that one. But you kept on blessing me. How come?"

A Bible verse Rich had memorized long ago bubbled through his misery: *"I have loved you, my people, with an everlasting love. With unfailing love I have drawn you to myself."*

The truth of the gospel; the truth of life.

The truth of God.

His love—a love that never failed, no matter how much a sinner did. No matter how much Rich failed. Tears slid down his cheeks.

"Thank you, Father, for your faithfulness. Even when I wasn't as faithful as I needed to be. And thank you for being here, even now."

Other memories played through his soul: songs and choruses from Sunday school, snippets of sermons, pertinent Scriptures. The strength of Rich's Christian heritage flowed into him, supporting him at this lowest of times.

He thanked God for the gift of faith. With his financial resources gone, his mother's fate uncertain, he could go on only by the Almighty's grace. What would he do if he didn't have the Father's love? What would someone who didn't know God do?

Rich thought of Lark, and he prayed. He prayed for the woman who, unwittingly, had brought him down. Low enough to find his spiritual knees and humble himself before

God in heaven. The woman who didn't realize she could do the same. The woman he loved.

The last scales over his eyes finally dropped.

Devastated, Lark was only able to take Mycroft home well past midnight. And Rich thought her good at asking questions. She was a rank amateur compared to those Secret Service guys.

Under the circumstances, she should be glad she could still make her way home, feed her dog, get herself to bed. The strain and the reality of Mariah's disappearance had brought her down lower than she'd ever been.

She was responsible for the danger her friend faced. She'd been so busy protecting herself from the glare of the town's gossips and trying to prove herself more than they'd ever feared she'd be that she hadn't acted quickly enough to keep Mariah out of harm's way.

True, she'd also been dealing with Rich, admittedly her greatest weakness. And no matter what he said, he was proud. "Don't you agree, Mycroft?"

A soft puppy snore was his only response.

"Great. What good are you? I need to talk and you leave me all alone to my ugly thoughts, my guilt . . . my fear."

And there it was. Fear had taken over her mind since the day she'd returned to Bellamy. Fear of again being branded the weird Blossom. Fear of again being mocked for her feelings for Rich.

Oh, yeah. Those feelings for him were back. Full strength and mature this time around. She loved him—even though she wanted to strangle him.

Her life was a mess. And Mariah's life was at risk.

Lark had no clue what to do next, even though she agreed

with some of what Hobey had said. She *was* proud of her accomplishments, her capabilities, her self-sufficiency. But now, when it really mattered, none of those things could help.

They couldn't protect Mariah, couldn't bring her back. The cops were stumped. So was the Secret Service. So was Rich. So was Lark.

She'd never faced a darker reality. Or a grimmer truth.

No matter how capable she was, she couldn't bring Mariah back. Not on her own. Not even with the help of those who were stuck here with her in the dark.

But if Hobey was right, if Rich had been right that day down by the creek, and if she'd been wrong all those years ago, then there *was* someone who could keep Mariah safe. Who could bring her back.

"God?" Lark asked tentatively. "If you're really out there . . . if I was wrong and Granny Iris, Mariah, Cammie, Hobey, Maggie, and Rich are right . . . could you help me? Please? Keep Mariah safe. Go with me out there. Help me find her. Not for me, but for Mariah. I'm the one who messed up. Not her. Could you . . . please?"

EIGHTEEN

LARK FELL ASLEEP AS SOON AS HER HEAD HIT THE PILLOW. In the middle of her slumber, however, a cold muzzle nudged her face. It made an effective wake-up call.

"Whaddaya want?" she said, then glanced at her alarm clock and groaned. "At four o'clock in the mornin'?"

Mycroft's energetic soft-shoe routine suggested that renaming him Fred—as in Astaire—would not be a problem. Yielding to the inevitable, Lark donned her terry-cloth robe and went for her pup's leash.

"All right, all right," she groused when his steps grew more frantic in the kitchen. "You can't be that desperate. You went no more than three hours ago."

No amount of griping deterred Mycroft. He tugged her to the back door and, once she'd opened it, lunged down the steps to the yard. There, he dipped his nose into the grass and set off after who knew what scent.

Then it hit her. If Mariah had been taken from her own kitchen, she must have left some kind of olfactory trail in her wake. Maybe Mycroft could help find her. Unless whoever took her did so in a car.

"Phooey!" After so many hitches, Lark wasn't about to pass up a possibility. "This is the first good idea anyone's had about findin' Mariah," she told her dog, "and I'm goin' to check it out."

Then she remembered her prayer of sorts. "Is this your answer, God?"

Nothing came from the velvet-dark night, but something inside Lark told her she was finally on the right track. Looking skyward, she called out, "Thanks," and yanked the reluctant pooch back inside.

True, her pet was a puppy still, and he'd never been trained to track, but surely the ability to follow a scent was inborn. "You can do it, boy, can't you? You can find Mariah for us."

Mycroft looked up at Lark, devotion in his eyes. He sniffled and gave a soft howl.

"That's right, kiddo," she said, hugging his solid neck. "We've got a job to do, and we're goin' to do it. We're goin' to find Mariah."

A raspy slurp across her cheek made her laugh. "You know, big guy, you're pretty much terrific. I'm so glad your Auntie Maggie gave you to me."

He offered his belly for a scratch.

Lark complied. "I owe her a great big apology and an even bigger thank-you, bud. She knew what she was doin' when she decided I needed a dog."

Her humor faded. "But I was sure actin' like a proud idiot when I switched her weddin' flowers. Even though my choice looked great, I should never have let my self-righteous side presume I knew better. I need to talk to her as soon as she gets back from her honeymoon." She groaned. "And Cammie, too. She doesn't need to wait to hear me confess to an excess of pride."

Pride. She'd never given it much thought before coming

back to Bellamy. Now it seemed like the only thing she thought about. Besides Mariah.

And Rich. Lark couldn't help remembering his kiss. Had he begun to see her as a woman? as a date? as a possible mate?

She admitted—finally—that she still wanted the same thing she always had: a future with Rich.

Had her pride pushed him away? It just might have cost her the greatest desire of her heart.

From the cobwebs of her childhood, phrases emerged. Take delight in the Lord, and he will give you your heart's desires. Commit everything you do to the Lord. Trust him, and he will help you.

Could it be true? Was that all she had to do? Delight in God, and he would give her her heart's desires? Commit her every action to God, trust him, and he would help her?

Although Lark was tempted to challenge God to prove himself by bringing Mariah safely home, she remembered Granny Iris saying one should never challenge the Almighty.

Trust him, and he will help you.

Was that it? Was that the way to belief? to that relationship Rich, Mariah, Cammie, Hobey, even Maggie now claimed to have with God? If Lark placed her trust in God first, would the faith follow?

Her heart picked up its beat. Well, she'd asked for God's help. Less than three hours later, her dog had given her an idea. Was it Mycroft who'd done so or . . . had God used the dog to reach her?

"Only one way to find out," she said. After taking a deep breath to settle the butterflies in her stomach, she went on. "OK, God, I've decided to trust you. I'm goin' to find somethin' of Mariah's, let the dog sniff it, and then I'm headin' after her. You're the one in charge here, so please take care of Mariah while I'm lookin' for her. Oh, and take care of my pooch and me, too. We're not sure what we'll be walkin' into out there."

Seconds later she added a belated "Amen."

"Now you be careful," called Reenie from just inside her front door. "We don't want you gettin' lost, you hear? We can't spend time lookin' for you an' Mama."

Lark patted her dog's pointy head. "I've got a secret weapon. Mycroft's nose'll never let us down. Now you get back to bed, pregnant momma. It's early."

And it was. After the insightful constitutional she and the pup had taken at four o'clock, Lark had gone back to bed. But she hadn't managed to catch another wink. Thoughts and memories, Scriptures, sermons, and Sunday school classes, not to mention conversations with Hobey and Rich, chased each other in her head.

Had she let her pride separate her from God? Had she demanded his actions instead of seeking his comfort, his support, his peace? His will?

Had she turned from him when, in his unfathomable wisdom, he had maintained his constancy? Remained ever the same? Remained holy, all-powerful, sovereign?

Lark's stomach tightened and her heart ached. She sighed. It looked that way. She *was* guilty.

She knew the Bible said God waited for his prodigals with open arms, but did that mean her, too? After all the things she'd said against God, her rebellion, her defiant refusal to return to him . . . would he even want her back now? Had her transgressions been too many for forgiveness?

Finally, as the rosy glow of dawn blushed the white tab-top curtains on her eastern window, she quit trying to sleep. She dressed for a hike and went downstairs. Anxious to start her mission, she skipped her daily scrambled tofu and opted for oj and a piece of whole-wheat toast instead. That would have to tide her over until after she found Mariah. And with her secret weapon, Mycroft, it should be well before lunch.

But finding Mariah didn't prove quite that easy. The bloodhound had responded to the scent in the baby quilt Reenie had lent Lark. And he'd wriggled in delight at the door to Miss Louella's, Mariah's, and Miss Sophie's little colonial.

After that, he'd darted off, nose to the ground, pulling on his leash. He'd led Lark straight down to Langhorn Creek, past the picnic bench where she and Rich had shared that unforgettable South-of-the-Border repast of tacos and burritos, and into the woods five hundred yards away. That had been ages ago.

Now Lark's stomach kept reminding her that the oj and toast had landed hours before, and it wanted a refill. But she wouldn't—couldn't—quit. She had to find Mariah.

It was the least she could do, since her friend had become some mobster's prisoner because of Lark. She had to make restitution for her sins. Maybe then—

A squishy slurp to her right caught Lark's attention. After so long searching the woods, she had come to recognize most of its normal sounds. That mushy noise was not one she'd heard before.

Mycroft growled softly, his body poised. Lark tensed, held her breath. She covered her dog's muzzle to avoid drawing the attention of whoever—or whatever—had made the sound.

She noticed the approaching dark. It was late. It had to be somewhere around seven-thirty or eight o'clock at night. Since she never wore a watch, Lark wasn't exactly sure. But by the position of the sun dipping below the trees around her, she figured she'd been searching for Rich's mother for over twelve hours.

No wonder she was hungry.

Then she heard another slurp, this one coming from the thicket to her rear. She froze.

Someone—or more than one someone—was out there, with her and her dog. Could it be . . . the mob? Was she getting close to where they were holding Mariah? Was that why they were surrounding her?

Lark's heart banged against her ribs—at least, that's how it felt.

Where was Mariah?

Lark didn't know. She hadn't found a trace, even though she felt as if she'd already searched the whole Shenandoah National Park instead of just the bare edge. She now doubted Mycroft had a clue what he was doing.

And she was alone. Totally alone in the growing darkness. Lark had never known such fear, such loneliness. She lost her footing and fell. A sob tore from her heart. What a hash she'd made of things. And this time, it was of her own making.

She'd thought she was trusting God earlier that morning. But in reality, she'd gone ahead, consumed by guilt, hoping to atone for her sins by finding Mariah, again thinking she had all the answers. All she'd done was get lost.

To her left, a light flickered. Salvation or doom?

Finally accepting that in and of herself she could do nothing, she turned to heaven. "Dear God . . . I blew it again. This self-thing seems to be a habit I can't break. I've learned my lesson. I can't save myself, and I'm lost. You, and you alone, can save me from myself . . . and from my sins. Please, Lord, I need your help. I need you."

Where was the crazy redhead? Rich had spent the worst day of his life looking for her in the woods down by Langhorn Creek. Not only had his mother been kidnapped, but Lark and Mycroft also appeared to be lost. He'd seen them racing toward the trees around six that morning. He'd had a bad feeling about their excursion.

He'd prayed. Then something inside him had urged him to go after her. So he'd gone. Good thing, too—even though all attention should have been focused on finding Mama and her kidnapper.

After all, that was exactly what Rich feared had sent Lark into the woods in the first place. Knowing her as well as he did, he was certain she'd gone after his mother.

After a fruitless few hours, Rich had dashed out of the woods and to the store shortly after ten. He'd packed sandwiches and sodas in his old backpack, arranged for Sophie to man the cash register until he returned, called Wiggon to let him know the latest, and left Mama and the mob to the cops while he went after Lark.

He'd resumed his search. Inexplicably, it seemed as though Lark had been going in circles. Her footsteps led him in wide spirals, sometimes vanishing in areas where leaves made a springy cushion that didn't take a print, only to reappear on nearby stretches of soil heading off into yet new circles.

Now the sun perched low on the western horizon. Rich was tired of walking, tired of searching, tired of eating the sandwiches he'd packed. He wanted to go home, have a decent meal, go to bed.

But he couldn't. Lark was out there with only her dog for protection. He had to find her.

"Father, you know exactly where she is, what shape she's in," he prayed. His shoulders tensed again, as they had each time he thought of what might happen to her. He couldn't stand the thought of her hurt, alone, lost, in the dark. "Please protect her, Lord. Lead me to her. Keep her safe."

He now knew that the first thing he'd do once he found

her—after hugging the stuffing out of the contrary creature—
was to share his recent spiritual revelations with her. Again
and again.

Somehow, he'd show her what a mess he'd made of things
by relying on himself, by letting his pride take the lead, by
taking his eyes off Christ. He'd persevere until she understood. "With your help, Father."

He didn't want Lark to struggle through the toughest
moments in life without God's comfort, love, support, and
help. He loved her too much—in fact so much that it hurt
because he knew she wasn't a Christian. And that, unless she
became one, they couldn't have a future together.

He kept on looking, fearing he might have to follow the
entire Appalachian Trail to find the woman and her dog.

Just as the sun slipped down past the treetops around him,
Rich heard a moan. Then a snuffle, followed by the whisper
of leaves. Not wanting to scare Lark—if indeed it was her in
the dark—he called out her name. "If that's you out there,
don't be scared, honey. It's me. Rich."

A sob. Then, "Rich?"

He hurried in the direction of the panicky voice. "I'm here.
I've been looking for you all day. Are you OK?"

"Hush!" she hissed. "Don't talk so loudly. There's . . .
someone out here besides Mycroft and me. I don't want them
to find you . . . hurt you. . . ."

Following her restrained voice, Rich reached Lark's side
and fell to his knees, relief robbing him of strength.

"Are you hurt?" he asked, his pulse thundering in his
temples.

"No. Just tired and hungry and scared."

"I'm tired, too, but we'll get through this together. And I
have food in my backpack. How about water? Have you had
anything to drink recently?"

She nodded. "I brought a large canteen with me. It's empty now, but I'm not dehydrated, if that's what you mean."

"Thank you, Jesus," he whispered skyward.

Even in the dim light, Rich saw Lark stiffen and regretted his audible prayer. With Lark, he'd have to approach the matter of faith cautiously, letting the Holy Spirit lead the way.

Then in an awed voice she said, "He answered my prayer. He sent you to me. . . ."

Even though the concept of being the answer to Lark's prayers appealed enormously, Rich focused on the first part of her comment.

"You . . . prayed?" he asked, holding his breath.

"Yes," she said. "I'd reached the end of my rope. I realized how badly I'd messed up and recognized that I was lost, literally . . . and, I have to admit, spiritually, too."

"So . . . ?"

"So I remembered some old Sunday school lessons and something you said."

"What did I say?"

"You told me people give up on God when things don't go their way, even though he's still there. That's what I'd done all those years ago, and since it hadn't worked, I prayed. If he wasn't there or who the Bible said he was, a prayer wouldn't make much difference. But if he was who he said he was, then I stood a chance. So I told God that I trusted him and that I needed to be forgiven for how I'd messed up. Just a short while later, I heard you call my name. So that's what you are—the answer to my prayers."

After a statement like that, what was a guy to do?

Rich kissed Lark with all the pent-up emotion that had pushed him the whole day. To his delight, she responded with equal fervor, wrapping slim arms around his neck. Their lips clung; tenderness and passion mingled in their caress.

Although they needed to find their way home—something

sure to prove easier said than done—eat a meal, and recover from the day, Rich was reluctant to release Lark. He enjoyed her presence in his arms, the curls that stuck to his five-o'clock shadow, the soft, warm whisper of her breath on his neck. He didn't want to let her go.

Not now.

Not ever.

Then a damp blob jabbed his ear. He pulled away from soft, sweet lips. "Hey, Mycroft. I know you're here, too, but I'm not about to kiss you."

Lark giggled and patted her dog. Then she grew serious again. "I owe you an apology, and if I remember correctly, I need to ask your forgiveness."

"For . . . ?"

"For the way I let my pride get the better of me. For how rotten and obnoxious I was as a kid, for how nosy I still am as an adult. Take your pick."

Bringing her close again, he said, "You know I forgive you. I guess I always have."

"Really?"

"You're alive and kicking still, aren't you?"

"Thanks a lot." She punched his shoulder with a bit more verve than he thought his comment merited.

Rich chuckled, then grew quiet. He remembered his promise to God. "I have some things to share with you."

"Go ahead," she said, surprisingly compliant.

"It's about God and my relationship with him. And you."

"I know. You're goin' to tell me I have a lot of fence to mend with him. I figured that out. And I have you and Hobey to thank for the nudge that led me to it."

"I'm glad. And I want you to know I'm here to help you along the way. I don't want you to fall into the trap I made for myself."

"What trap's that?"

"The one of spiritual pride. I had a problem with pride to begin with, one I refused to think I had. To make matters worse, as I learned more about God, I grew in my faith, and became cocky about my knowledge, my salvation, my relationship with Jesus. Notice all those *mys*?"

When she nodded, he continued. "I took my focus off God and what he was teaching me, and I put it on me and what I'd gained. I forgot that without Christ, I gain nothing."

As Rich spoke, Lark snuggled against him, silent, listening. He wished the darkness weren't so thick; he wished he could see her face as he spoke.

He went on. "I knew I was a Christian, saved from my sins by Christ's sacrificial death. But then I took that a step further and began to see myself as a holy man. Worse, as a man holier than others."

Lark lifted her head, and he saw the gleam of her smile. "So I was right, wasn't I?"

"Righter than you knew." He curved his hand around the back of her head and pressed her close again. He could grow addicted to the pleasure of having her there; she fit against him as if she'd been made precisely for him.

He continued his confession. "You have to remember something else. I've always been kind of reserved. I reached the point where I chose to hide from others because I didn't want to become the center of attention. Embarrassment was big in my fears, thanks to you and your crazy schemes when we were kids."

"Oh, please, don't bring that up again."

"OK. Not now." He chuckled. "Some other time. Anyway, when I told myself I didn't want the acclaim for my work and hid behind my pseudonym to avoid that limelight, I felt I was better than others—a better Christian. They did everything they could to draw attention to themselves, their accomplishments—"

"Uh-oh. Those *they*s sound a lot like me."

"A little. And I was no better than you or them. I just let a sneaky, corroding kind of pride seep in. It wasn't the kind of thing where I said, 'Look at me; I'm holier than you.' I'd have hated myself for thinking that. It was more of a satisfaction with my spiritual achievements. I couldn't help but see how far I'd come in my faith walk, and I kept measuring it against that of others. In my mind, hey, I always came out ahead."

"Not just in your mind, but in your attitude toward others, too."

"You don't have to agree with me so readily."

"When you're right, you're right."

Scooping her onto his lap, he tickled her under her chin with his nose. "You're still a brat, you know?"

"Oh, no," she answered—too solemnly. "I'm just agreein' with your superior intellect."

He laughed. "Anyway, what I wanted to say is that I realize now that I need to grow in humility, to make myself nothing so that God can be everything."

"Why are you tellin' me this?"

Could he bare that corner of his heart? This soon? True, she seemed content on his knees, but was she ready to hear how deeply his feelings for her ran?

Then he remembered what he'd face back in town if they weren't certain this was the real thing. He couldn't stand the thought of becoming an "item" with Lark, only to have the relationship explode in his face.

Talk about gossip and attention and scandal.

Help me, Father. What do I tell her? I don't want to scare her away.

"You know," she said, "I think I figured it out. You know I have a problem with pride—just as you did—and you're sharin' your experience so I don't repeat your mistakes. That's so sweet of you, Rich."

She reached up an arm, pulled his head down, and planted a kiss on his cheek. Then she gasped. "That must be what Hobey meant about a servant's heart. You're doing this for me, for my benefit. Why, Rich, thank you, thank you. I don't think anyone has ever cared enough for me to do that."

Oh, dear. She'd gotten it all wrong. Rich had been speaking for himself, confessing his sins to someone he'd wronged, and here Lark had seen it as a gesture on her behalf.

Rich was dumbstruck. He'd asked God to give him the words to reach Lark so that she wouldn't go through life without knowing the Lord's goodness. Now it seemed God had answered those prayers.

"Father," he prayed aloud, "you are so generous, so faithful, so loving, and good."

"Amen," Lark whispered. "You know, I'm goin' to need help fixin' things with God. Would you . . . ?"

"I thought you'd never ask." He kissed her again—to seal their bargain, of course.

Then he heard a wet, thick noise about a hundred feet to their right. It brought his thoughts back to where they were and why they'd originally set out.

In the dark, Lark's eyes glowed eerily large. Mycroft whined. Rich waited, praying for safety.

Minutes crept by. He heard nothing more.

A muted flash pierced the dark up ahead.

"Come on," he said, shifting Lark off his knees and scrambling upright. "We'd better get out of here."

She joined him, sticking an arm through the shoulder strap of Rich's backpack. "Not until we find your mother."

"Are you crazy?"

"No, just determined. She's out here and in danger. We have to find her. Besides, there are two of us now, and we have God on our side, so who's goin' to keep us down?"

"Look," Rich said, trying to reason with Lark, "it's dark, we're tired and hungry—"

"Oh, yeah. You said you had food, so give me something. I'm starved. And let's get movin'. I have a baby quilt your mama made for Reenie's little one, and the dog goes nuts every time he sniffs it. He sticks his nose to the ground and chases after that trail like a house afire."

He couldn't have heard what he thought he'd heard. "Are you telling me you came here to this wilderness, looking for my mother based on what this mutt does?"

"He's not a mutt, as you so sagely pointed out, and he's very good at sniffin'."

Rich smacked his forehead. "Of course, he is. He's a dog. A bloodhound, even. But he hasn't been trained. He doesn't know what he's doing."

"I say he does. That tracking talent has to be inborn. God-given. And I'm trustin' God to use Mycroft's natural abilities to find your mama. Now hand over some food. All kiddin' aside, I haven't eaten since a piece of toast this mornin'. Before that, all I had for supper was that stale donut at the PD last night. I need to eat."

Rich paused to rummage through his pack and withdrew one of his last two sandwiches.

"Here."

"At last." Silence followed as she took a bite.

Then she sputtered. "Yuck! Gross. You didn't tell me it had dead animal in it. How could you, Richard Desmond? You know I don't eat meat."

"Look, Lark. That's all I have. The other one's a ham sandwich, too. If you're so determined to find Mama, you'll have to eat. Or else we give up the search and find you some sprouts."

In the dark Rich allowed himself a triumphant grin. In fact, he came close to giving himself a pat on the back for his ingenuity.

The silence grew.

Neither moved.

Then, "OK. Let's call it a truce," Lark said quietly. "How about if I just eat the bread from the two sandwiches, and leave the meat for you?"

Rich blinked.

A reasonable compromise? Lark?

Who woulda thunk?

NINETEEN

RICH HURRIED TO CATCH UP WITH LARK, WHO WAS QUITE clearly heading toward the light they'd seen. "Can you keep the dog quiet if we find something?" he asked.

"I think so. Well, actually, I hope so. He's kind of unpredictable."

"I wonder whom he resembles?"

"Oh, hush! We don't want whoever's out here to hear us."

Rich laughed softly. "I'd be willing to bet they've known where you've been the whole time. You marched just like Sherman across this place."

She said something under her breath that he didn't catch—and figured he was better off that way. Then she added, "If that's the case, then, let's hurry up. I want to find Mariah and bring her back home—"

Crack!

The hairs on the back of Rich's neck rose. Mycroft growled. Lark's cold fingers reached for his.

"They're out there," he whispered in her ear. "We have to be quiet. We don't know how many there are."

She nodded, her soft hair tickling his nose.

"Want to go get Wiggon?" he asked. "It could get nasty out here."

She shook her head and resumed walking. Admiration for Lark's courage swept through Rich, and he again sought God's blessing and help for their endeavor.

A heartbeat later, they heard another smooshy sound, this time ahead of them and to their left. He tugged on Lark's hand, pulling her toward the noise. She squeezed his fingers and followed his lead.

Another light wavered briefly farther left than where the sound had come from. They stood still, waiting, praying.

"*Woo-hoo-hoo!*"

Rich's heart leaped into his throat.

Lark staggered into him. "What was that?"

"An owl. I think." *I hope.*

The eerie cry sensitized Rich to their surroundings: the robust scent of decaying vegetation, the moist leaves grazing his cheeks. He heard the impenetrable silence, now broken only by their breathing—and his pulse. In the darkness, he could only make out looming shapes; tree trunks, he knew, but their ghostly outlines took on a frightening quality at this time of night.

Where was Mama? Who had made that loud noise? What did the lights mean? Were he and Lark any closer to finding the perp?

"Let's go," Rich murmured. "It was just an owl."

As he spoke, the nocturnal bird called out again, reinforcing with its spectral call his assessment of the situation.

"Onward," Lark replied, but Rich noted that her voice wavered.

They wended their way through a tight stand of trees that, after a bit, thinned out. The slender sliver of new moon peered out from behind the clouds to see what they were up to.

"There!" whispered Rich. "Do you see that sort of square shape up ahead?"

"Am I seein' things, or does it seem to have thin threads of light runnin' through it?"

"I see them. Could that be a cabin? With windows?"

"Bet you that's it. Let's go find out."

"Do you understand the danger we might be facing?"

She clasped her other hand around his. "Yes, Rich, I do. And that's why I have to keep on. Your mother's been facin' this terror long enough."

"Then there's something else you have to know."

"What?"

"That I . . . I lo—"

Snap!

Lark's fingers convulsed around Rich's. "Let's get her. We don't want to wait until their reinforcements arrive," she said as she slipped forward, bearing down on the squarish shape before them.

With clammy sweat beading his forehead, his back, and slicking his palms, Rich took a different tack, hoping the approach from two angles would give them the benefit of surprise.

As he came closer to their goal, Rich verified it was a shack. The old, dilapidated wood barely stood after suffering through a century of time. But the structure provided shelter, and Rich was glad his mother had had at least that much, if she was indeed inside.

Then he focused on the shards of light. The closer he came, it seemed that someone had gone to the trouble of covering the glassless windows with what looked like cardboard. Yet, despite their efforts, the light shone through.

When Rich reached the warped door, he said a quick prayer. Then he raised a foot, kicked in the slab of wood, and dashed inside, prepared to face the perp.

"Richie!" his mother exclaimed. "What are you doin' here, son?"

"Mariah?" Lark asked, pressed up against Rich's back.

Then, before they could look farther, a sound like a stampeding herd of buffalo descended upon them. Rich and Lark turned toward the door . . . and faced the most ludicrous spectacle they'd ever seen. In front of the shack ranged a mob of camouflage-garbed commandos, their faces underlit by flashlights. Olive, black, and hunter green blotches rendered their features unidentifiable.

To Rich's further confoundment, the militia members appeared engaged in some form of skirmish among themselves. Knees and elbows jabbed. Shoulders shoved. Bodies darted before others, and all the maneuvering was effected to the tune of stifled squawks and, presumably, commands.

"See?" one said loudly. "I *told* you we'd find Mama."

Rich studied the grunt who'd spoken. "Reenie?"

"Don't mind me, Richie," his sister chided. "How's Mama?"

Reminded of the reason for the day's stupefying events, Rich looked around inside the cabin—if one cared to dignify the handful of splinters with that name. As if attending a ladies' tea party, his mother sat upright at a rickety table across from a deathly white Frank Vallore.

"Hello, son," Mariah said, not at all nonplused by the situation. "I didn't expect you to be the one to find us, and certainly not to break down the door."

He blinked. Had he heard right? Evidently so, seeing as Mariah wore a frown.

"Mother. You've been kidnapped, the Dream Squeeze records were demanded in exchange for your release, Lark and I've been trudging in these woods all day trying to find you, and the only thing you have to say is that I shouldn't have kicked in the door?"

"Why, Richie," Mariah said, "I do believe you've gone a bit crazy. Calm down, son. Take a seat. I've been havin' a mighty important talk with Frank here. Did you know he's never met the Lord?"

Rich grabbed his pounding head. His mother had been witnessing to Frank, who must be her would-be kidnapper?

"Oh, Mariah, what a wonderful thing to do," commented Miss Louella. Rich recognized the voice, even though he couldn't tell one wrinkled, war-painted face from another.

"She's a saint, that's what she is!" exclaimed another soldier.

"The truest of witnesses for our Lord," added a third.

Another *crack!* rent the air. Leaves rustled wildly. Footsteps approached. Mycroft yowled with all his heart.

"Humph! I wouldn't go that far if I were you, ladies," grouched Myrna Stafford, who always managed to pop in toward the end of any of the Garden Club ladies' excursions. "She didn't even have the sense of a duck to keep from gettin' herself taken prisoner. What kinda saint bollixes up like that?"

Rich's eyes opened wide as Mrs. Stafford appeared at the fringe of the gathered gardeners . . . er . . . troops. If the commandos looked odd—to be most charitable—then Myrna looked nothing short of preposterous.

She'd taken to the woods in an ancient trench coat and an equally geriatric fedora, which she was using to fan herself. Her purply hair rolls looked like damaged, droopy Slinky toys.

Still, she appeared undaunted—or perhaps unaware of the picture she painted, not that it was any better or worse than the invasion force that had preceded her—and stepped closer to Rich.

Then he caught sight of her footwear. And he lost it. Totally. Instead of normal, comfortable walking shoes, Myrna had opted for combat boots: big, black, clunky things at the end of her spindly shins.

Rich howled with laughter, and Mycroft joined along. At his side, Lark chuckled, and from the table, Mama snickered in a ladylike way. Frank Vallore, however, looked ready to faint.

Looking at his mother's operations manager sobered Rich. "What do you have to say for yourself?" he asked the man.

Vallore only clenched his jaw.

Instead, Mama spoke. "Oh, Richie, it's the saddest thing. Frank told me his mama died when he was a tot, and his awful, awful mobster father raised him. Nothin' Frank ever did satisfied the man. He was always demandin' Frank make more money, too. You know how that is, son. Our Lord says the love of money's the root of all evil, you know."

Rich nodded, his gaze frozen on the man who'd betrayed his mother's trust.

Mama went on. "Well, that's it. His father gave him an ultimatum. Frank needed to set up his own business, turn a profit—with no help from his father. Now what kind of a parent is that?" His mother settled back into her worn chair. "As I was sayin', it was Frank's last chance to make things right with his daddy—although why he wanted to by then, I'm not rightly sure. Frank knew a man who had a team of women who lifted things from stores using ladies' stretchy undergarments to hide the merchandise. And seein' as my Dream Squeezes are the absolutely best girdles *ever,* why, he was clever enough to get me to hire him."

"Clever," Rich gritted out.

"Of course, he used his cleverness in a sinful way," Mama continued, "but seein' as he doesn't know the Lord . . . I was just tellin' Frank he has to get right with God, when you showed up," Mariah said.

"Amen!" cried Miss Louella.

Over his shoulder, Rich saw a smattering of bereted heads bob in agreement. "Fine, Mama," he said, "let's get him to Wiggon, and you can send Pastor Melbourne over to help him through the Sinner's Prayer. It's past time you were home."

"We *were* gettin' around to the Sinner's Prayer, son." She shook a finger at Rich. "You interrupted."

"That'll keep for another time, Mariah," Lark chirped, obviously fighting the urge to laugh again. "We really should go home. Especially since Reenie is out there and must be tired by now. You know, this kind of late-night outing can't be good for the baby."

At that bit of unexpected wisdom, Rich's mother squeezed by him and Lark and hurried outside to check on her daughter.

Myrna interrupted, "If it hadn't a'been for that big fat branch that tripped me earlier, I'd a'found them first—before Rich and Lark and the rest of you girls. And to think Mariah 'n him were havin' themselves a churchy prayer talk. Him a crook, even."

"You know, Myrna," Lark said, "I recently learned that sinners come in all kinds. What's important to know is that in God's eyes we're all plain vanilla sinners. We have to come clean with God, or we'll keep on ruinin' our lives."

Rich slipped an arm around Lark's waist. "Well said," he whispered.

A shrill whistle sliced through the night. Heavy footsteps ran forward, and a black blur dashed past the cabin. More men in dark garb surrounded the motley gathering outside. Handcuffs clicked on camouflage-covered elderly wrists.

A chorus of discontent burst into further discord.

"You take your paws off me, you young pup!" one gardener cried.

"I cain't believe you'd subject a decent, law-abidin' woman of *a certain* age to such indignity," another complained.

"Just wait 'til I tell your mama what you've gone and done this time, Wiggon," hollered Myrna, as she fought against her constraints.

"What in blue blazes is goin' on around here?" asked Wiggon. "Oh no, don't tell me. Not the Garden Club ladies again."

"'Fraid so," answered Rich. "Is that the Secret Service out there?"

"Sure is."

The aged troops picked up their hue and cry; the agents ignored the noise.

By the light of Wiggon's giant police-issue flare, Rich saw

Wiggon wince. "Is that Lark Bellamy there with you, Rich?" the cop asked.

"The one and only," he replied and squeezed her waist.

"Oh, man," Wiggon said, removing his regulation hat from his white blond head. "I should've known it'd be somethin' like this. Déjà vu all over again. Didn't you women learn anythin' that last time?"

"Wiggon, dear," Mama said, slipping her arm through the cop's, "do you remember back in Sunday school? How we learned it was more blessed to give than to receive?"

Wiggon wrinkled his brow, then, turning to the agents holding the Garden Club members captive, he said, "We got the wrong ones, fellas. Let 'em go. They're only guilty of felonious nosiness."

The gardeners liked that no more than the handcuffs, but they generously allowed the Secret Service to release them. Once freed, the ladies began to pick their way back to Bellamy through the pitch-black woods, their penlights giving off brief bursts of brilliance, as the losing agent charged with ensuring their safe and swift return home shepherded them toward the most direct route to town.

Grinning, Lark nudged Rich. "Can you believe how lost I got, goin' in circles all day, to wind up not more than half an hour away from Hollings Park?"

He gave her another squeeze. "It may be funny now, but it sure wasn't then."

In accord, they watched Sophie Hardesty and Florinda Sumner bring up the rear and vanish into the dark.

Once the gardeners were gone, Wiggon turned to Mariah. "What *does* the givin' lesson have to do with the Garden Club's doin's?"

"Why, everythin'," offered Miss Louella, taking the officer's other arm.

"Poor guy," said Lark in Rich's ear. "He doesn't stand a chance between those two."

In eloquent tones, Miss Louella expounded. "You see, Wiggon, we just want to *give* of our wisdom, our talents, our help. . . ."

Rich and Lark laughed at the distinctly Louella brand of logic.

Of course, the last lady to leave the area around the cabin was Myrna, who was busy giving the young agent stuck with the misfortune of uncuffing her a piece of her churlish mind. Not to mention repeated smacks with her beat-up old fedora.

Lark and Rich roared, while Mycroft gave an enthusiastic howl. But their laughter died when a pair of dark-clad men led Frank Vallore away, his hands in metal bracelets.

"I can't believe he did that to my mother," Rich said as the trio melded into the shadows of the trees.

"I don't know," Lark answered. "You can do an awful lot of stupid stuff, tryin' to prove yourself."

As Rich led her back toward town, he considered her comment. "You know, Red, you're getting smart in your old age."

"I'll have you know, Mr. Desmond, I've always been smart. And I'm younger than you."

He wrapped his arm around her shoulders. Nuzzled the hair at her temple. "Truce?"

"Oh, yeah."

"Praise God."

"Amen."

Late the next afternoon, even though her internal clock insisted on calling it early morning, Lark rose and smiled at the world. They'd found Mariah. They'd caught the crook. And, for all she knew, the Secret Service had by now rounded up everyone who was involved in the scheme, including the elder Vallore and Tony Alberti, one of the two who'd nearly killed Frank.

Even better, Rich had held her and kissed her as though he really meant it. There was even that one time when he'd started to say something, which in retrospect sounded suspiciously like the most beautiful three words in the English language. If only Myrna hadn't chosen that moment to trip and break a dry old tree branch.

Lark chose a bright emerald pair of walking shorts, a green-and-white-striped cotton T-shirt, and clean undies, then headed for the shower. The interruption last night didn't matter. If she hadn't imagined the kiss and Rich's embrace, another opportunity for those lovely words would soon arise. She would trust the Lord.

As Lark leaped out of the shower, a silly song kept teasing her tongue as Mycroft cheerfully followed her to the kitchen. She took a fresh container of tofu from the refrigerator, drained, then crumbled it before scrambling it in the skillet.

After eating, Lark went to the living room and took Granny Iris's old Bible from the bookshelf. She sat on the sofa and let the book fall open on her lap.

She read for a while before a disturbance outside distracted her. Peering out the side window, she noticed a throng on the Desmond front porch and yard. To her surprise and dismay, they looked like a crowd of reporters, with tape recorders, mikes, and cameras at the ready.

A sick feeling lodged in her stomach.

Lark placed her Bible on the table behind the sofa and ran to the front door. "Hey!" she called out. "What's happenin' over there?"

She really didn't want to have her suspicions confirmed, but a second later, a dozen voices cried, "We've discovered Des Richter!"

She closed the door, thinking, *Poor Rich.* He'd been found out. True, his hiding had been silly, but Lark was certain he didn't want his identity revealed like this.

She decided to call and see how he was doing. "Rich?" she asked when he answered the phone.

Dead silence.

"Rich? Are you there? Are you all right? It's me, Lark."

"I know who it is, and I'm fine. I suppose you're finally happy. Tell me, how much money did you get for the scoop this time?"

"Money?" she asked, refusing to register his harsh words. "Scoop?"

"Wasn't that what you were after all this time? Well, now you have it. I hope they made betraying me worthwhile." He hung up with a definitive *click.*

Lark's earlier cheer vanished. She felt cold. Numb. Dizzy.

"It can't be," she told Mycroft when he slipped his head under her dangling hand. "Rich can't really believe me guilty of betrayin' him. Not after last night."

The pup whimpered in sympathy and licked her fingers. He wriggled, calling for her attention, but Lark felt ill. Ice weighted her middle. It was impossible. Rich had to know she hadn't done anything but sleep since they'd returned from the woods.

But someone had alerted the media. They were now camped out on Rich's doorstep. His worst nightmare had come true.

And he believed her to be the cause of his misery.

A lump in her throat made it hard to swallow. A burning behind her eyelids made it difficult to watch the mike-jockeys outside. The ringing in her ears made it impossible to—

Oh! That wasn't her ears ringing; it was the phone.

"Hello."

"Lark?" Reenie asked in greeting. "How bad is it? Miss

Louella called a minute ago, an' she says Richie's house is crawlin' with reporters. Is she right?"

Lark collapsed onto the couch. "'Fraid so."

"Oh, dear."

"That's puttin' it mildly."

"Oh?"

"Yeah. I just talked to the recluse himself—"

"Ooooh! Tell me all about it. I saw him huggin' you an' holdin' your hand last night. Did he kiss you?"

Something private in Lark ached at her best friend's question. She took a moment to compose herself. "There's nothin' to tell, Reenie. I was frightened, and Rich was reassurin' me."

"Uh-huh. An' I'm Leonardo DaVinci himself. Fine. Be that way. But remember, he's my big brother. I'm gonna learn all about your romance anyway."

Reenie's words jabbed into Lark, making a tear overflow her eye. "There is not—and won't be—any romance. Rich thinks I sold the story of his identity. He made it perfectly clear right before you called that he's havin' nothin' to do with me."

The air on the other end of the phone remained empty for a minute. Two.

"You didn't . . . did you?"

"Do you think I'm crazy? Of course I didn't rat on your brother. Why, after all he said last night, I would've cut my tongue off before I'd have told on him."

Reenie sighed in relief. "Well, then, Lark, you're just gonna have to tell him you didn't do it."

"Don't you think I tried? It's worse than when we were kids."

"Oh, no! An' things were goin' good there for a while."

"No, Reenie. We were workin' together to help your mama. Nothin' more." Unfortunately.

"Oh, well. I guess I'll have to see what I can do."

"Do? What do you mean 'do'?"

"Oh. Why . . . about Richie and those reporters," Reenie answered, clearly flustered by Lark's question.

"Oh no you don't," Lark said.

"Don't what?"

"Don't act so innocent, for one. And for another, don't you go messin' with Rich and me, tryin' to match us up or anything. It's never going to happen, and it's best you admit it."

"Why, Lark, honey, would I do somethin' like that?"

"In a flash."

"Why, I would not, dear. I'll just mind my own business. I'm so busy what with the baby, an' did I tell you I joined the Garden Club? Made Mama so happy, she cried at the installation meetin'."

The thought of Reenie as a Garden Club member didn't offer Lark much comfort, but she didn't feel like pursuing the matter right then. "Good. I'm glad you're so happy and busy. But I'm still tired from last night. I feel a nap comin' on."

"Take care of yourself, Lark. I'll come by real soon."

"See you then."

When Reenie had hung up, Lark cuddled deeper into the couch. The comfortable furnishing had seen her through many a crisis, including all the times she'd been hurt by Rich. Lark hoped God would again use the old piece to soothe her, because this time she knew the true meaning of a broken heart.

And this time she hadn't done a thing to bring it on herself.

TWENTY

No self-respecting, full-grown male needed his mother to help him survive a siege, as Rich told Mariah the day after her rescue when she showed up at his front door, bags in hand.

Since the authorities were still sifting through evidence at Dream Squeeze, Mama had too much time on her hands—a frightening state of affairs. She'd decided to turn her efforts toward protecting her son from the media vultures camped outside his front door.

To Rich's further dismay, she came replete with reinforcements: the Garden Club. He didn't need an elderly guard. He needed peace, quiet, time to pray, think, grieve.

Lark had broken his heart. He'd thought she understood his feelings, and even though he'd recognized the error in his reclusiveness, he hadn't expected betrayal to be her way to "fix" things.

He'd thought she'd learned she didn't have to fix anything. That God was best left in control. How could she have done this to him?

He remembered her sweet response to his embrace in the woods. She'd curled up against him, holding him, returning his kisses, listening, sharing. He'd begun to think she might really love him. Not with that crazy infatuation from her childhood but with real and mature love—what he felt for her. He'd thought her a gift from God.

He should have known better. After all, she was Lark Bellamy.

Now his life was a nightmare. He'd become a prisoner in his own home. And he didn't have a clue how to escape these bars of Lark's making.

Then a thought occurred to him. Was he again acting out of his old pride and arrogance? Was Lark solely to blame for this situation? Had he done something to push her toward betrayal?

He remembered the day she'd mentioned the lack of children at Desmond's Country Store after Rich had taken over. Had he done something arrogant to chase her off as he'd obviously done to the kids?

"Lord God," he prayed aloud, "check out my heart. If there's something else rotten in there, something that makes me push people away instead of drawing them near and serving them in your name, please just take it away. I can never trust Lark again, but I can certainly make things right at the store. With your help, maybe I can lead someone to you."

For the first time since the invasion in the woods, Rich felt calm.

He added to his prayer. "And, Father, could you take away the pain of losing Lark? I really do love her, even though I should have known better. I thought I had her love, too. But I guess I never really did."

He'd known she was trouble. And she'd proved him right.

Moving aside the curtain on the front window, Rich nearly

swallowed his tongue. For the first time since early morning, there wasn't a soul in sight. His front yard, grass trampled beyond repair, was vacant. Not a microphone-bearing leech could be found. Instead, however, an army of geriatric gardeners crawled over every inch of once-green lawn, spades, hand rakes, gloves, topsoil, fertilizer, seed, and potted seedlings in hand.

Good. They'd found another target for their energy. Rich had been in danger of death by sympathy through their coddling, overmothering, and comforting. It'd been simply stifling.

But his yard would benefit from the attention of his mother's gardening friends. He could go back to nursing his broken heart.

And figuring out what God wanted him to do with the rest of his life.

Lark had a heavy heart. As heavy as it had been since that awful morning three days ago when she'd called Rich, only to have him accuse her of betraying him.

She'd never have done that. She loved him.

"Don't I, Mycroft?" she asked her pooch, who opened one eye, rearranged his chubby body across his favorite pillow on her bed, and went back to his nap.

"Hey, mutt. I need to talk here. Wake up."

Mycroft opened his other eye and sighed.

"One eye's better than none, I guess. Don't you think Rich should just go public, explain his good and sincere reasons for refusin' to sign a contract that goes against his convictions, then get on with his life?"

Mycroft snuffled.

"I'll take that as a yes. And you know Rich even has the

best person for that interview livin' next door. Lovin' him, too. I'd make sure the piece was balanced. Logical. And gave witness to Rich's devotion to Christ."

Two closed eyelids told Lark the dog considered the matter settled.

Well, it wasn't. But she wished it was.

She cared about the article, but not as much as she cared about Rich. It really mattered to her how he came across. And his faith.

Her faith, too.

Because, after three days of leaning in the dark on a God she hadn't trusted for far too long, Lark had fallen in love with a second man: Jesus Christ, God's Son.

Recognizing the reality of answered prayer, she'd devoured the Gospels in the hours of pain after Rich's rejection. She'd renewed her acquaintance with the story of the Savior's sacrifice. She'd remembered the many rejections Jesus had suffered during his thirty-three years on earth. She'd revived their relationship.

Although she could barely stand what had happened between her and Rich, she now knew she wasn't alone. She'd asked God's forgiveness, had welcomed Jesus back where he belonged: in her heart and in her life. She'd invited the Holy Spirit to be her guide again, knowing he would do a better job of leading her than she'd ever done.

In her recognition of God's all-powerful wisdom and genius, Lark had finally taken a good look at herself. He'd made her just as she was. True, she had a lot of learning and growing to do, but he hadn't made a mistake when he'd made her a redhead. Or freckled. Or Southern, impulsive, imaginative, or any of the other things that she'd always believed set her apart from others.

Those things she'd tried so hard to deny. Those things she'd considered so ugly, but hadn't been. Not nearly as ugly as her rejection of God, her family, herself—a child of the King.

She'd also accepted her share of the blame for the broken relationship between her and her sisters. Now she couldn't wait until Maggie got home from her honeymoon. She had so much to tell her.

And Cammie. Lark now knew she had hurt the youngest Blossom very deeply the day she'd shown her disdain for her sister's life.

"Father," she prayed, "I don't know how to fix this— ooops! Forget that. Let me start all over again, and this time I'll get it right."

She knelt. "Lord, I hurt my sister. I thought of myself as better than her. Please forgive my pride, and heal me. Show me, Father, how you want me to mend the fences I tore down with my sin."

That was better.

Oh, yeah. "And another thing. If there's any way I can make up for the pain Rich has suffered these last few days, please show me. But I want your will done, not my mule-headed notions. And I'll try to wait on your answers patiently. Thanks, Lord God."

Lark smiled despite her sadness. Prayer really did make a difference. It brought hope to a hopeless situation, and it took the weight of her world off her shoulders.

A strange buzzing sound outside interrupted Lark's quiet time. What were those reporters up to?

She went to the window and saw, instead of the media, Bellamy's garden militia. The members of the club had spread out across the Desmond property and were diligently working on the landscaping. The buzz came from the trimmer Miss Louella was using to trim the hedge between Lark's and Rich's homes.

"What a relief," she told Mycroft, who'd woken from his

doggy nap. "At least they're tryin' to beautify somethin' rather than tryin' to patch Rich and me back together again."

The hound yawned loudly, then trotted down the stairs. Lark followed, knowing he'd need one of two things. He either wanted o-u-t, or food and water were on his clever little mind.

Evidently, Mycroft wanted nourishment, and Lark supplied it. As she watched Mycroft crunch, swallow, wiggle his tail, then slurp water to chase down his meal, Lark decided it was time to get her work back on track.

But what was she going to do next?

She hadn't scooped the Des Richter/Rich Desmond thing—that had been splattered all over CNN and the networks for the past three days. And she didn't have the heart to review the latest gift from the next-biggest writer, the "king of horror," as the man's representatives were pressing her to do. She'd generally stuck with literary fiction for her magazine, but she'd lost the taste even for that.

"What am I goin' to do with myself, Lord?" she asked, then corrected herself. "Sorry about that. What do you want to do with me next?"

At seven-thirty that evening, Mycroft's earsplitting yowl jolted Lark out of her enjoyment of the psalms. She'd found the only thing that held any interest for her was her granny's Bible, and so she'd spent the day rediscovering the blessings of Scripture.

"Hang on, buster," she said, putting down the aged book. The dog skittered all over the kitchen floor while Lark leashed him and opened the door. As always, he tore down the back steps and began sniffing the minute his paws touched grass.

Then Lark froze.

"The hedge," she wailed.

It was gone. The dense forsythia growth between the Desmond and Bellamy homes had been replaced by a white picket fence, just like the one across the front of her home.

She approached the raped land and touched a freshly painted picket. Mycroft went mad sniffing, obviously finding too many fascinating smells for one single puppy's nose. He howled.

"What have you done *now,* Red?" called her next-door neighbor. "Where are my shrubs?"

"I haven't done anything, you crazy man. And I want to know what you did with the hedge."

"I've been inside all day."

"Guess what? So have I."

"But you've taken Mycroft for w-a-l-k-s, right?"

"Sure. And we went as far as downtown at lunchtime, but never came out this side of the house."

"A likely story. After all, you left the window open in my car, and the dog sneaked into the warehouse."

"But Alberti and his thuggy buddy broke the window Mycroft used to get inside when Frank refused to hurt Mariah, as they felt he should."

"That's right, Lark. Shove the blame off on someone else. Just like you did when your chums descended on me."

"What chums?"

"The media."

"I had nothin' to do with them."

"Right, Snoop-Scoop. And I'm Queen Elizabeth's pet Corgi."

"Well then, hi there, pup."

"Quit being cute."

"Why, thank you Mr. Desmond . . . er . . . Richter—just who are you?"

"Rich. The guy whose life you've spent yours ruining."

"I've never done anythin' to you, just as I never ever called in the press. I had nothin' to do with the reporters. I was exhausted after our tramp in the woods; I slept that whole day."

"I don't believe you. You wanted that story bad enough that you'd have betrayed anyone for it. Of course, I was fair game."

Lark approached the new fence in fine battle form. "Listen to me, Richard Desmond, and listen to me good. I'm goin' to tell you this only one time. I had nothing to do with the media buzz. Please believe me, I'd never hurt you like that. I . . . I care about you, and besides, it's not my place to decide when or how you tell the world your secrets."

Something in her denial must have pierced his obstinacy, since he didn't fire off another accusation. She took advantage of his silence. "Rich, remember that day in the store? When I heard you and Storey talkin'?"

"Yes."

"You told me neither of you were mobsters. I took your word for it then. Can't you do the same for me now?"

In the soft mauve of dusk, Lark saw Rich blanch.

She continued. "I've made my peace with God. I'm speakin' as a Christian, Rich. I'm not lyin'. I won't ever sin against God on purpose—not anymore. And lyin' to you would be just that. I didn't betray you. I'd never, ever do that. Not to anyone, but especially not to you."

His Adam's apple bobbed as he swallowed hard. "You didn't sell my story?"

"No."

"And you didn't cut the hedge?"

"Not me."

"Then who did?"

Lark shrugged. "Beats me, but I think I kinda like the fence."

"You do?"

"Mm-hmm. We're actually talkin' over it, whereas with the hedge, why, we had a wall built up. Kind of like the wall I built between God and me. I've decided I'm not one for wall-buildin' anymore."

"Then what are you up to these days?"

"Fallin' in love."

Rich turned a sick shade of pea green. "Oh, that's nice," he said in a voice that suggested it really wasn't.

Lark placed a hand on his tense arm. "With Jesus, Rich. I've spent the last three days in prayer and in his Word."

"Funny, so have I."

"I've been prayin' about my future, my career."

"Me, too."

"Come up with any wonderful insights?"

"No insights yet."

"Me neither. Just to be patient and wait on the Lord to show me what to do next."

"Sounds familiar."

"Hey," Lark said, hoping she wasn't making yet another mistake with Rich, "why don't you hop over the fence and come sit on the porch swing awhile. It's a nice evenin' for that."

Rich hopped, watching out for the still-wet paint. "Sounds good to me."

As they set the swing rocking, Lark thanked God. She'd wanted to smooth things over with Rich, even though she knew all hope of romance was gone. It now looked as though God would make them friends. And that was better than nothing, she guessed.

"What do you think of the way Mama's case turned out?" Rich asked.

"Pretty sad, don't you think?"

"Poor Frank. What a way to grow up. In the mob, expected to pursue a life of crime since it was the family business."

Lark shuddered. "And to have his very own father threaten him, just because he'd never become rotten enough for those bloodthirsty mob tastes."

"Just goes to show how men can ruin the gifts God gives them."

"You know," she said, an idea taking form. "That would make a great story—you know, the human interest angle. Maybe I should contact the *Sun,* see if they want me to do an in-depth piece."

"Instead of an exposé on a boring, small-town store owner who also writes?"

"Nah." Lark grinned. "Along with the thoughtful piece where the fascinatin', small-town merchant explains why he walked away from what many called the deal of the century."

"Is that what you'd like to do?"

"Very much. But only with you, Rich. No exposé. Just a chance for you to speak your heart. There's a Scripture I wanted to mention to you. I can't remember where I found it but it talks about God's people bein' the light of the world. It tells us not to hide our lights under baskets, but to let them shine for all to see."

"It's in the Gospel of Matthew. Chapter 5."

"So you know it, then. There was another one, farther on in the New Testament. Maybe you know this one too? It says that although our hearts were once full of darkness, as Christians, we're now full of the Lord's light. Our actions should show it, because this light produces what's good, right, and true. Since you want to write for God's glory, then I think you should tell the world. I want to help you do it."

"That one's in Ephesians, Lark. And I'm glad you reminded me of it."

"So, you'll do it? Work with me on an interview?"

"You mean—" he shuddered theatrically—"you want us to work together again?"

She punched his bicep. "It wasn't that bad. After all, we found Mariah and caught the creep."

"Oh, no, it wasn't that bad at all. Only slightly worse than root canal."

Lark stood. "I've offered you an olive branch, givin' you the chance of a lifetime to tell the world what you want it to know about Richard Desmond, and all you can do is make fun of me?" She marched off the porch. "I don't need this, Rich. Mycroft? Where'd you get off to? Let's go inside."

Mad at Rich, she searched the yard for her dog and finally found him digging around one of the newly installed fence posts. "There you are—"

"And here we are," Rich said, placing a hand on her shoulder, "arguing again. I'm sorry. I was only joking. I think your proposal is great. I'd like to tell my story, my way. And if you're willing to help me do that, then, yes, I'll take you up on your offer."

Lark looked up into earnest gray eyes. She'd put so much hope in her plan that when he'd laughed at her, she'd feared she'd blown it again.

"Thank you, Jesus," she whispered, then smiled.

"Amen."

Rich's other hand came to rest on her vacant shoulder. Lark caught her breath. Was he going to hold her? Pull her close? Would he kiss her again?

Something in Rich's gaze set her heart racing. Something in his gentle smile sent a ripple of warmth through her body. Something in the way he slipped his arms around her brought a new, unfamiliar brightness to Lark's heart.

Is this real? Is it possible? Is it . . . joy?

Rich kissed her, and the brightness burst into Roman candles in her head. Lark's ears hummed, her heart danced.

Her lips welcomed Rich's passionate kiss. She wrapped her arms around his neck, running avid fingers through his hair, down his back, up and over his wide, solid shoulders.

Most of all, she spoke her love in her kiss. Lark returned the caress with the same need and fire Rich had revealed, letting all of her walls finally collapse. She loved Rich Desmond, always had, always would, and if it was in God's will, she might, just might, someday have him for her very own.

For the moment, simply knowing she'd built a bridge between them—one steady enough to withstand this kind of kiss—was enough. She would trust God with the rest.

Rain began to fall, unexpectedly.

Rich ended their kiss—with obvious reluctance, she noted—and said, "What's this?"

"Rain," she answered, perfectly content to stay where she was, even if she wound up soaked in the process.

"But it can't be—"

Footsteps approached, followed by a *humph!*

Lark and Rich groaned simultaneously.

"Myrna!" he cried.

"What's this world a-comin' to," she brayed, her purple curls in regimental rows on her head, "when a body cain't even take her constitutional without bein' forced to watch all sorts of intimacies while she's walkin' right down city streets."

"Myrna Stafford," chided Miss Louella, coming from behind Rich's house, "after all our hard work to get things goin' again between these two since you went and sold Rich's story to a tabloid, you go and turn the water on them just as they were finally gettin' it right."

Mariah joined Miss Louella on the Desmond side of the fence. "Myrna, dear, they weren't doin' anythin' unseemly. My son was just kissin' his lovely . . . "

Lark moaned.

Rich groaned.

Mycroft bayed.

"Neighbor, Mama," Rich said. "I was kissing my lovely neighbor."

"Oh. But she's so right for you and—"

"And if you want her to be more than my lovely neighbor, Mother, I suggest you gather up your cronies and leave us alone."

Lark felt like dying. Here she and Rich were, once again the focus of the town's gossipmonger, surrounded by the greatest busybody matchmakers anyone could ever know.

"I'd better go inside," she said to Rich.

He tightened his hold around her. "You're not going anywhere yet. They're the ones leaving. Right, Mama? Miss Louella?"

A whispered consultation followed. Then, from the rear of the Desmond home, Reenie called out, "I think we'd better be doin' as he says, Mama. It doesn't look like he's lettin' her go right quick. Looks like we've done our job, ladies, so why don't we leave my big brother to do his?"

The unenthusiastic contingent trudged to the sidewalk and dispersed in various directions. In the distance, Lark heard Mariah say, "Didn't I tell you all? It's just like the Word tells us: 'We know that God causes everything to work together for the good of those who love God and are called according to his purpose for them.'"

Lark laughed. "She's right."

"Mama knows best?"

"Hmm . . ." She thought of Mariah's multitudinous efforts over the years to bring her and Rich together. "Sometimes."

"Yes, I'd say sometimes she's right."

All this while, Rich's arms held Lark securely, comfortably, lovingly.

"You know," Rich said with a chuckle, "if I were to write

all this as a play—the girdles, the fraud, you, Mycroft, the Garden Club—no one would buy it. They'd never believe it."

"That's it!" Lark cried, taking Rich's much-loved face between her hands. "That's God's answer to our prayers."

"Huh?"

She dropped a soft, tender kiss on his lips. His arms tightened around her, and he deepened the kiss. Quite nicely, too.

When they finally surfaced, he said, "Run that by me again?"

Since pinwheels still sparkled before Lark's eyes and breathing remained a chore, she fanned her heated cheeks. "Wow," she breathed.

Rich grinned. As his lips came back toward hers, she slipped a hand to her mouth. He kissed her palm instead.

Tingles running through her, she finally managed to say, "The story . . . the case. Mariah's case would make a fabulous play. Don't you think?"

Rich blinked. "You may have something there."

"Oh, no. Not me. It's God's idea all the way."

"You figure?"

"Mm-hmm."

He studied her, a faint smile on his lips, arms holding her close. "How so?"

"Well, we've both been prayin' for God's leadin' on our future these past days, right?"

He nodded.

"Well, we're both writers, right?"

This nod was more brief. "And . . . ?"

"And we proved we could work very well together, right?"

He choked. "Well, I wouldn't put it in those terms, exactly."

"How would you put it?"

"Both of us got out of this alive?"

She socked his shoulder. "Get serious, Rich. Wouldn't it be

wonderful if we collaborated on this project? You said an article about you was a great idea, so why shouldn't we carry that
forward into a writin' partnership? I bet we'd be good at it."

He shook his head.

Her heart dropped.

"I gotta hand it to you, Red. You do come up with some
wild ideas."

"Oh."

"But that partnership deal has merit. I think we'd better
give it serious consideration."

"Oh?"

"Yes. I think we would make good partners . . . if we didn't
wind up killing each other first."

"We'd have to set up ground rules. . . ."

"And agree to discuss things thoroughly. . . ."

"Plus, no more of this Red business. Or Snoop, either . . ."

"And you're not allowed to hang out with the Garden
Club. . . ."

"Why would I want to?"

"Reenie's a member now."

"Yeah, but she's married."

"You could be, too."

"Me?" she squeaked.

"You."

"To whom?"

He gave her a gentle shake. "Who else would put up with
you?"

"You?"

"Of course!"

"Are you askin'—"

"You to marry me."

Tears swam in Lark's eyes. "For real?"

"No, honey, forever. In God's eyes, and in those of every
snoopy Garden Club member in Bellamy."

"Oh, Rich . . ."

"I love you, Larkspur Bellamy."

"I love you, too, Richard Desmond."

"We have a deal?"

"We have a deal."

"Good. How soon?"

"As soon as you'd like."

"Then it's goin' to be very soon."

"Why the hurry?"

"Because I don't want to have to worry about Myrna Stafford and the sprinkler when we kiss again."

"Myrna's not here now."

Rich grinned. "I know."

And he kissed her.

It was joy.

A Note from the Author

Dear Reader,

As a former newspaper reporter, I loved the challenge of telling Lark's story. Not only was she a successful newshound, but she had an abundance of courage . . . to the point of blinding herself to caution.

Guess what?

I can relate. Completely!

Shortly after I became pregnant with my fourth son, I was assigned a zoning-ordinance story that on the surface seemed cut and dry. Because of my tendency to leap where angels fear to tread, though, I raked up a number of threatening letters, harassing phone calls, and the worst case of morning sickness in history—caused by nerves, of course.

The Lord used my husband to rein in my exuberance for truth and a story, for which I'm truly grateful. As a high-risk-pregnancy mom, I might have wound up with a tragedy otherwise.

Sound familiar?

Lark also needed the voice of reason, provided by Rich. She learned that God's ways are *always* balanced and perfectly wise. And just as Lark does, I gained valuable knowledge all those years ago.

In the end, my research brought to light a number of dirty dealings, and the authorities handled the outcome. I concentrated on being joyfully pregnant and writing fiction to my heart's content.

I'd like to thank those of you who read *Magnolia* and invite those who haven't to do so! In the meantime, I'm having a great time with *Camellia*. Look for it soon.

Ginny

About the Author

A former newspaper reporter, Ginny Aiken lives in south-central Pennsylvania with her husband and four sons. Born in Havana, Cuba, and raised in Valencia and Caracas, Venezuela, she discovered books early on and wrote her first novel at age fifteen. (She burned it when she turned a "mature" sixteen!) That first effort was followed several years later by her winning entry in the Mid-America Romance Authors' Fiction from the Heartland contest for unpublished authors.

Ginny has certificates in French literature and culture from the University of Nancy, France, and a B.A. in Spanish and French literature from Allegheny College in Pennsylvania. Her first novel was published in 1993, and since then she has published numerous additional novels and novellas. One of her novels was a finalist for *Affair de Coeur*'s Readers' Choice Award for Best American Historical of 1997, and her work has appeared on various best-seller lists. Ginny's novellas appear in the anthologies *With This Ring, A Victorian Christmas Quilt, A Bouquet of Love,* and *Dream Vacation.* If you missed *Magnolia,* the first novel in the delightful Bellamy's Blossoms series, be sure to pick it up soon. And watch for book 3, *Camellia,* due to be released in summer 2001.

When she isn't busy with the duties of being a soccer mom, Ginny can be found reading, writing, enjoying classical music while indulging her passion for needlework, and preparing for her next Bible study.

Ginny welcomes letters written to her in care of Tyndale House Author Relations, P.O. Box 80, Wheaton, IL 60189-0080, or by E-mail at GinnyAiken@aol.com.

Visit www.HeartQuest.com for lots of info on
HeartQuest books and authors and more!

www.HeartQuest.com

HEART QUEST

Current HeartQuest Releases

- *Magnolia*, Ginny Aiken
- *Lark*, Ginny Aiken
- *Camellia*, Ginny Aiken

- *Sweet Delights,* Terri Blackstock, Ranee McCollum, and Elizabeth White

- *Awakening Mercy*, Angela Benson
- *Abiding Hope*, Angela Benson

- *Faith*, Lori Copeland
- *Hope*, Lori Copeland
- *June*, Lori Copeland
- *Glory*, Lori Copeland

- *Freedom's Promise*, Dianna Crawford
- *Freedom's Hope*, Dianna Crawford
- *Freedom's Belle*, Dianna Crawford

- *Prairie Rose*, Catherine Palmer
- *Prairie Fire*, Catherine Palmer
- *Prairie Storm*, Catherine Palmer
- *Prairie Christmas*, Catherine Palmer, Elizabeth White, and Peggy Stoks

- *Finders Keepers*, Catherine Palmer
- *Hide and Seek*, Catherine Palmer
- *A Kiss of Adventure*, Catherine Palmer (original title: *The Treasure of Timbuktu*)
- *A Whisper of Danger*, Catherine Palmer (original title: *The Treasure of Zanzibar*)
- *A Touch of Betrayal*, Catherine Palmer
- *A Victorian Christmas Cottage*, Catherine Palmer, Debra White Smith, Jeri Odell, and Peggy Stoks
- *A Victorian Christmas Quilt*, Catherine Palmer, Debra White Smith, Ginny Aiken, and Peggy Stoks
- *A Victorian Christmas Tea*, Catherine Palmer, Dianna Crawford, Peggy Stoks, and Katherine Chute

- *Olivia's Touch*, Peggy Stoks
- *Romy's Walk*, Peggy Stoks

Coming Soon—Fall 2001

- *A Victorian Christmas Keepsake*, Catherine Palmer, Kristin Billerbeck, Ginny Aiken

Other Great Tyndale House Fiction